The Dalliances
of
Monsieur D'Haricot

Luna
Press
PUBLISHING

First published by Luna Press Publishing, Edinburgh, 2021

www.lunapresspublishing.com
ISBN-13: 978-1-913387-39-6

To all Sagittarians,
especially my sister Kathleen.

Contents

Chapter One

Monsieur D'Haricot did not approve of automobiles. He could not understand the modern fascination for them. He had risked life, limb and big toe defending his country against the Germans, and he would not be mown down in a Paris street by a French car driven by a Gallic lunatic who believed they were on the finishing straight at Le Mans.

His father had presented him with a spanner, a steel tube and two wheels of differing sizes salvaged from a scrapyard on his twelfth birthday. Since that day, twenty-six years ago, the bicycle had been Louis-Philip D'Haricot's main mode of transport, other than his feet (now down a toe due to gangrene, but the government compensated for the loss with a medal of honour). His current bicycle was a state of the art, 1935 roadster, fitted with the latest pneumatic tyres, derailleur gears and a bell, which Monsieur D'Haricot had no compunction in using.

'Sacré bleu, have you no eyes?' His bicycle wobbled as he thrust a clenched fist in the direction of the driver. 'Mad men like you should not be allowed on the road.'

The car stopped and Monsieur D'Haricot blushed. The driver was not a madman, but a mad lady. She stuck her pinned blonde hair, powdered cheeks and centimetre long eyelashes out of the window. 'I do not give a bean what you think. Unless you want your contraption flattened, I suggest you move it.'

'Contraption? Contraption!' The veins on Monsieur D'Haricot's forehead bulged, but despite losing his big toe at Charleroi he had not lost his sense of humour. *Not give a bean* – that was droll. But why was her voice familiar?

He took a moment to retrieve his monocle from his top pocket, wiping the lens on his sleeve before positioning the glass in front of his right eye.

'Mon dieu! C'est Madame Chapleau.'

'Monsieur D'Haricot. I didn't recognise you with your clothes on.'

Louis-Philip glanced round and waved a hand to indicate she should lower her voice. The incident was the result of a simple mistake, and nothing improper had occurred in the hotel room, but the minds of Parisian citizens could, he found, be quick to assume 'hanky-panky' – which he believed was the case even in England.

The lady put a gloved hand over her mouth to suppress a titter. She stepped out of the car and inspected the twisted wheel of his bicycle.

'That does not look good,' she opined.

'It will mend, I am sure,' Monsieur D'Haricot answered.

'As did your trousers, I hope,' the lady said. 'I haven't seen you in the salon since the Bastille celebrations. Do tell me what you have been up to.'

The manners of the drivers behind Madame Chapleau's vehicle were no better than goaded rhinos. Horns sounded and fumes rose. The lady did not intend budging until she heard the latest tit-a-tat. There was nothing for Monsieur D'Haricot to do except secure his bicycle to the back of her Delahaye 135 cabriolet and clamber into the car. The seat was in use and he found himself squashed between the door and a turquoise portmanteau.

'Please be careful,' Madame Chapleau warned. She returned to her seat and adjusted her hair pins. 'The contents are fragile.'

It was on the tip of Monsieur D'Haricot's tongue to claim that he too was of a delicate constitution, but that was not the image he wished to portray.

'Where are we heading?' he asked instead.

'Oh, nowhere, unless you have somewhere in mind.' Madame Chapleau had the habit of fixing her eyes on her listener when she spoke. The sapphire one had a slight squint. The emerald one was steady; nonetheless Monsieur D'Haricot suspected their sole attention being on a passenger was contrary to the rules of the road.

'I have business in Montmartre,' he said. 'It is a hush-hush affair.'

The lady pretended to shiver in an exaggerated manner. 'I do love it when you are on a case, Louis.'

'I fear, Madame, the case is on me.' He nudged the portmanteau with his elbow. 'Why have you a need of luggage when you are going nowhere?'

'Touché, Monsieur.' Madame Chapleau tapped the side of her nose. In doing so, she jerked the wheel and the car swerved, missing a nursemaid pushing a perambulator on the pavement by half a centimetre.

Monsieur D'Haricot had his suspicions about Victoire Chapleau. Even before the unfortunate incident in the hotel room, he had a notion that she was employed in shady business.

'You can drop me off at the corner,' he said, recognising a lane leading to the Sacre Coeur basilica. 'There's no need to go out of your way.'

'It is no inconvenience. There is a bistro I should like to visit.' Madame Chapleau stopped the car and was out before her passenger could reach for the door handle. Her parking left much to be desired and Monsieur D'Haricot feared the owner of the handsome red Terrot 175 LU motorcycle would not be amused when he returned to find his vehicle scratched. 'Would you mind awfully?' She gestured towards the portmanteau.

Monsieur D'Haricot gritted his teeth. The case had cost him significant inconvenience during the short car trip, banging against his elbow and causing a bruise which he felt was darkening as they spoke. Not to be taken for a wimp, however, he manhandled it from the car.

'Where would you like it deposited?' he asked.

They were at the entrance to a run-down bistro. The sign was in need of a fresh coat of paint and a Parisian joker had rubbed over the lettering. Instead of what Monsieur D'Haricot took to be 'Café de Canard Rouge', The 'Red Duck' café, the name read 'Café de la Canaille Rusée', the 'Wily Rabble' cafe. On entering Monsieur D'Haricot revised his opinion – the clientele were indeed a shifty crowd and there was no evidence of fowl, red or otherwise.

He stumbled towards the bar counter with the portmanteau knocking against his ankles. It was a relief to set it down. Turning to enquire if his companion would like a drink, he was surprised to see she had taken a seat at one of the poorly scrubbed tables. Did she not know that her drink would cost decidedly more at a table than at the bar?

'A coffee for me and one for the lady,' he addressed the barman.

The man was standing idly, taking his time to wipe a glass with the bottom of his greasy apron. Although no more than a metre

3

from Monsieur D'Haricot, he ignored the order. Monsieur D'Haricot repeated his request. The customer leaning against the corner of the counter glared at him. His expression conveyed not only annoyance, but anger. Thankfully the only dagger on his person was tattooed on his right arm. It took a moment for Monsieur D'Haricot to realise a gramophone was playing in the background. Straining his ears, he could make out the crackling notes of La Marseillaise sung by a male voice, possibly Chevalier. He clicked to attention and stood in silence until the tune ended. Madame Chapleau was seemingly unaware of the anthem playing. She was fingering her driving gloves in a lackadaisical manner.

'Encore,' the patriot at the bar demanded.

Monsieur D'Haricot supposed he would have to wait for his beverage until the record played once more, but the barman poured the coffee from a steaming jug before replacing the stylus. Monsieur D'Haricot retreated with his cups to the table where Madame Chapleau was examining her hands with despair.

'Feel how rough my skin is.'

Not wishing to offend, he stroked a finger against her knuckle. The skin was smooth and pale. 'It seems fine – more than fine, magnifique.'

'You are kind, but it is no use. I shall have to apply cream to my fingers.' She stared at Monsieur D'Haricot, expecting him to act. 'My moisturising cream is in my portmanteau.'

Monsieur D'Haricot set his cup down with a clatter. 'Ah, I see.' The portmanteau was sitting where he had left it and was attracting curious looks from the other patrons. He stood up and walked to the bar to retrieve it.

'Marchons, marchons…' The man at the counter was close to tears during his rendition of the song, half a key lower than the recording.

'Marchons, indeed.' Monsieur D'Haricot was careful not to bump him with the portmanteau, which he guessed contained more than hand cream. He placed the case beside Madame Chapleau, but did not retake his seat.

'I can't emolliate my hands here,' Madame Chapleau said. 'Would you mind carrying the case upstairs for me?'

'Upstairs? Here?' Monsieur D'Haricot was taken aback.

'François will show you where.'

The barman gesticulated to an exit at the back of the bar. Monsieur D'Haricot picked up the case and struggled with it to the door. The

4

singing patron sniggered and Monsieur D'Haricot heard words that questioned his virility. He chose to ignore them.

There was a design fault in many of the older properties in the area and this one was no different. The iron staircase was narrow, winding and screeched a protest at every step. The portmanteau banged against the railings. By the first floor landing, Monsieur D'Haricot was convinced whatever was inside had shattered into a thousand pieces. The barman had followed him up and nudged him towards one of the bedrooms.

The door was not locked. The bedchamber was sparsely furnished and a stale odour lingered on the bedclothes. Monsieur D'Haricot had an excellent sense of smell, an attribute which had seen him through the war. On two occasions he was able to detect mustard gas and alert his comrades before they came to harm, earning him the nickname of 'le canari'. He regretted it now as, depositing the portmanteau on top of the worn bedspread, he sniffed an incongruous mixture of cigarillo and lavender.

'Does Madame Chapleau stay here often?' he asked.

'She comes when she comes, and goes when she goes,' the man mumbled. Monsieur D'Haricot thought he said 'where' rather than 'when' and glanced towards the open fireplace, which had metal rungs placed at intervals heading up the chimney.

The barman held out a palm, expecting a tip despite not having helped with the case. Monsieur D'Haricot reached in his pocket for a small coin. The man clenched his fist over it, then made his way downstairs. Monsieur D'Haricot hesitated before following him. He glanced at the turquoise portmanteau, at the door, then back to the case. There was no clanging to indicate Madame Chapleau was on her way up. The case would be locked, of course, he told himself, sliding his fingers along the fasteners. The metal clicked and the bars sprung up. A quick peek could do no harm.

He eased the top cover of the portmanteau up to prevent creaking and averted his eyes from the pair of ladies' red silk drawers. A glimmer of steel below the underwear caught his attention and he lifted the knickers, which had been poorly disguising a machine with valves, wire coils and complex circuitry. He didn't recognise the specific equipment, but had an idea it was for sending telegrams. The identification marking on the side was not French. There was only one reason Madame Chapleau would have an alien instrument in her possession. It explained her otherwise inexplicable lack of enthusiasm for La Marseillaise.

Victoire was a foreign spy.

'Oh, you've found it.' Madame Chapleau had ascended the stairs like a nymph and entered the room without him hearing. Monsieur D'Haricot turned, still holding the underwear. 'I didn't expect a gentleman to handle a lady's private vestments.'

Monsieur D'Haricot blushed. 'I was looking for your hand cream. I didn't expect a French lady to have foreign telegraph equipment in her portmanteau.'

Madame Chapleau moved closer and took a seat on the bed. 'What will you do? You won't report me, will you?' She retrieved a handkerchief from her pocket. Monsieur D'Haricot noticed a long-haired, long-necked goatlike animal embroidered in one corner. She dabbed her eyes, then blew her nose.

'I'm afraid it is my civic duty,' he replied.

Madame Chapleau stretched a hand to grab his wrist, then looked away in a flourish she had copied from a second-rate movie. 'These are difficult times, Louis-Philip. A girl must do what she can to survive.'

Monsieur D'Haricot drew back. 'I'm sorry, Victoire.' He marched to the door and down the stairs, tripping on the bottom step and tumbling into the bar area to bump into François's protruding belly. 'Excuse me.' He sidestepped the barman and exited the bistro.

He hadn't realised the café was dim until he stood in the sunlight and squinted along the street in search of a public telephone kiosk. There was one on the corner. He hurried towards it, only to find the booth occupied by a fur-clad Madame. The faux fox head was crushed against the glass, pleading for release.

Sensing he had been followed from the café, he glanced down the street to see the drunken patriot stagger against a shop front. He tapped on the glass to encourage the lady to finish her conversation, but she was not to be hastened. He opened the kiosk door and grappled the receiver from her hand.

'The country's need is greater than yours,' he explained.

The lady's indignation was about to spill out into bad language.

'Vive la France!' Monsieur D'Haricot declared, punching an arm in the air. His movement was curtailed by the enclosed space of the box.

'I am from Belgium,' the lady answered.

'That cannot be helped.' Monsieur D'Haricot managed to edge her out of the booth. He grabbed the door and pulled it closed, keeping hold of the inside handle to prevent the lady reentering.

He dialled the number and asked to be put through to his contact. The call did not take long. Returning the receiver to its holder, he felt a pang of regret. Madame Chapleau was an old acquaintance, but that counted less than a sou when it came to the defence of his country.

The Belgian lady was speaking to a policeman. Her crooked nose poked into the officer's notebook as if it could write the report for him. Monsieur D'Haricot had no desire to explain his actions to a traffic official, but it was either walking past them or facing the now not-so-drunk patriot marching towards him. His quick wits came to his rescue.

'Fire, fire,' he yelled, pointing across the street at a patisserie.

Three pedestrians, a woman and two gentlemen panicked, getting in each other's way. Monsieur D'Haricot slipped down a side alley and emerged in a familiar part of the arrondissement. He waited a moment outside a bookshop, then went on his way.

The following day he received a telegram requesting that he attend headquarters. It came directly from the General. Confident he would receive a commendation, he dressed in his best suit. There was no wait. An aide showed him into the General's office on arrival. The General was seated in his favourite armchair. His ample form expanded to fill the space in the same way his personality took over the room, but he was not alone. Madame Chapleau was seated, cross-legged, on a couch drinking pastis.

'Come in,' the General encouraged. 'Take a seat.'

Madame Chapleau patted the cushion beside her. Monsieur D'Haricot remained standing.

'Don't be like that, Louis.' Madame Chapleau pouted.

'I do not understand why you are not in handcuffs,' Monsieur D'Haricot blurted out.

The General forced a laugh. 'Victoire is one of our best agents.'

'A double-crossing one,' Monsieur D'Haricot insisted.

'Madame Chapleau was on a mission set by me.' The General stood up to refill Victoire's glass from a bottle on his desk. He poured himself a drink and offered one to Monsieur D'Haricot, who refused.

'Have a drink, man. You passed the test.'

'What test?'

The General looked to Victoire to explain.

'There have been rumours of double agents and spies who babble under pressure. When your name cropped up—'

'My name?'

'I knew it was utter nonsense,' the General continued. 'It doesn't matter now. You passed.'

'You reported a friend whom you believed was a traitor,' Madame Chapleau said. 'That shows true loyalty to your country. It means you can be trusted.'

'It means I was set up. How long have you been working for the agency?'

Madame Chapleau batted her fancy eyelashes, but didn't answer.

'Don't take things personally,' the General said.

Monsieur D'Haricot's moustache twitched. His eyebrows lowered and he clenched and unclenched his fists. Finally, fearing he would say or do something that would not only ruin his career, but also jeopardise his liberty, he marched out of the room.

Halfway along the corridor he stopped. His nose never betrayed him. It was not the aniseed of French pastis he had smelled from the General's bottle, but the wormwood of German Kräuterlikör.

Chapter Two

Monsieur D'Haricot strode along the bank of the Seine, fuming at how he had allowed Victoire to humiliate him without recourse. Two city waifs dived, semi-clad, into the river and he moved aside to avoid the splash although the time of year, as well as his temper, warranted the cool down. In a heated moment his grandmother, a noted music hall singer from Saint Denis, had downed a glass of champagne laced with arsenic intended for a taunting rival. She collapsed into the orchestra pit and died in the arms of the lead violin, teaching the young Louis-Philip that revenge was a dish best served cold.

His grandfather, a poilu in Napoleon III's infantry, imprinted on the young Louis-Philip the need for adequate means of transport. A speedy exit was likely at least once during a young man's dalliances.

He contemplated his grandparents' teachings and watched the boys duck under the water.

Zut.

He had abandoned his bicycle hitched onto the back of Madame Chapleau's Delahaye 135. Considering Madame Chapleau's driving, even in a day, anything could have happened to it. Retrieving it was top priority. He continued his walk home, his mind engaged in devising a plan that would not only result in the recovery of his bicycle, but would also score a point back on Victoire.

Madame Chapleau was a lady of the salon. It amused her to entertain the Parisian elite; politicians, intellectuals, philosophers, artists, writers, poets, musicians, people with pimples on their noses, even organists. No doubt there would be one or two agent provocateurs among her devotees and valuable information could be had when fine wine and expensive cognac loosened tongues. Heretofore, he had not been invited to such a soiree. Given the current situation, he doubted that should he present himself at her apartment while a gathering was in swing, and innocently request the return of his bicycle, she would refuse him entry.

With a firm idea in his head, Monsieur D'Haricot increased his pace. Once he reached his apartment, a telephone call to a school friend, who also happened to be a music hall singer, was all it took to be in possession of the date and time of Victoire's next cocktail party.

Madame Chapleau's apartment was in the 5th arrondissement. There were considerations to be made. Was it wiser to dress for a society reception or simply for a cycle ride? On the grounds that a gentleman should be prepared for any potentiality, he settled for a lounge jacket with breeches and long hose, which served neither purpose. He completed his couture by positioning his cycling cap on his head and pulling the brim down to ensure it didn't fall off.

Monsieur D'Haricot rapped on Madame Chapleau's front door. He handed his card to the major-domo and explained the need for his impromptu call. The man twisted the card between his fingers, giving time for Monsieur D'Haricot to hear the laughter streaming from a side room. With the merest upturn of his lips, the manservant conveyed his approval of the visit. Monsieur D'Haricot was invited over the threshold and escorted into the lady's parlour, where he removed his cap and stuffed it in his pocket.

A cloud of blue smoke hovered in the air and it took a moment for Monsieur D'Haricot's eyes to adjust. The room was filled beyond decency. Blurred figures pressed against him. The ladies smelt of rose water and the gentlemen of cigars and opium – at least that was the way round he imagined. A figure of a gentleman in a maroon velvet jacket and matching cravat came into focus, seated at an upright piano, stretching his fingers over lime green keys. The ample soprano resting an elbow on the piano lid was smoking a slender cigarette from a holder, forming circlets of smoke from puckered lips.

Victoire was nowhere to be seen. Monsieur D'Haricot scanned the room, ears primed to pick out her throaty accent. He noticed the scantily dressed young lady approach out of the side of his eye.

'Tell me, are you a Chartreuse man or a Benedictine?' she asked.

Turning to answer, he realised that "scanty" did the lady too much justice. The silver feather boa failed to cover what it should and the lady was not as young as he first imagined.

'I am not and never have been a servant of the cloisters,' he answered, keeping his gaze three centimetres above her head.

'Heavens no, darling, I'm talking about your cocktail.'

'He must have a Calvados sidecar,' another voice said. Monsieur D'Haricot felt a hand on his right shoulder. 'I have no idea who you are,' the second person tittered, 'but I know you will love one of those.'

Monsieur D'Haricot expected from the lightness of pitch to confront a young lady, but beneath the face paint, more suited for the Moulin Rouge than St Germain, he recognised masculine canine teeth and a prominent Adam's apple. The vampish young man flicked ash from his cigarillo onto Monsieur D'Haricot's spit-and-polished brogues. He lifted his gloved hand from Monsieur D'Haricot's shoulder to snatch a Martini glass from the tray of a passing maid and pushed it towards Louis-Philip's chest.

'Salut,' he said.

Monsieur D'Haricot accepted the glass, but didn't drink. He was overwhelmed by the scent of orange peel and he hated orange peel more than he detested being patronised by young men who hadn't learned their manners. It was impossible that this cluster of misfits had information other than the latest fashion craze. His head told him he had made a mistake in coming, yet a sixth sense persuaded him that things were not what they seemed.

Placing the untouched cocktail on a wrought iron table with a flawless onyx top, he made his way deeper into the room. The smoke had cleared or his eyes had adjusted, because he was able to identify details. The pianist began playing and Monsieur D'Haricot realised that the man was a war veteran like himself. He could count himself fortunate that he had sacrificed merely a big toe. The man tinkling the ivories had lost an arm, which had been replaced by a prosthetic. It was difficult to say whether the new limb was a result of a surgeon's genius or an engineer's. The lustrous metal was not one that Monsieur D'Haricot was familiar with. From the flair with which the musician played each note, he suspected that the lightweight, strength and adaptability of the material would make it ideal for a bicycle frame.

He advanced towards the piano. The pianist's natural arm looked less than flesh and blood. The skin was pale and the veins bulging across his knuckles looked like they might burst. Monsieur D'Haricot searched for his monocle, but before he could position it he was waylaid by Madame Chapleau. He had not recognised her in a red wig and Sub-Continental shawl. The manner by which she snatched his elbow, causing his monocle to fall back into his pocket, reinforced his mistrust and a backward glance as she drew him towards the balcony suggested that the piano was the source of the blue smoke.

The balcony window was framed by silk damask curtains that shimmered as the late afternoon sunlight tried to break into the party. A manservant moved to close the curtains behind them.

'I did not expect to find you here,' Madame Chapleau scolded.

'I simply came for my bicycle.' Monsieur D'Haricot had the wits to keep to his story. Madame Chapleau eyed his breeches and hose, then gave a high-society snort of amusement.

'Oh, you mean that jumble of metal and rubber? I had my man deliver it to the scrap merchant.'

Monsieur D'Haricot's face turned white then purple. Words failed him. He stamped one foot and then the other, bringing it down hard on the toes of a statue of a naked maiden, hoping to break them. 'Madame,' he spluttered. 'That was a 1935 roadster.'

'So-o-o last year,' Madame Chapleau smiled. 'We can provide you with more suitable transport.'

We.

The personal pronoun was not lost on Monsieur D'Haricot. He took a step sideways and his hostess had to reach out an arm to prevent him toppling over the low balcony wall.

'You are being "un cul".'

'Pardon me madam, but I am no four-legged fool. If I were I would have no need of a bicycle.' Monsieur D'Haricot thought his answer somewhat droll and, despite the shock of being informed his bicycle was soon to be no more, he allowed an inkling of a smile to curve his lips. His hostess, however, seemed bored of his company.

'You should not be here, Louis-Philip. You must leave immediately. Do not fear, I shall have a new bicycle delivered to your door.'

She pulled back the curtains and glided into the room. Monsieur D'Haricot stood for a moment, then followed in her wake. He noticed the pianist turn to give Madame Chapleau a glance of annoyance. The man jerked his head towards the door in a mechanical manner. Until that flicker, Monsieur D'Haricot had been eager to leave the debauchery, but being ushered away, he felt inclined to stay. Something was afoot, and it was his duty as a French patriot to discover what.

He bowed to his hostess and made his way towards the door, waving farewell to his new friends. He sensed Victoire's eyes on his back. Calculating his speed with the precision of a lizard flicking its tongue at a fly, he reached the door in time to block the maid carrying the cocktails. Monsieur D'Haricot had never been on the stage, but from his grandmother's tales he knew how to achieve a Shakespearean actor's 'points'. A puff of the chest, a rise of the chin, a squaring of the shoulders and he was ready to give his final address. He thrust both arms in front of him. The maid's tray was lifted from her palm. Glasses of colourful, sticky alcohol hurled through the murky air to spill their contents on false nails, wigs and gowns.

The guests froze. As their throats thawed, gasps rose like the whistling of steam from an overboiled kettle. Monsieur D'Haricot brandished a silk handkerchief which he swiped from his top pocket and proceeded to wipe at sleeves and skirts, dashing from one to another, causing irredeemable damage to the delicate fabrics.

'No, no, please stop. This dress is Paris chiffon.' A lady waved her fan at him. Monsieur D'Haricot's trained eyes spotted writing on the silk. He snatched it from the lady and pretended to cool the air. A uniformed manservant advanced towards him and he stuffed the fan into the opposite pocket from his cap, swirled on his heels and dashed out of the room.

Scurrying along the street, he was disappointed to find the only creature following him was an alley cat. He put that down to the fish paste on his breath from lunch. The thought of the fan in his pocket made Monsieur D'Haricot's fingers itch. He was too close to Madame Chapleau's apartment to pull it from his pocket and examine it, but there was sufficient distance between where he stood and his pied-à-terre to check the lettering on the fan. If necessary, he could dispose of it before he reached his front door.

This would not have been possible were he riding his bicycle. Monsieur D'Haricot was not the type of sentimental gentleman who afforded a mode of transport a name, like 'la belle Clodette' for instance, but he felt a pang of sorrow knowing he would never again feel the smooth workings of his roadster beneath his thighs.

Absurdité.

Victoire had promised him a new model and, although he did not trust her on matters of national security, he had no reason to doubt she would honour her word. The new Clodette, he pictured, would be sleeker, speedier, more responsive to the touch than his previous bicycle. Madame Chapleau would not skimp on performance or comfort; a padded seat, spacers on the stem to give a handlebar height suited to his back, pedal extenders.

Monsieur D'Haricot had barely completed his wish list when he found he was on his avenue in Montparnasse.

Sacre bleu!

Monsieur D'Haricot did not consider himself a snob, despite there being a hint of English nobility on his mother's side. He was happy to live and let live with his neighbours, some of whom he would swear in court were cranky, obdurate and pigheaded, but it had been agreed on signing the lease that the pavement outside his apartment should be kept clear. He, and he alone, had permission to chain a vehicle to the wrought iron railings.

His nostrils sealed, forcing his puckered lips to release his rage. Monsieur D'Haricot stormed towards the diabolical monstrosity that was blocking the entrance to his apartment. If he had brought his umbrella he most certainly would have stuck it, bayonet-like, into the 'thing'. Granted, he would have required the reach of a professional boxer to do it damage. The wheeled machine – he could not bring himself to call it a bicycle – was over twice the size of a normal vehicle. It had two wheels of equal diameter, but the tyres were thickened to unnatural proportions, resembling the rear wheels of some new-fangled agricultural tractor. The seat was a plush, velvet covered armchair taken from the lounge of a gentleman's smoking club, with the pedals situated in a box in front, similar to the swell box of a pipe organ. A closer inspection of the workings showed them to be pneumatic.

'One must assume this… this… cranked sideways ship's helm is used for steering.' Monsieur D'Haricot spoke aloud. There was no-one in the street to answer him. He grabbed hold of the wheel and yanked it clockwise. It responded with the smoothness of a curling stone over ice. The front wheel shifted to the right. A female voice from somewhere beneath the steering mechanism informed him, with the tone of a schoolmistress, that less force should be applied while the vehicle was stationary.

'It is an abomination,' he spluttered. 'It is not "ma belle Clodette". It is "une répugnant Mathilde".' He addressed the nearest lamppost. 'It is most damnably not French.'

An urge had been growing since he set eyes on the machine to mount it and, despite his indignation, he could not resist. An inconspicuous iron step was set in the framework to assist a rider onto the 'bicycle' and Monsieur D'Haricot climbed aboard. The padded chair had a firm back to support his posture and the steering wheel was set so that he needn't lean forwards to such an extent that it discomforted him. The pedal box could have been measured by a tailor to fit the length of his legs. A dish on his left contained white pebbles smelling of peppermint and on his right he noticed a polished mahogany stick rising from the framework to a height at hand level. There appeared no clear reason for it being there, unless it served as a braking device and indeed he could see no other. He would have to set the vehicle in motion to test it.

The key to the padlock securing the machine to the gate was in the lock. Monsieur D'Haricot tutted.

Why, anyone could steal it.

Although not to his taste, it was certainly of value. He unchained the machine, recovered his cycling cap from his pocket and put it on before easing his feet against the pedals. The vehicle started with a screech that threatened to burst his eardrums. He grabbed a handful of the peppermints and stuffed them into his mouth. The sucking action popped his ears and he was able to continue. The screeching died down and he familiarised himself with the steering. The machine jerked and jolted onto the treelined avenue, and it took all of Monsieur D'Haricot's cycling skills to avoid a collision with the lamppost.

He had safely negotiated his way past three of his neighbours' houses and was gaining in confidence when he noticed a blue smoke swirling around him. A rapid glance down showed it was emanating from the underside of the vehicle. He assumed it was smoke, but there was no smell of burning. It grew in thickness to blur his vision and he grabbed at the mahogany stick to halt the machine. Instead it veered into a cavalry charge. He thrust the lever in the opposite direction. The smoke did not clear, but he was given a window through the haze to see ahead. He was approaching a corner.

Monsieur D'Haricot stuck out his right arm to indicate the direction he intended travelling, but his hand and fingers were lost in the smoke. He could not locate the bell on this new machine to give warning. Ahead of him, stepping out to cross the street directly in his path, were a young lad and his mother.

'Attention,' he called out. He swung the steering wheel to pull la répugnant Mathilde into the centre of the street, hoping no oncoming vehicles were travelling faster than the regulations permitted.

The bicycle swept past the pedestrians and he heard the boy turn to his mother and say. 'It isn't windy. Why is that cap floating in midair?' Monsieur D'Haricot snatched the cap from his head.

'What cap are you talking about?' He heard the mother ask. 'Are you making up stories again? Your father will not approve.' The boy was pulled by the hand across the road, out of the way of the monstrous machine.

Monsieur D'Haricot scratched his head. The mother and child had reacted as if the weird contraption didn't exist – only his cap, which rose above the blue smoke. It was odd the mother hadn't commented on the smoke. He steered the répugnant Mathilde round the corner with no further incident and relaxed into the chair. Strange as the machine was, riding it did bear a resemblance to cycling, without the need to adjust his balance on the pot-holed street thanks to the wide tyres. Confident he was in control, he ran his left hand beneath the steering wheel to investigate and felt a handle, which he grasped. Without warning, the machine pulled up. The forward momentum knocked him out of the armchair and onto the steering column, where he dented his nose on the helm.

He should have expected sensitive controls and muttered a curse at his stupidity. He dabbed his nose with his handkerchief, convinced that it was about to spout blood like a geyser. It didn't. He dismounted to stand on the pavement, replaced his cap on his head and looked onto the road.

Where was the bicycle?

He could see across the street towards the patisserie with fresh croissants in the window, but when he sniffed the air, he wasn't rewarded by the buttery smell that he had anticipated. An acrid, metallic, decidedly blue odour choked his throat. He was sure even the most erudite language professors would not have a word to describe the smell.

He continued to gaze at the empty space where the bicycle should have been. Gradually the top of the armchair appeared, floating in midair like a magical carpet from the tales of Scheherazade. Monsieur D'Haricot rubbed his eyes and the rest of the vehicle materialised. He approached it with caution. The blue smoke had vanished. The bicycle was as it had been when he freed it from the unlocked chains.

Impossible!

Monsieur D'Haricot had the benefit of a French education. He had read books written in America as well as Europe. Furthermore, thanks to his experience in the trenches, he was horribly familiar with the effect noxious gases could have on the human body and on the mind. He examined his hands for burns and paused to consider his breathing. Apart from an increased heart rate, which was to be expected after his ordeal, his body's physiological functions were normal. His eyes were not streaming with tears, his throat was not aflame and there were no dancing green elephants obscuring his vision.

While he was deconstructing what had occurred, he saw a police officer stride towards him. The man had his eyes set on Monsieur D'Haricot and it was pointless trying to evade him.

'Is that your vehicle?' the officer asked.

Monsieur D'Haricot was unsure of the answer. He had assumed it was the bicycle that Victoire had promised him, but on consideration, she couldn't have provided it in the short time it had taken him to walk home from her apartment.

'I have ridden it,' he responded.

The police officer made a show of examining the machine, walking round it and tapping the wheels with his baton. A puff of blue smoke rose and circled the officer's feet before evaporating into the surrounding air. Monsieur D'Haricot's eyes bulged. The man's legs had disappeared below the knees.

'Perhaps, officer, it would be wiser not to touch the machine,' he offered, fearing he would lose sight of the man entirely.

The officer frowned. 'I shall be the judge of that, monsieur,' he said, leaning into the vehicle. He stretched out an arm to push a button beside the seat, which Monsieur D'Haricot had not previously been aware of. A bell sounded, not unlike the ringing of a normal bicycle bell. Monsieur D'Haricot gaped at the policeman's hand, expecting the fingers to melt or turn blue.

The policeman produced a huffing noise which rose from deep in his chest. 'Everything appears to be in order,' he said with obvious disappointment. 'But you cannot park your machine there.'

'Oh?'

'No. You are blocking the entrance to the residence of Monsieur Otocey.'

Monsieur D'Haricot turned to look at the house in question. Although it was less than a kilometre from his own apartment, he had not realised that the town house of Nicolas Otocey, the notorious astrologer, was here. He noted that the police officer, like the great man himself, did not use Otocey's title of Vicomte.

'I shall move it at once, officer.' Monsieur D'Haricot tapped the brim of his cap. He did not instantly mount the machine, waiting for the man to depart, but the policeman was keen to make sure his instructions were carried out. 'Yes... well...' Monsieur D'Haricot made grunting sounds as he considered his exit. Feeling he could delay no longer, he mounted the machine under the police officer's eye and wriggled in his seat.

How was he to drive the vehicle, under the scrutiny of the French law, without producing the smoke that would cause the effect of invisibility?

'Bless my soul, what a magnificent chargeur.' A voice spoke from behind the police officer. Monsieur D'Haricot saw a gentleman in a green, double-breasted woollen overcoat complete with silk scarf and emerald Fedora. The smell of sandalwood eau de cologne wafted from the gentleman towards the street corner, cloaking the unpleasant odours rising from the sewer grate. The speaker carried a walking cane of a red wood that may have been American. He twirled the handle with flair. Monsieur D'Haricot imagined the figures carved into the wood were performing a native ritual and glanced at the clouds, anticipating rain.

'Is there a problem, officer?' the man asked.

The stranger was shorter than the policeman, but he carried himself with a confident air. The officer automatically cowered to assume an inferior attitude. 'The owner is moving his bicycle on, Monsieur,' he assured the gentleman.

The newcomer took a step back to get a better view of Monsieur D'Haricot seated above him. Even without his monocle, Monsieur D'Haricot recognised the man's face from photographs in the newspaper. It was Nicolas Otocey himself.

'You are the owner of this fine beast,' Otocey said. It was a statement rather than a question.

'I explained to the officer—' Monsieur D'Haricot began, trailing off so that he did not need to answer.

'Indeed. Then we shall have plenty to talk about.' Monsieur Otocey glanced at his wrist, pulling the sleeve back to reveal his timepiece. It was unlike the wristwatches Monsieur D'Haricot had seen worn in the trenches, where having the time to hand, so to speak, was vital. The bracelet of Otocey's watch had a feminine feel. Monsieur D'Haricot did not doubt it was pure gold. Embossed in the metal were zodiac figures. The ornate strapping left little room for a face to display the time.

Otocey paused, giving Monsieur D'Haricot adequate opportunity to appreciate the ostentation on show, then with a deliberate movement he adjusted the side button to move the hands forward four revolutions. The watch clicked four times. With each click the light around them darkened. Otocey raised his wrist to present the watch face towards Monsieur D'Haricot. It would not have been possible to tell the time in the fading sunlight, were it not for the fluorescent glow from the hands.

'I'm afraid we do not have time today,' Otocey said brazenly. 'Are you free tomorrow morning?'

'I don't believe I have any appointments in my diary,' Monsieur D'Haricot replied, trying to copy the other man's air of superiority without laughing. The result was a lion's roar followed by a mouse-like squeak.

'Good, we can have coffee or something stronger—'

'Coffee would be acceptable.'

Monsieur Otocey tapped his cane on the ground three times, then turned to enter his house. The police officer had been standing motionless since the sky darkened, but at the taps he stirred. He stared at Monsieur D'Haricot with glazed eyes.

'Can I help you, sir?' he said.

'I was looking for a spot to park my bicycle for the evening,' Monsieur D'Haricot said.

The police officer looked both ways along the street. 'I would leave it here, if I were you,' he answered. 'It will be perfectly safe. This is my beat and I shall be on patrol all night.'

Monsieur D'Haricot ran his fingers along his moustache, regaining his composure before thanking the policeman. It didn't seem wise to argue that he was the one who had ordered the bicycle to be moved in the first place. Instead he climbed down and made a show of rubbing his handkerchief against the wheel that the policeman had prodded. He gave several backward glances as he made his way, on foot, along the pavement towards the corner and his apartment.

The clock on his mantelpiece registered the time to be fifteen minutes past ten o'clock, which fitted with the setting of the sun, but not with the fact that he had left Madame Chapleau's cocktail party shortly before five. He had heard the bells of Saint Sulpice declare the hour on his walk home. His pace had been no slower than normal, and the incident with the weird bicycle, plus his encounter with Otocey, could not have taken more than forty minutes. It should be quarter past six or half past at the latest.

It had been a strange day, he decided. He unbuttoned his waistcoat. Decidedly strange. He settled in his armchair with a cognac. Something hard poked into his thigh. Reaching into his pocket he pulled out a lady's fan. The dalliance with the bicycle had caused him to forget his victory of snatching it at the party. To his disappointment, the ink spot he had noticed was not an address or telephone number. It was nothing more than a drink stain. He tossed the hand fan on the table.

So much for his great attempt at infiltrating Victoire's secret society.

The fan fell at a crooked angle. Monsieur D'Haricot did not like crooked angles. He put his glass on the table and reached to straighten the accessory. The stain took on the shape of a childish drawing and he realised he had seen the design before, that afternoon in fact, carved into the red wood cane belonging to the mysterious Vicomte Otocey.

Chapter Three

The Vicomte had not specified a time for Monsieur D'Haricot to visit, but ten thirty seemed a polite midmorning hour for coffee. The sky was clear and there was no need for an umbrella, but Monsieur D'Haricot felt unarmed without one. He strode along the street swinging it in front of him like a sword stick. The répugnant Mathilde was parked outside the Vicomte's house where he had left it the previous evening. He noted it was now attached by a golden chain to a fire hydrant on the edge of the pavement. Oddly, the key was in the padlock, as it had been before.

He skipped up the three steps to the door and chapped the lion-headed knocker. The door was opened by a manservant, who claimed not to have been made aware of the invitation, and had not seen fit to roll down his shirt sleeves or put on his jacket before answering. Monsieur D'Haricot was requested to wait in the hall while the master of the house was informed of his arrival. Under normal circumstances, Monsieur D'Haricot would have made use of the opportunity to have what Madame Chapleau would call 'a nose around', but he had the eerie suspicion that he was being watched by numerous pairs of eyes hidden behind pictures – indeed not only pairs, but trios and quartets of telescopic organs. The oil painting of the one-eyed Wotan, the stuffed grizzly bear in the corner, the statue of the three-headed Cerberus, even the aspidistra had whatever it was they had primed against him. Monsieur D'Haricot edged away from the Grecian urn with its naked Olympians to knock against the carved American totem pole which was doubling as a coat and hat stand. He slotted his umbrella into the

21

appropriate compartment, although he had not been relieved of his outer clothing by the manservant.

'Nicolas will see you in the sunken garden.' The manservant descended the stairs with the stealth of a monitor lizard. Monsieur D'Haricot was taken aback by the butler's use of Otocey's given name, but hoped his face did not show lines of snobbery. He waited to be directed to the aforementioned garden. The man stood rigid, unflinching as the marble surrounding them. Monsieur D'Haricot's moustache twitched. The collection of artefacts, reinforced by the smell of furniture polish, transformed the hallway into a museum. He averted his gaze from the manservant and his eyes fell on a slender grandfather clock, which he believed was a style favoured in Normandy.

'You're admiring Nicolas's clock?' the butler said.

'A fine instrument,' Monsieur D'Haricot agreed. 'But the time is wrong.'

'The time is never wrong,' the butler answered. 'Nicolas constantly reminds me of that. The clock may be,' he conceded.

'Of course.' Monsieur D'Haricot pretended to laugh. 'My father kept his mantel clock fifteen minutes fast. He was never late for an appointment.'

'That is of no concern or interest to me,' the butler replied. He turned to retreat up the stairs. Monsieur D'Haricot hesitated, then decided to follow the man. He was stopped on the first step by a snigger from a side room.

'You won't find the sunken garden on the first floor,' a voice said.

Monsieur D'Haricot looked round. A young person in their mid-twenties was lounging against the doorway of the room. It was impossible to tell if he or she was male or female, but it seemed unimportant. He or she wore an orange robe made from silk and patterned with dragons, reaching from their neck to their ankles. The arms were covered, but from the little Monsieur D'Haricot could see of the person's skin he could tell that they suffered from a terrible eczema. Soft boils had burst to ooze a yellowish fluid that stuck to the person's hands, bare feet and face. Monsieur D'Haricot didn't want to stare at the afflictions, but looking away seemed rude. He avoided eye contact.

'My name is Mala Kai,' the person said, holding out a bony hand. The fingers were a deep purple with blisters and open sores. The nails, those that weren't cracked, lifting from their beds or lost completely, were painted a mustard colour.

Monsieur D'Haricot was not squeamish and he had seen worse wounds caused by gas gangrene in the trenches. He accepted the outstretched hand, somewhat afraid to shake it too vigorously.

'What if I told you my boils were highly infectious?' Mala Kai said.

'I would say you were either a liar or a scoundrel,' Monsieur D'Haricot retorted. Mala Kai laughed again.

'Fortunately I am neither.'

Monsieur D'Haricot was about to ask what he or she was, but before he could think of a polite way of doing so, Nicolas Otocey appeared on the upstairs landing and leaned over the banister. He was dressed for bed, with a scarlet dressing gown wrapped around fern green satin pyjamas and a yellow nightcap perched on his head.

'I appear to have come at an inconvenient time,' Monsieur D'Haricot said, his face aflame. There was no point trying to hide his embarrassment.

'Not at all,' Nicolas Otocey assured him, making his way down. 'I hope my... secretary... has been entertaining you while I dressed. That will be all for now, my weasel.'

Mala Kai shrugged his or her shoulders and puffed a sound reminiscent of a spitting alpaca before sidling past Monsieur D'Haricot. He or she rubbed against Otocey as they slunk up the stairs.

'Forgive Mala – it's a little early for human form. Was there something I can do for you?'

Monsieur D'Haricot's gaze couldn't help following Mala Kai's spine up the stairs until it reached the landing, where it disappeared along a corridor. 'We met yesterday,' he reminded Otocey once Mala Kai was gone. 'You invited me here to talk about my... bicycle.'

'Ah.' Otocey snapped his finger and thumb. 'Of course, Monsieur—'

'D'Haricot. Louis-Philip.'

'Well, Louie, we call it a chargeur.'

'We?'

'We connoisseurs,' Otocey answered. 'Can I ask where you got your machine? It is one of the finest I have seen in Upper Paris.'

'It belongs to a friend,' Monsieur D'Haricot answered.

'Come, you can speak plainly. You are a Taurean.'

Monsieur D'Haricot's birthday was in late November, making him a Sagittarian, but he kept that information to himself.

'You can trust Taureans,' Otocey continued. 'Unlike Scorpions. Not that Scorpions will lie to you – most are scrupulous to a fault. It is just that they only tell you what they feel you should know, which is usually very little, if anything. Indeed they would rather cut out their serpentine tongues than answer a direct question. I, on the other hand, am a Leo. Leos delight in telling complete strangers everything they know – which is usually very little, if anything.' Otocey gave a hearty laugh and thumped Monsieur D' Haricot's back. 'Robert will serve us coffee in the sunken garden. It is this way.' Otocey put out a hand to indicate a narrow, spiral staircase leading down from behind a rusty suit of armour.

Monsieur D'Haricot allowed his host to lead the way, following at a respectable distance. He expected the sunken garden to be laid out with flowerbeds, potted plants or at least some small water features, but when he spotted the bar counter, billiard table and shelves of bottles lined up in rows he realised his mistake. Tables and chairs were laid out in the manner of a traditional hostelry.

'Coffee, or something stronger?' Otocey asked. He had made his way behind the counter while Monsieur D'Haricot finished descending and was shaking a bottle containing a pink liquid. The air bubbles sank to the bottom. 'What's wrong?' Otocey noticed his astonishment.

'Nothing. I'm merely taken by the colour.' Monsieur D'Haricot looked round to see a bee vanish inside the trumpet of a sun-coloured daffodil in a violet vase on a table. 'Your garden is… vibrant.'

'I hadn't noticed,' Otocey answered. His voice betrayed a hint of pride.

'Isn't it deliberate?' Monsieur D'Haricot asked.

'You have read me well. Perhaps you have a touch of Cancer rising in your chart,' Otocey said. 'The colour is simply a counterbalance to the grey of Lower Paris.' He selected two glasses hanging from an oak panel above him and poured the drinks. 'Do you think your friend would be willing to sell me her chargeur?'

'Her?' Monsieur D'Haricot picked up on the pronoun.

'That is undeniably the chargeur of a lady,' Otocey said with the same conviction he displayed when declaring Monsieur D'Haricot to be Taurean.

Monsieur D'Haricot felt justified in his chagrin. He had no wish to be seen riding on the chargeur of a woman. 'The vehicle belongs to Madame Chapleau, I believe,' he said.

'Ah, you mean the vivacious Victoire, a Gemini – as you know.'

Otocey was toying with him like a tyrant would with a traitor. Monsieur D'Haricot had not considered Victoire's astrological sign, but he resisted the urge to ask the question Otocey was hoping he would. 'I haven't met Victoire's twin,' he said, accepting the glass of pink liquor and allowing the sugary bouquet to waft under his nose.

Otocey raised his right eyebrow. He crossed his eyes, sending a probing beam through Monsieur D'Haricot, then chuckled. 'I can assure you that you have, although I do not believe you are trying to deceive me.' He swallowed a mouthful from his own glass while he waited on a response. Monsieur D'Haricot did not reply. Otocey licked his lips with his tongue. The muscle was either larger than most or semi-detached, because it reached below the bottom of his chin with ease to catch a drip.

Monsieur D'Haricot had a desire to push past Otocey and leave the building. His pride would not allow him to do so without first procuring a victory, however trivial. He took a sip of the drink and was pleased to discover it was premium quality champagne. The bubbles bounced down his throat and sprang into his stomach, soothing his nerves, firing his resolve and loosening his own tongue. 'I was drawn to your walking cane yesterday,' he said. 'The carvings on it are quite unique.'

'You are mistaken,' Otocey answered. 'They are common symbols in the Americas.'

'I am not familiar with the Americas. There was one symbol that especially intrigued me,' Monsieur D'Haricot persisted. 'It looks like a matchstick dog.'

'The coyote,' Otocey put his glass down on a table and rolled up the sleeve of his dressing gown in delicate movements, making sure no fold was greater than another. The profile of a coyote's head was tattooed on his forearm. The animal's eye burnt blood-red, but its half-lip was parted in a smile. One ear was cocked at a quizzical angle. 'The teacher or the trickster – take your pick. It is the bringer of good fortune or of mischief, but ever with a smile. Laughter, as they say, is a better medicine than laudanum.'

'I have not heard that adage,' Monsieur D'Haricot said.

'I am sure there are many sayings your delicate ears have not permitted to enter your skull,' Otocey replied, moving on before Monsieur D'Haricot could take offence. 'What particularly interested you about my coyote?'

'I saw the same design a few hours before I met you. It was scribbled onto the hand fan of a lady.'

'Aha, we come to the crux of your visit,' Otocey snatched upon his words. 'You believe it was no coincidence. It is true I have a number of lady fans, but not ladies' fans.' He tittered, showing his off-white teeth. A slither of ham hung from his upper wolf fang.

'I have the fan in question,' Monsieur D'Haricot announced.

'You have a lady's fan,' Otocey mocked. He sat down and rested his chin on the palm of his right hand, keeping his elbow on the table. 'You must tell me more.'

'It is not what you seem to be inferring. I am a French gentleman. What is more I am a patriotic French gentleman. I suspect there is a plan to somehow disrupt the running of our great country. You are a Vicomte, from a noble family. I look to you for guidance.'

Otocey puckered his lips. He changed hands to lean on his left. His eyebrows did a dance, resembling a cross between a quickstep and a tango. Finally he lifted his glass and drank the dregs, swirling the liquid around his mouth before spitting it into a spittoon. He stood up, appearing to grow in height until he towered over Monsieur D'Haricot. 'Since you are a friend of Victoire Chapleau, I must trust you,' he said.

Monsieur D'Haricot waited. Otocey moved to check the door they had entered through was shut. The room had no windows and Monsieur D'Haricot felt uncomfortably confined. Otocey approached close to him, breathing sour alcohol onto his face.

'Juan will be performing in Le Crochet on Friday evening,' he whispered.

'Le Crochet? This Friday?' Monsieur D'Haricot repeated the details. Otocey nodded, fearful of raising his voice. 'Le Crochet in Montmatre?' Monsieur D'Haricot strove to clarify.

'In Rouen, fool,' Otocey hissed. 'You said you were given the fan.'

Monsieur D'Haricot thought it wiser not to mention that he had taken the item without the owner's consent. 'Thank you for the information.'

'Given in strict confidence,' Otocey reminded him.

Monsieur D'Haricot tilted his head in agreement. 'I should leave. There are matters I have to attend to before I set out.'

Rouen, he calculated, was 120km from Paris if he flew like a crow, but nearer 135km by road since he couldn't. Even if he still had La Belle Clodette he could not, in his present physical condition, have cycled there to arrive by Friday evening, it being Wednesday morning. He would be forced to break the habit of a lifetime and take a train to his destination, assuming there was a railway station in Rouen.

'There is no need for you to go yourself. Juan can be handled by an aide,' Otocey said.

'I like to do things properly,' Monsieur D'Haricot asserted. 'As I said, I am a French gentleman.'

'So am I, but I have never done anything proper in my life.'

'That is because you are a Vicomte.'

'It is because I am a clown.' Otocey forced a nasal snigger. 'Allow me to read your horoscope before you depart.'

'There is no need. I shall meet a stranger who will speak in a foreign tongue, most likely Spanish, and whom I should be wary of trusting.' Monsieur D'Haricot moved to the door and opened it. 'I can find my own way out.'

As he departed he heard Otocey mutter, 'How the deuce could he know that?'

Chapter Four

Monsieur D'Haricot's professional remit was safeguarding the country's German border, which involved the unsavoury task of keeping tabs on the National Socialist German Workers' Party. Being an educated man of the world, he was aware of Spanish politics, but the situation in Spain seemed less straightforward. It was like a flamenco dance, tapping heels one way then the other. King Alfonso XIII's abdication, elections and riots served to make the country volatile. He believed Casares Quiroga led a Republican government, but that could have changed during the short time he had spent with Otocey.

The enigmatic Juan could belong to any of the vying factions, or none. The business could have nothing to do with politics. He suspected Madame Chapleau of having her fingers in various pies – fine, silk-gloved fingers – but nonetheless entrenched in different aspects of private and public life. Furthermore, despite his assumption, Otocey had not confirmed that Juan was Spanish. Names could be misleading.

He did not ride his chargeur home. There was a great deal of the serpent in addition to the coyote about Vicomte Otocey, and the meeting had proved irksome. He was in no mood for battling with the mechanical monstrosity. The brisk walk would allow him to order his thoughts and consider his travel plans. Journeying to Rouen by train did nothing to soothe his nerves. He had heard from a medical friend that going through tunnels could leave a person permanently deaf and he knew a spinstress who would not travel by rail without first anointing herself in calming lavender oil. The thought concerned him, but worse was the fact that the self-styled trickster Otocey – why else would he have a wild dog tattooed on his arm – had deliberately got his birth sign wrong. An astrologer of the Vicomte's calibre would know immediately that he was no Taurean. It seemed a slight matter, but life was peppered with trivial minutiae that constantly niggled Monsieur D'Haricot.

Once home, he retrieved his case from beneath his bed and dusted it down. He was not sure how long he would be out of Paris and decided he should tell his neighbour where he was going, in case of a delay or mishap. The lady in question was hard of hearing, perhaps due to her love of railway journeys, and it took him two cups of coffee and a ginger tuile biscuit to explain. Thankfully, after checking railway timetables back in his apartment, he concluded that there was no requirement for him to leave Paris before Friday morning. He would be gone no more than two or three days, depending upon what Juan had to say. This thought pleased him because he only had two clean shirts and three starched collars.

Settling down to read the newspaper, he heard a knock at his door. On answering, a livery-clad messenger boy stuck an envelope into his hand and left his palm out to receive his tip. Monsieur D'Haricot rewarded him with no more than a sou. The envelope overpowered Monsieur D'Haricot with aromas of the East. He carried it at an arm's distance into his stuffy bachelor study and laid it on his desk. His silver letter opener was not where it should have been, but was located beneath a cushion. Its design, the shape of the Grand Tower designed by Monsieur Eiffel, was pointless. He could see the top of the monument by walking a few metres from his apartment, which no doubt was the reason the opener had been gifted to him by a cousin. Despite the novelty, the blade sliced open the envelope with professional ease.

He had deduced the missive was from Otocey. The contents were harder to fathom: a boat ticket and a map of the Seine as it flowed through Paris. A red ink dot punctured the map. The scrawled instructions read:

'My fine Piscean, you will find Gustav waiting for you at 12 noon, but do not delay. NO.'

He was being offered a puzzle and, working out that 'NO' was Otocey's initials and not a reinforcement of the prior instruction, Monsieur D'Haricot felt equal to it. He wore a pocket watch in his waistcoat, in preference to the more effete wristwatches which were the fashion among gentlemen like Otocey, and consulted it, making swift mental calculations. It was already past eleven thirty. There was insufficient time to pack then walk to the allocated spot, which was over 3km away. Unlike Otocey, he could not turn back the hands and expect the sky to lighten. Fortunately he had a plan.

Madame Chapleau would have advised him to toss the necessary items of clothing into his case in whatever haphazard fashion they landed, but that was not Monsieur D'Haricot's way. He wondered as he folded a black tie, in preparation for any eventuality on his assignment, why it had been Victoire's advice that had sprung to mind. He had been thinking of the lady a little too often, even before bumping into her on his bicycle.

There was space on top of his shirts for a book, which he selected at random from his shelf. The lid was closed, the locks snapped shut and the case propped on a chair while he changed into his cycling breeches and socks. He was out of his apartment and had locked the door ten minutes after reading the letter.

The répugnant Mathilde was where he had left it outside Otocey's door. He spotted Otocey's manservant spying on him through a ground floor window. Spying was not the correct word – the man made no attempt to conceal himself. Monsieur D'Haricot marched up the steps to the door and knocked. It took considerably longer than Monsieur D'Haricot expected for the manservant to answer. He put his case on the step while he waited and looked along the street at the growing traffic. The door opened.

'Did you forget something? Your umbrella, perhaps?' The manservant held it out for Monsieur D'Haricot.

He took it with more force than was necessary. 'I am taking possession of my chargeur and driving it here.' He had intended unfolding the map to show the butler, but holding the umbrella made the task awkward. He sheepishly handed the umbrella back to the manservant. 'Here,' he repeated, indicating the red dot. 'I would be obliged if you could arrange for someone to collect it.' Monsieur D'Haricot allowed the butler ten seconds to register the location before refolding the map.

'I shall confer with Nicolas to see if that is convenient,' the butler answered, somewhat put out. He shoved the umbrella back towards Monsieur D'Haricot. Monsieur D'Haricot accepted it and the manservant closed the door in his face.

He made his way to the chargeur and secured his case to the back before mounting with the dexterity lacking on the previous occasion. He wriggled into the seat and made his feet comfortable in the pedal box. There was no way of stopping the blue smoke, despite pulling every handle and pressing every button. He waited until the chargeur was enveloped, then moved the lever at his side to provide the allotted vision.

The Parisian streets were filling and he had not become accustomed to other drivers ignoring him, but he was an experienced cyclist and his confidence grew. Mathilde, although incomparable to Clodette, was not as repugnant as the name he gave her implied. The meeting station on the Seine was on the left bank, further down river, past the Jardin des Plantes. The grand bells of Notre Dame were chiming the hour. Monsieur D'Haricot parked his chargeur, recovered his case and hastened towards the riverbank in search of the man called Gustav.

A gauche lad dressed in rowing shorts, a faded white collarless shirt and a blue blazer belonging to a larger and older man, was leaning against the railing looking towards the river. There was a paint stain on the elbow of the blazer, which appeared to have been there before the added patch. Nobody else was in sight.

'Bonjour, Monsieur Gustav?' Monsieur D'Haricot said. He had taken time before leaving his apartment to pick up his bowler hat. He removed it to address the young man. The lad turned round and Monsieur D'Haricot noticed he had the same haggard expression as Mala Kai, without the skin impairments.

'You're not what I expected,' the lad said in a disagreeable manner. He spat on the pavement to clear his throat and Monsieur D'Haricot noticed there was blood in the saliva.

Monsieur D'Haricot reached in his pocket for his handkerchief to offer to the lad. The boy pulled a knife from his pocket and flicked it open. He jerked the blade at Monsieur D'Haricot.

'What is the meaning of this?' Monsieur D'Haricot set his hat back on his head. He raised his clenched fists to his face to protect himself. 'I was sent here by the Vicomte Otocey.'

The lad laughed. 'That old geezer.'

Monsieur D'Haricot had suspected the boy was not French, not only by his lack of bespoke tailoring, but by his disregard for flair and finesse. 'You have made a mistake and so have I,' he answered, in English. 'I am not the man you are expecting. I was sent to meet

Gustav.'

'Gustav is—' the boy began. Before he could finish he slumped towards Monsieur D'Haricot, who stepped aside and allowed him to fall to the paving.

'—behind you,' a voice said. Monsieur D'Haricot saw a hatted head, neck and upper body above the railing. One hand held a wooden baton. He nodded at Monsieur D'Haricot. 'You were warned not to be late.'

Monsieur D'Haricot was about to plead his case, but with a flick of his baton Gustav indicated there was no time for talking. The lad was beginning to stir. Gustav's head descended towards the river and Monsieur D'Haricot sidestepped past his assailant to peer over the side. A ladder was attached to the bank and a flat-bottomed boat was moored to it. Gustav was on board untying a rope.

A hand reached for the leg of Monsieur D'Haricot's breeches. It fell short, but managed to seize his ankle and tug at his sock. Monsieur D'Haricot kicked out, feeling a squishiness as his shoe made contact. The barge was floating away from the mooring. He freed himself from the boy's grip.

'You will have to jump,' Gustav called. 'It isn't far.'

Giant cogs ground against one another, drowning out the hissing from pistons. Three quarters of the deck was covered by machinery. The remainder was loaded with wooden crates, marked with letters, mainly 'O's and 'P's but there was one larger crate marked 'V'. Monsieur D'Haricot had scant knowledge of the inner workings of an elephant's body, but if asked to sketch a mechanical version, it would look somewhat similar. There was a square metre of free space for him to jump onto. He closed his eyes, but realising immediately that was foolish he opened them and held onto his nose as he jumped from the bank towards the barge. He landed on a tarpaulin at the stern of the boat, which broke his fall. The canvas, miffed by his unannounced introduction, folded itself around him and he was unable to get to his feet without being dragged towards the deck. He could hear Gustav laughing.

'Welcome to the Souslamer, or Susie as I prefer to call her. Here, take my hand,' he offered.

Monsieur D'Haricot eschewed the aid. He swept aside the tarpaulin and got to his feet, wiping down his jacket and taking the extra seconds to brush sawdust from his sleeve. 'Who was the boy?' he asked.

'One of Caprice's kids,' Gustav answered. 'They aren't the brightest

– no better than a herd of goats.' Gustav gave an un-French guffaw.

Monsieur D'Haricot didn't appreciate the humour, but he smiled thinly. 'Where should I put my things?' he asked, holding out his travelling case.

'You'll need to stack them below deck.'

Monsieur D'Haricot looked for a hatch. The machinery wheels were accelerating, metal grinding metal and spitting out purple sparks. A lad in dirty dungarees hosed the pistons down with water, releasing steam that swirled between the crates. Monsieur D'Haricot watched the steam and Gustav watched Monsieur D'Haricot.

'What are you looking for?' Gustav asked.

'Nothing. Are you sure this vessel will get us to Rouen by Friday evening?' Monsieur D'Haricot asked. There was time, he calculated, to abandon ship at the next mooring and resume his planned itinerary.

'Have no fear, Monsieur.'

Monsieur D'Haricot knew that if he listened to Gustav's chuckling a minute longer, he would throttle him before the barge passed under the Austerlitz railway viaduct – ship's captain or not. 'How do I get below deck?' he asked, expecting the reply to be accompanied by amusement at his ignorance of nautical matters. Gustav stopped laughing and narrowed his eyes.

'Susie is no different from other aquatrans.'

'I didn't mean to insult your craft,' Monsieur D'Haricot said. 'I haven't been on an… aquatran,' he paused to consider how to play the situation, 'for some time.'

Gustav furrowed his brows until they tied themselves in a Celtic knot. 'How did you get here?' he asked.

'By chargeur.'

Gustav blew air through his teeth. He removed his captain's cap and scratched his bald scalp. 'You must be one of the stagers,' he said.

Monsieur D'Haricot tapped the side of his nose with a finger. Gustav puckered his lips, then nodded. He looked round the deck of his aquatran. 'Not exactly shipshape, is it? It's not my fault. The committee dumped this stuff on me at Fontainebleau.' He used the side of his foot to shove aside the box marked 'V'. Monsieur D'Haricot heard a creak from inside.

'It is all right. This one has already been emptied,' Gustav explained. 'Here.'

Monsieur D'Haricot saw the trapdoor, a square of salt-seasoned wood standing out against the varnished boards. A twisted length of rope was attached to a rusty ring set in the wood.

'Do you take this boat out to sea?' Monsieur D'Haricot asked.

'Are you serious?'

Monsieur D'Haricot decided not to pursue his query. He bent to lift the rope and pulled. Nothing happened.

'Do you need a hand?' Gustav asked.

Monsieur D'Haricot turned his shoulder on him. After two more attempts, he realised the door slid across. He had to move the box further to the side to free the rollers. Metal steps led down to the innards of the boat.

'Take the second room on the left,' Gustav said. 'You'll have it to yourself, until Giverny.'

'You are picking up more passengers?'

'Regular omnibus service, we are,' Gustav replied, his hilarity returning.

Monsieur D'Haricot stood looking down, contemplating the descent. Gustav reached for his case and took it from him. Before Monsieur D'Haricot could object, Gustav tossed it down the hatch. Monsieur D'Haricot turned and put his foot on the first step without speaking. He lowered himself down with his eyes on the ship's captain. There were twelve steps.

By the time his toe touched the eighth, Gustav was out of sight. At the bottom a narrow corridor ran the length of the boat. Monsieur D'Haricot picked up his case and teetered along the passage to find the room. It was unlocked. He opened the door and entered. The cabin was narrow, with half the space taken up by bunk beds. The bottom bunk had less head room, but it gave access to the round porthole window. He set his case in the corner and looked for a peg to hang his jacket. Finding none, he took it off, folded it symmetrically and laid it on the top bunk with his bowler hat. He jackknifed his back to squeeze onto the bottom bunk with his toes banging against the back board.

The mattress was as thin as mille-feuille pastry and covered in crumbs. The blankets, one per bunk, were grey, woollen and damp. There was one pillow between the two bunks and he seconded it. He wriggled to make himself comfortable, regretting his failure to ask Gustav where the washroom was on board the boat. After five minutes he disentangled himself from the bunk and opened the door. His idea to return above deck was halted by the noise of a battering ram rattling the ceiling wood. The metallic clawing made him fear they had hit one of the Paris bridges. Gustav's legs and waist appeared on the ladder.

'Is everything in order?' Monsieur D'Haricot called along the corridor.

The remainder of Gustav's body appeared. 'Oui, oui, I was adjusting the tarpaulin. We can't pick up speed until we are clear of the Eiffel Tower, but according to my mother, hell is the only finality it is best not to prepare for. She was a Cancerian and liked to think she knew about such things.'

'Indeed,' Monsieur D'Haricot agreed. 'I was looking for the washroom.'

Gustav stiffened. 'You won't find namby-pamby pampering on board this boat.'

Monsieur D'Haricot assumed Gustav had misheard what he said, but let the matter rest. 'I shall be reading should you need me,' he said.

'You do that, sir. I'll make sure you know when lunch is served.'

Despite the gastric rumblings, Monsieur D'Haricot was not convinced his constitution would cope with a midday meal. His feet had not managed over the threshold and his head and neck recoiled, tortoise-like, into the shell of the room. He moved to his case and opened it to pick up the book. He examined the cover. It appeared to be a fantasy adventure, 20,000 Leagues under the Sea by Jules Verne, which was not at all the type of book he would choose to read. He wondered how it had bargained its way onto his shelf. The explanation came when he opened it and examined the frontispiece. Written there, in green ink was:

> To my dearest Louis-Philip,
> Enough! Enough!
> Victoire.

He supposed that he should know what was meant by Madame Chapleau's entreaty. A coded message, no doubt. Reading the book might offer a clue.

He sat on the edge of the bunk with his feet on the floor and read the opening chapter. His eyes flickered towards the door. His inattention didn't surprise him. The artwork was sufficient to tell him the book would not be of interest. Prototypes for underwater crafts had been in existence since the seventeenth century. Monsieur D'Haricot appreciated their unique advantage when it came to espionage, and he was acquainted with their technological design, but he did not see the point of the detailed description of a super submarine that was no more than the figment of a writer's imagination. How could that serve the country? From what he gathered, skipping through the chapters, Captain Nemo's 'Nautilus' would have its enemies die from uncontrolled laughter rather than pose a military threat.

He put the book down and peered out of the porthole window. The glass was steamed up and, disregarding the patterned water droplets, there was nothing to see. His ears were experiencing an unpleasant humming and his head was fending off sharp thrusts of pain. Sticking one finger in each ear canal helped ease the pressure. The boat rolled. There was a thwack at the window and Monsieur D'Haricot looked to see what appeared to be a giant catfish knock its head against the glass. He fell short of sharing it, but he was aware of the revolutionary temperament of Parisians. Even so, tossing catfish at passing boats was new. He rubbed the glass. The view remained blurred and watery.

The humming went, and his stomach returned to its proper position, but he remained nauseous. He needed fresh air. He got to his feet and left the cabin, travelling five rapid steps along the corridor before Gustav appeared from behind a blue door of what Monsieur D'Haricot believed, from the hissing within, was either a snake pit or the engine room.

'The dining room is in the other direction,' Gustav informed him with a smile. 'Cook has prepared catfish with green beans followed by delicate fruit tarts spiced with ginger.'

'I didn't realise the boat had a chef,' Monsieur D'Haricot said.

'Chef is too coarse a word, monsieur. The man is a sorcerer with sauces, a pastry perfectionist, a fish fanatic,' Gustav declared. He reached his right hand to grip his left shoulder and for a moment Monsieur D'Haricot feared Gustav was about to twist off his own joint. The shoulder clicked and Gustav let go. 'His speciality is crab,' he finished, raising his left arm in the air in a victory salute.

'I shall forego lunch, if you don't mind,' Monsieur D'Haricot apologised. 'I need to get air.'

'We won't be surfacing before Giverny, I'm afraid.'

'I'm sorry?'

'We are submerged, swimming beneath the water like a giant shark.' Gustav placed his greasy palms together and wiggled them in front of

Monsieur D'Haricot.

'I know what swimming is,' Monsieur D'Haricot flicked them away before they hit his nose. 'You mean to tell me this barge is an underwater machine.'

'The finest in Ecnarf.'

'Sorry? I'm not hearing well.'

'Perhaps your ears haven't popped from the descent,' Gustav suggested. 'Why don't you rest or finish your book? I'll let you know when we have docked in Giverny.'

'Giverny must be seventy kilometres from here. I shall need to use the bathroom before then.'

'Susie is not only the finest vessel on the Seine, she is also the fastest. We shall be in Giverny in an hour, give or take.'

'Give or take what?'

Gustav did not reply. Monsieur D'Haricot tried to sidestep past him, but Gustav managed to bend his body like a sideshow contortionist, with arms, legs and neck blocking the passageway. It was impossible for Monsieur D'Haricot to go anywhere except back to his cabin. He collapsed on the lower bunk bursting with frustration – no, it was unadulterated anger. This was not an emotion he was familiar with, but there was no other explanation for the racing of blood through his veins and the throbbing in his forehead. He was being treated like a recalcitrant child, screaming for a lollipop when he was being offered a Latin dictionary. He was convinced that Otocey and the people he was dealing with – despite them appearing to be true-born French citizens – were not on his side.

He needed a plan, but first he had to be better informed about his 'enemy' before initiating the rules of engagement. If his alimentation had been up to it, he would have accepted Gustav's offer of lunch and questioned him over the catfish and green beans. Since it wasn't, he would have to make do, a virtue decried by his mother. Gustav could not guard the corridor while he was eating, making exploration a possible option while he was thus occupied. He waited five minutes, marked by his pocket watch to the last second, before opening the cabin door to peek along the corridor. He could hear singing from the direction of the galley, a bawdy cabaret song about a down-on-his-luck sailor and a fallen woman. The chef, culinary maestro that he was, did not have a singing voice, caught somewhere between a baritone and a bathtub squawk, but he thrust the words out with gusto. Occasionally his voice cracked, like a chipped phonograph record, which Monsieur D'Haricot put down to a catfish bone.

He kept a foot in the door to make sure it didn't bang shut as he exited, then made his way on tiptoe in the opposite direction from the singing, towards the blue door. A buzzing sound was coming from inside, murmuring through the walls and causing the hinges of the door to vibrate. Monsieur D'Haricot stood outside, listening for voices. He heard none. Centimetre by centimetre, he eased his right hand to the door handle and felt the metal in his palm. It was surprisingly cold, forcing him to rethink his notion of there being a boiler in the room. Curiosity got the better of him and he turned the handle. The door slid open further than he intended. Immediately ten pairs of hands stopped working, ten heads looked up and nineteen eyes were upon him. The tenth worker was wearing an eye patch with a tricolour painted over the cover. No-one spoke.

Chapter Five

'Excuse me, I am looking for the captain,' Monsieur D'Haricot said.

The workers were all men, he assumed, although it wasn't obvious from the blue overalls and gloves that covered their bodies and the caps pulled low over their foreheads, concealing their eyebrows. What he did see appalled him. The pale skin on their shaved chins melted like wax on heated candles. Noses were at odd angles and ears slid down necks to jut out from collarbones. His sight adapted to the immense light in the room and he saw that certain individuals lacked limbs, while others had a grotesque excess.

The workers didn't move except to blink or breathe. The machines they stood beside were shining engines with pistons bobbing, belts turning and wheels whirling. The effect was hypnotic. Monsieur D'Haricot took a step into the room. The workers shuffled a step towards him in time to the hissing from a fan in the corner.

The movement reminded Monsieur D'Haricot of a chess game. He was not a master, but he had the notion that pawns did not move backwards. Then again, he was not a pawn. While he was thinking this, the army of amorphous engineers moved another step closer. He expected to smell decaying flesh over the odour of engine oil. Instead the room had the dankness of a cave.

A cave full of living corpses.

Monsieur D'Haricot gulped the saliva gathering in his throat. He put up his hand to stop the advance.

'Can I help you?'

Monsieur D'Haricot swung round to find the smiling captain

standing behind him. 'Who are these people?' he demanded.

'What people?' Gustav asked.

Blue smoke was drifting from the blades of the fan. It engulfed the room, swallowing the men but leaving the machines visible.

'There were men here,' Monsieur D'Haricot insisted. 'You can't fool me. I know about the blue smoke, although these engines seem immune to its effects.'

Gustav took hold of the door handle with one hand and gestured for Monsieur D'Haricot to leave the room with his other. Monsieur D'Haricot didn't move.

'It is not as it seems,' Gustav said. 'These sailors are not galley slaves, ha ha. They are not being ill-treated or forced to work against their will.'

His moustache was itching to twitch, but Monsieur D'Haricot kept his face stern.

'I thought you knew,' Gustav said. 'Didn't Otocey explain?'

'Non. There are several things Otocey forgot to tell me. Perhaps you would like to fill me in,' Monsieur D'Haricot answered.

Gustav laughed again, but the chortle stuck in his throat. 'There is nothing to tell. Some Upcomers find it easier to acclimatise than others.' He paused, then snapped his fingers. 'What you need is a cup of cocoa.'

'I'm sorry?' Monsieur D'Haricot assumed he had missed part of the conversation due to his unacclimatised hearing. 'What has cocoa to do with this?'

'We need to make an unscheduled stop to unload part of the cargo. I received news a minute ago. Unloading can be noisy. Cocoa helps.'

None of what Gustav said made sense. What communication had he received in the galley? How could they unload cargo if they couldn't surface until Giverny? How could cocoa help?

Monsieur D'Haricot said nothing. He allowed Gustav to escort him back to his cabin and waited until the captain brought him a mug of steaming cocoa with a dollop of pink cream floating on the surface froth.

'It smells delicious,' he said, wrapping both hands round the warm mug.

'Finest in France,' Gustav agreed. 'The cacao is from Côte d'Ivoire, but the secret ingredient is courtesy of yours truly.' Gustav formed a ring with his thumb and index finger, then kissed the tips, the way chefs did in humorous films.

Monsieur D'Haricot pretended to sip, then blew on the surface. 'I'd better let you get on with your duties. Thank you for the cocoa. I'm sure it will… do its job.' Gustav was standing outside the doorway and Monsieur D'Haricot used the side of his foot to slide the cabin door closed in his face.

Operating within the spatial confines of the cabin was a trick Monsieur D'Haricot learned from studying cine reels of Houdini. He knelt to set the mug on the floor, jutting his left leg in front of him in a move from a Cossack dance in order to open his case. He drew out the items he required – blotting paper, tweezers and a selection of paper strips held together by a piece of wool. Closing the case allowed him to use its flat surface as a worktable. It didn't take long to realise that if he wanted to preserve the cuffs of his shirt he would have to roll up his sleeves, a fashion he did not approve of.

He laid out the sheet of blotting paper, untied the wool to separate out the strips of paper, then, using the tweezers, he lifted the first strip and dipped it into the cocoa.

Zut!

He had forgotten to leave out his pocket watch to time the operation. He crumpled the paper and stuck it in his pocket, then retrieved the watch. Setting it on the case with the face visible, he began again with a new strip, picking it up with the tweezers to avoid contamination, dipping it in the drink, waiting thirty seconds before transferring the strip to the blotting paper. It was a slow process. Insisting on precision meant he could do no more than one strip a minute. After five minutes he had ascertained that the cocoa did not contain arsenic, strychnine, morphine, cyanide or barbital barbiturate. After ten minutes he suspected that the cocoa was indeed safe to drink. He had still to repeat the initial, wasted test. This involved opening the case to find another set of strips, a tricky manoeuvre with his experiment laid out on top.

Never slack a task or it could be your last.

His spy master instructor had repeated the phrase like a mantra and it would have been better for him if he had taken his own advice. While engaged in a mission to a pesticide development laboratory in Germany, Monsieur Bisset had dropped his toxin indicator in a wash basin. He ignored the squeaking warning, believing it to be due to water in the workings. Monsieur D'Haricot had visited Monsieur Bisset in the hospital before he died and he shivered at the thought. He rearranged his experiment to enable the safe opening of the case and removal of the test strips.

Success.

After thirty seconds the strip changed colour. His drink had been spiked with... he checked the chart... valerian.

That was disappointing. A medicinal sleeping potion with limited action didn't warrant the fifteen minutes spent testing for it. He had no time to reflect on this. His case started to shake a fraction of a second before the onslaught of banging in his ears. The boat listed, then righted itself. It repeated the action until Monsieur D'Haricot wished he had taken the cocoa and was asleep on his bunk.

Non.

That was not the attitude of a French special agent. He must find out at once what was going on. Gustav had mentioned unloading cargo. Monsieur D'Haricot assumed he meant the boxes on deck, but as he listened at the cabin door the thuds came from deeper in the vessel. Before leaving his apartment, he had had the sense to pack the smaller items of the espionage equipment he used on a regular basis. This included miniature binoculars, an invisible ink pen, a blade concealed as a moustache comb and a sound magnifier. The sound magnifier was what he needed. It was similar in appearance to a stethoscope and worked in much the same manner. He retrieved it from his case and wiped the earpieces with a cloth before positioning them to stay in place. When he was satisfied, he put the metal bell-shaped magnifier against the floorboards and listened.

He heard the creaking of wood, the grating of metal being rolled along a floor and the clicks of a door being opened and closed. A crash was followed by an expletive from Gustav and someone warning him to keep the noise down. Monsieur D'Haricot didn't recognise the second person. When a third, softer voice showed concern for Gustav's big toe, he let go of the sound magnifier, letting the end dangle by the rubber tubing from his ears.

'Victoire,' he said aloud. His heart beat faster. That complicated matters. Should he make his presence known to her, try to escape the vessel while the others were occupied, or play along with their game by pretending to be asleep?

Again, no. He would not run away, play along or expose himself to Victoire. He would find out what they were up to without being seen.

Monsieur D'Haricot was a patriot – Vive la France – but he did not swallow the gung-ho bravado of his instructors. Some of their ideology smacked of brainwashing. Believing that being French was sufficient for success was the easiest way to an early grave. Spying on Victoire and her colleagues would not be a Sunday cycle ride in the Bois de Boulogne. He repositioned the listening device and waited until the noises receded. He was tempted to allow another minute, but feared the unloading would be complete and he would miss the opportunity.

Assuming that the cocoa would do its work, Gustav had seen fit not to lock the cabin door. Monsieur D'Haricot was a teensy bit irritated that he wouldn't get to try out his latest gadget, the skeleton lock picker. It was an instrument he had made himself, which to the untrained eye appeared to be a lady's hatpin. Purchasing it had caused more than a slight degree of embarrassment when the shop assistant had asked the circumference of the lady in question's head. He considered locking the door, to prove that unlocking it could be achieved in less than thirty seconds, but that seemed a rather English thing to do.

He opened the door with care, glancing both ways along the corridor before stepping out. His eyes registered the exact positioning of the rooms, in case he needed to slip out of sight. His heels tapped on the wooden floor. He switched to walking on his toes and increased his speed to reach the end of the corridor. The aroma of seafood bubbling in red wine wafted from the room on the right, indicating that this was the galley. The singing he had heard earlier was now snoring. He turned to the left, where a wooden box, about a metre in height and width and one and a half metres in length, took up the remaining space. The top of the box had a metal handle, painted orange.

Apart from a miniscule pair of nail clippers and the hat pin that he still held, Monsieur D'Haricot was unarmed. Before opening the lid he placed the pin in his pocket and practised a number of boxing moves, pounding the life out of the air in front of him. Since he needed both hands to open the lid the sparring proved pointless. Looking into the box, Monsieur D'Haricot could see the top of a staircase leading into the bowels of the boat. The grey fudged to black and he couldn't see beyond the first three steps. There was a torch in his case, which he had forgotten to bring. If his superior had known about this, it would have earned him a guillotine mark. These reprimands were a puerile amusement of the General's. Even before the incident with Victoire and the liquor, Monsieur D'Haricot had thought his commander's humour verged towards the Germanic.

He was about to hoist himself into the box and onto the first step when he heard the asinine giggling of a society lady. It was interrupted by a hiccup. 'Don't let me stop you,' the lady said, or so Monsieur D'Haricot interpreted from the slurred vowels and staccato consonants.

He turned, reaching for his head before realising he wasn't wearing his hat. There was no-one to be seen. He heard a further attack of hiccups followed by a snigger.

'Hello,' Monsieur D'Haricot said. 'Who is there?'

'Me, silly.'

The squeaky voice came from the space his missing big toe would have occupied. He looked down and jumped back. On the floor, a pincher centimetres away from his ankles, was a large crab. Its shell was a plump red, its legs rosy and its eyes black and sparkling.

'Have you been drinking?' Monsieur D'Haricot asked, sniffing the air.

'I have been marinating,' the crab replied.

'Ah,' Monsieur D'Haricot glanced towards the galley.

'You won't tell on me?' the crab said. She wiggled a pincher, but wobbled sideways. 'The chef threatened me with a chopping knife. What was a girl to do?'

'What did you do?' Monsieur D'Haricot asked. 'If that isn't a delicate question.'

'I pinched his nose and ran for the door. Will you help me?'

Monsieur D'Haricot was divided in his loyalties. He could hardly leave a lady in distress, but he wasn't impartial to well-seasoned bisque. The pockets of his breeches were not large enough to harbour an edible crab and he had left his case in his cabin. He could not even offer the lady a hat to hide under. While he was thinking, there was a stir from the galley. He heard a pig-like grunt and a chair was pushed back.

'Quick, hang on to my braces,' Monsieur D'Haricot instructed. He bent to pick up the crab and she obliged by hooking her pinchers round the strips of his suspenders. He didn't wait for the chef or whoever to appear. Sitting on the edge of the box, he swivelled his legs round to reach the stairs. He descended until his head was below the top of the box, then reached to replace the lid.

A light shone from beneath him. He continued to climb down until the space opened into a long room, which he assumed was the boat's hold. He halted to peer down on the scene below. Two rows of crates faced each other, ready to begin a dance, but most of the cargo had been unloaded. Two workers in blue overalls and flat berets slouched against the end crates, one on either side, smoking rolled-up cigarettes. A covered gangway was attached at right angles to the side of the

44

vessel halfway along the hull. From it Monsieur D'Haricot heard the distinctive voice of Victoire Chapleau.

'You are sure he is asleep?' she asked.

'Like a hibernating hedgehog,' Gustav answered.

'Still, we should be careful.'

Gustav appeared at the entrance to the gangway and signalled to the two workmen, who shuffled across. Monsieur D'Haricot thought about climbing up a step to be out of view, but moving might incite a groan from the ladder. The crab was swinging from his shirt front in an alcohol-induced stupor and he was afraid she was about to start singing – if crabs could indeed sing.

Gustav disappeared back along the gangway and the two men followed. Monsieur D'Haricot made his way down the ladder and sneaked behind the nearest crate, which was marked with a 'P'. He tapped the side. The wood was heavy. He heard an echo, but nothing to indicate what was inside. He broke three nails prising his fingers between the top and the sides. The lid didn't shift and he gave up. He was alone in the hold and hiding seemed stupid. He stepped out and stretched his legs, which had developed cramp from bending on his knees. The room was still. The low ceiling, dull light and shadows gave the atmosphere of a morgue, not helped by the smell of seasoned wood. He made his way to the gangway and flattened his back against the wall before peeking round to glance along the corridor. An orange light flickered from the far end and the silhouette of a figure jerked in slow motion like the undead in the silent movies he enjoyed in his youth. He was reminded of the engine room workers and resumed his camouflage position, holding his breath for forty seconds until his ears hummed. No-one appeared.

The aroma from the crab was overpowering and he took the opportunity to unhinge the pinchers from his clothing, not without resistance from the crustacean.

'You can't abandon me here,' she objected.

'Surely you can find a way into the water?' Monsieur D'Haricot answered.

'The hold is secure, but even if I dug my way out, bruising my delicate shell and ruining my beautiful pinchers, I am a creature of the sea. I cannot survive in fresh water.'

'I hadn't thought about that,' Monsieur D'Haricot conceded. 'I'm not sure how to help you.'

'The boat is going to the coast,' the crab said. 'I heard the chef say so. All I ask is that you keep me hidden from that evil man until we reach the Channel.'

'I can do my best,' Monsieur D'Haricot agreed. 'I have a mission of my own, though. I need to find out what is going on here.'

'Why don't you sidestep along the corridor and ask the people there?'

'I can't trust them.'

The crab huffed. 'It's always the same. People ask for advice but never take it.' One of the crab's claws was swaying close to Monsieur D'Haricot's nose and he thought it wiser not to remind the crab that he hadn't asked for guidance. Besides, she had a point. It was time for action. He waited until the crab had reattached itself to his braces, then made his way along the gangway with bold strides, allowing his footsteps to echo.

The orange light shone in his eyes and he tripped off the edge, tumbling into a stack of wooden boxes. The top boxes fell to the ground and he imagined he heard a grunt, as if the box was voicing its complaint. He extricated his limbs from between gaps and crouched behind the remaining pile to get his bearings. He was at the end of a short, covered jetty leading into a cave, lit by artificial lighting. The boat was moored by two lines to the side of the jetty. Behind the boat was a sealed metal door rising from beneath the water level to the top of the cave.

Monsieur D'Haricot rose and walked to the cave entrance. He stopped to look towards the far end, about twenty-five metres in front of him. There were several passages leading off, all except one marked by a glowing green light. A red warning light flashed at the entrance to the final passageway.

The memory of logic games he had been forced to play at spy school returned.

If one passage leads to the prize and the other to death, what question should you ask?

There were five passageways and no-one, barring the crab, to ask. While Monsieur D'Haricot was cogitating, Gustav and his two crew members appeared from the passage nearest to him. He slipped further round the side of the boxes, holding in his stomach to ensure he was out of sight. It meant he couldn't see the men, but he attuned his ears to eavesdrop on their conversation. Their voices were loud, but they spoke in a language which, despite Monsieur D'Haricot knowing a smattering of five European languages and two Indo-Chinese, he did not recognise. Every three seconds one of Gustav's arms would be flung into view. He was either teaching the labourers sign language or giving elaborate instructions. The hand swinging stopped and Monsieur D'Haricot heard two sets of footsteps trudge along the gangway and back onto the boat. He assumed they were those of the crew members. Gustav coughed and Monsieur D'Haricot sensed he was staring in his direction.

'Do you smell crab?' Gustav called in guttural French.

'No,' Victoire answered him from nearby. 'It is time you departed. You have valuable cargo to deliver to Rouen.'

Gustav chuckled in what Monsieur D'Haricot believed was a disrespectful manner. The captain continued to his boat and the laughter was replaced by a shout to the crew. The scraping of metal against solid rock tore at Monsieur D'Haricot's eardrums, then there was silence.

The crab had begun to sober up and was twisting her eyes to work out why she was clinging for sweet life onto the braces of a strange man.

'Ooh la la,' she exclaimed. 'Unhand me, you crazy human. My mother warned me about men like you.'

Monsieur D'Haricot raised a finger to his lips to shush her, but it was too late. He looked up to see Victoire peering over the top of the stack at him. He stood up and brushed dust from his shirt.

'Yes, well, delighted to see you, Madame Chapleau, but I'm afraid I really must be off. My boat, you know—'

His cheeks were bright red. Ignoring this, he took a confident stride towards the pier only to see the top of the boat disappear into the murky river water and the metal gate close behind it.

'No, wait,' he called, increasing his pace to a jog.

The crab had been struggling to unhinge herself from his clothing and at that moment succeeded in snapping his braces. Monsieur D'Haricot had been foolish enough to loosen his belt while he rested. He moved forwards and his breeches slipped from his waist to his ankles, displaying his patriotic, toile de Jouy undergarments. He heard Victoire snigger as he attempted to protect his modesty and realised the crab was dangling from his right wrist, making headway in a precarious direction.

'Would you like a hand?' Victoire offered in a somewhat risqué manner.

Chapter Six

'What are we going to do with you?'

The Vicomte's voice sounded cheerful. While Monsieur D'Haricot was rearranging his breeches, Otocey had joined Victoire and was standing next to her, with a finger poised centimetres from her hair. A strand had come loose and he was deliberating whether to replace it under her headband. By the time he had repeated his question twice, Monsieur D'Haricot realised he was referring to him and not the hair and he had picked up on Otocey's underlying annoyance.

Victoire, in comparison, seemed delighted by his unexpected presence. 'There is nothing for it,' she declared. 'We will have to let Louis-Philip in on our little secret.'

'Humpf,' Otocey grunted. 'Why do I get the feeling that was your intention from the outset?'

'Because you know me so well,' Victoire teased.

'I am not concerned with your "little secrets". What I would like to know,' Monsieur D'Haricot interrupted, 'is where we are.'

'Nowhere important,' Madame Chapleau answered at the same time as Otocey said, 'Classified information.'

'We, Nicolas and I, belong to a secret organisation,' Victoire took up the narrative. 'Our ultimate aim is to restore France to greatness.'

Monsieur D'Haricot could not disagree with the sentiment, but he doubted Victoire's idea of "greatness" was similar to his own. Indeed, he feared from her previous eulogies about Versailles that she would rejoice in seeing France return to being a monarchy. He inclined his head the way he had observed Clark Gable do in the movies.

'I understand you think it strange that we have our headquarters underground. Believe me, it is essential.' Victoire paused and Monsieur D'Haricot obliged with the expected, 'Why?'

'It is a long story. I suggest we retire somewhere comfortable.'

Madame Chapleau's suggestions were, in reality, instructions which she expected to be obeyed. She linked her arm through Monsieur D'Haricot's in a gesture more of ownership than affection and ensured Otocey was aware of the intimacy. Otocey frowned and led the way along the central tunnel. The passage was lit by strips of orange lighting attached by brackets to the stone walls. The paved flagstone flooring equalled the best in Paris and Monsieur D'Haricot's feet bounced from one slab to another.

'The material is ideal for the posture. Moving across it stimulates pressure points in the foot.' Victoire explained. 'A Chinese gentleman recommended it.'

The passage sloped down and as it did it widened to resemble an elegant avenue in the fifth arrondissement. Lime trees and rose bushes flourished in the artificial atmosphere of sunlight and shade, or perhaps the plants were also artificial. They had no perfume to tickle the nostrils.

'No birdsong,' Monsieur D'Haricot commented.

'Oh no,' Victoire answered. 'It would be too cruel to expect sparrows and blackbirds to live down here, and I can't abide the recorded squawking favoured in the deeper districts.'

The avenue led into a square with a marble fountain at the centre. The water spurted three metres into the air. It changed colour at its height, then tumbled down to gather in a rainbow pool and splash onto the polished stone wall enclosing it. A miniscule pink lizard tried to scurry away at their approach, but the suckers on its feet stuck to the wet stone. Victoire pinched her thumb and forefinger gently around the creature's abdomen to release it. Monsieur D'Haricot was not fond of reptiles and looked away as Victoire performed the manoeuvre, which he surmised she had perfected over time.

The natural rock of the cave's interior had been chiselled out and carved to resemble the fronts of well-known buildings in the city. Monsieur D'Haricot recognised the Pantheon, the Conciergerie and the Abbey of Saint Germaine des Pres.

'They look more lifelike than the originals,' he complimented.

'They are the originals,' Victoire answered, rubbing her lizard stained fingers on a silk handkerchief. When she finished, she handed it to Monsieur D'Haricot to dispose of. He stuffed it into his pocket. Otocey directed them towards the front door of the underground Louvre without speaking.

'Why, I was here only last week,' Monsieur D'Haricot said in a jovial manner.

'I very much doubt that,' Otocey replied.

Monsieur D'Haricot followed Otocey inside, not sure what to expect. He did not anticipate a replica of the inside of the Parisian museum, which was what now stretched before him. The interior hall was vast, burrowing deep into the rock face, with what looked miraculously like a glass ceiling.

'Crystals,' Victoire explained, following his gaze upwards. 'Naturally occurring...'

'...In the Dordogne,' Otocey completed the sentence. 'We had them shipped here.'

'A gargantuan task, but worth it, don't you think?' Victoire looked to Monsieur D'Haricot for approval.

'Exquisite,' he answered. His eyes darted from statues to carpeted staircases, potted citrus trees to rows of windows, lined like sentries on top of one another to guard the different storeys. Doors promised room upon room of wonders. Monsieur D'Haricot stood glued to the marble flooring, as helpless to move as the pink lizard.

'It is magnifique,' he exclaimed.

'A little warm and colourful for my taste,' Victoire answered. Monsieur D'Haricot had managed to escape her hold and she linked her arm through his again, with a tighter grip. 'Nicolas likes it and he paid for it. Come, we shall take tea in the garden café.'

Monsieur D'Haricot did not remember a garden café from his visit, but there hadn't been time to explore every room on every floor of the grand building and pastries, however delicate, were not on his list of artwork to enjoy. He did not doubt that Victoire was an expert on them.

The café was situated along a corridor guarded by a palisade of white plastered columns intertwined with honeysuckle. Once free of the decorative shield, the tables overlooked a square of symmetrical flowerbeds enclosed by a metre high buxus hedge. It was a plant that Monsieur D'Haricot appreciated, as much for its exotic bouquet as its ability to keep order, but there was no scent from the hedge. The café was unoccupied and it occurred to Monsieur D'Haricot that not only was the museum empty, but he hadn't noticed any citizens in the square or outside the elaborate buildings.

'Last week, I had to queue to see the Venus de Milo,' Monsieur D'Haricot commented.

'You only have yourself to blame if you visit a museum during public opening times,' Otocey replied.

'This area is too close to the surface for the more inexperienced,' Victoire answered, without explaining further. She chose a table at the back of the café, complaining of biting flies near the garden. Monsieur D'Haricot drew her chair out and held the back until she was seated. Otocey made a clicking noise with his tongue and wagged a finger at him.

'Old-fashioned manners have their place, I suppose,' he allowed before taking a seat next to Victoire.

Monsieur D'Haricot sat opposite them and reached for a copy of the menu. Victoire stopped him with a gloved hand on his.

'You must allow me to order for you,' she said. 'The apricot macarons are a house speciality. People have killed for them.'

'Ooh, j'adore les macarons.'

'Did that crab speak?' Otocey spluttered. The monocle he was wearing to inspect the menu fell from the Vicomte's eye.

Monsieur D'Haricot had forgotten about the crab, who had attached herself to his belt during their walk. Now that he was seated, she had crawled onto his knee. Standing on two pairs of back legs, she balanced her pinchers on the table in order to see what was going on.

'I believe it did,' Monsieur D'Haricot answered, unperturbed.

'Where did it come from?'

'It was on the boat,' Monsieur D'Haricot answered. 'I met it in the galley.'

Otocey replaced his monocle and examined the crab. 'Its tastes seem to include corporal readjustment accelerator biscuits, if I'm not mistaken.'

'It has been quite a glutton, by the sound of things,' Victoire agreed.

'Excuse me,' the crab broke in. 'I am a "she", not an "it".'

'I am terribly sorry,' Victoire apologised.

Otocey gaped at the crustacean, his mouth opening and closing like a goldfish.

'Are these corporal readjustment accelerator biscuits commonplace or something of a delicacy?' Monsieur D'Haricot asked.

'They are miniature galettes, with a soft texture and mild almond flavouring,' Victoire answered. 'Nothing compared to the exquisite Belgi galettes that Madame Bernard bakes in the Latin Quarter, but not unpleasant.'

'That is not what D'Haricot meant, ma chérie.' Otocey had found his voice. He spoke to Victoire, but his vulpine eyes were fixed on the crab.

The conversation was interrupted by the arrival of the waitress. She was a young girl in a black crepe dress, with a spotless white apron and hat both made from lace. She held a small notebook for taking orders and twiddled a pencil between her fingers with the agility of a drum major. Monsieur D'Haricot was drawn to her hands. The skin was pale, with a translucent quality, as though her fingers and palms were formed from the icy waters of Élivágar. The museum lighting reflected from them with a shimmer that amplified the vision. For a moment he was afraid to look at her face, although it was rude not to. He looked up to see the waitress smiling at him with the grin of a favourite niece in need of an allowance.

'Three black coffees and four macarons,' Victoire ordered for them. 'Two apricot, one almond and...' She turned to address the crab, 'Which flavour would you like, Madame?'

'I cannot read the menu. I have forgotten my pince nez,' the crab replied.

Otocey gave an ungentlemanly snigger. 'You have your pince pied.' He pointed at the crab's pincher.

'Ignore him, my dear,' Victoire said.

'We have vanilla, pineapple, mango, passion fruit, kiwi, papaya, kumquat, cherimoya, horned melon...' The waitress could have taken ten minutes to complete her list as the choices became more exotic. Monsieur D'Haricot was irked that she had not listed the flavours in alphabetical order, but presumably there was a method to her seemingly random sequence. Victoire raised a hand to stop her.

'Allow me to recommend the samphire,' she said to the crab. 'It has a delicious balance of salt and crunch.'

'I am not sure.' The crab swithered.

'It doesn't need balance, it is a Cancerian, not a Libran.' Otocey looked to regain lost ground with his astrological humour.

'You can't go wrong with apricot,' Victoire decided. She addressed the waitress. 'That will be three apricot macarons. Cancel the almond one. The Vicomte's behaviour does not deserve one.'

The waitress took the order, curtseyed and left.

Monsieur D'Haricot had listened to the conversation with growing impatience. 'You were about to tell me of your secret order,' he reminded Victoire.

Otocey banged a fist on the table. 'Shh, keep your voice down man,' he reprimanded.

There was no-one to hear, and Monsieur D'Haricot suspected Otocey's irritation was at losing his macaron, but he lowered his voice to a whisper.

'Our order was founded in 1789,' Victoire began, 'At the height of the Revolution. Our forebears feared for the future of France.'

'They feared for their lives and property,' Otocey corrected.

'You will insist on reducing matters to their basest.' Victoire gave his knuckles a mild rap. Monsieur D'Haricot feared he would die of old age before they stopped squabbling and told him what was going on. Before Victoire could return to her account, the waitress appeared with the coffee, side plates and macarons. She had taken the liberty of providing a saucer of sea water for the crab.

'Merci,' the crab said. Her voice had turned squeaky and she put an arm across her mouth to hide her embarrassment.

'It seems the effect from the biscuits is wearing thin,' Otocey said.

'Like my patience,' Monsieur D'Haricot muttered.

'Paris wasn't safe,' Victoire continued once the waitress left. 'A group of intellectuals decided to go underground.'

'Quite literally,' Otocey said. On cue there was a rumble overhead and Monsieur D'Haricot felt the plaster ceiling was about to crumble. His chair trembled towards the table leg for shelter. Monsieur D'Haricot caught a flash of fear on Victoire's face before her muscles slackened.

'Victoire is afraid of waking the mythical Core Worm, but the tremble is simply from the Metro,' Otocey explained. 'The Worm lives much deeper,' he whispered an aside to Victoire, who rapped him hard with a menu. He returned his attention to Monsieur D'Haricot. 'There is nothing to worry about. We are far enough below the tunnel system to experience few significant disruptions.'

'Louis-Philip is not interested in the mechanics,' Victoire said. The snap had returned to her voice, but Monsieur D'Haricot realised there was something different about her face. He could not say what, but he had a feeling it was her eyes.

'To cut a centuries-long story down to ten words, our ancestors built their own Paris beneath the one you know,' Otocey finished.

'That is eleven words,' Monsieur D'Haricot said.

'Pedant – that is so unlike an Aquarius.' Otocey's smile could have been a jackal snarling. Monsieur D'Haricot did not rise to the bait and declare himself a Sagittarian. 'I suppose it comes from having an unnecessary 'H' in your name,' Otocey continued.

Monsieur D'Haricot smarted. He was about to retort that Otocey was lacking a necessary brain cell, but before his rage subsided sufficiently to allow him to get the insult out, Victoire began speaking.

'We did have a primitive base to work on,' she continued the saga. 'Refugees from struggles dating back to the Hundred Years' War had built tunnels and caves and dug out fresh water springs. It has taken time to reach the stage we are at now.'

'Which is?' Monsieur D'Haricot asked.

'Time to give something back,' Victoire said with a flourish.

'Give what back exactly?'

'Don't you pay attention to current affairs?' Otocey said. 'Hitler is polishing his jackboots in Germany; the situation in Spain is no better than a bullfight and the results of their upcoming election could see the bull escaping; Mussolini has an iron fist round Italy. France is caught in the middle.'

'That is not to mention the atrocities Stalin is reported to be responsible for in Russia,' Victoire said with a shiver.

'You believe your order can solve these problems?'

'Certainly, but…we have discovered a difficulty,' Victoire said. 'You met my twin.'

Otocey had declared the same, but Monsieur D'Haricot was no better informed as to who the person was. 'I don't believe we were officially introduced,' he answered.

'I made the introduction myself, when you called at my residence,' Otocey said.

Monsieur D'Haricot pictured the stairway. 'You mean the—'

'Mala Kai isn't used to being on the surface for extended periods,' Victoire said.

Monsieur D'Haricot had been about to say, 'the butler', but he kept quiet about his mistake.

'Mala Kai takes a strange reaction to the readjustment biscuits,'

Otocey finished.

'I would say 'exceptional' rather than 'strange',' Victoire corrected him.

'Allow me to summarise and correct me if I have misunderstood,' Monsieur D'Haricot said. 'Your families have lived underground for the past a hundred and fifty years.'

'Yes. We have evolved to thrive in the artificial light and reduced oxygen. Unfortunately that means that when we surface, our specialised metabolisms are compromised.'

'Which is why you need these readjustment biscuits,' Monsieur D'Haricot said. 'Is that what Gustav was delivering to you?'

'No,' Otocey snapped. 'Gustav's business with us is unrelated.'

'And unimportant,' Victoire gave a sweet smile. She leaned over to put a hand on Monsieur D'Haricot's. 'What we need are agents from the surface, au fait with the atmosphere above ground, to work with us.'

'Initiated into our order, you understand,' Otocey said. 'You would have to swear our oath of loyalty and obedience.'

'Wait one moment.' Monsieur D'Haricot snatched his hand away and drew back his chair. 'I didn't say I wanted to join your order, and frankly I believe it would infract upon my professional obligations.'

'We understand,' Victoire agreed with a condescending nod. She had eaten her own macaron, taking bites while Otocey spoke. Assuming that Monsieur D'Haricot didn't want his, she reached out to take it from the plate. Before her fingers reached it the crab flicked a pincher and snaffled the macaron. 'We really should return this crustacean to the sea,' Victoire said.

'Perhaps if I were able to see what it is you do down here,' Monsieur D'Haricot suggested. Otocey and Victoire exchanged quick glances. 'That is, if you aren't required to kill me afterwards if I don't join you.' Neither of his companions laughed at his humour.

Otocey took up the conversation. 'You will have heard of Fraumy?'

'Upper or Lower?' Monsieur D'Haricot answered without hesitation.

Otocey's grimace begged the use of fisticuffs to relieve its misery. 'It is a small, independent duchy bordering our country and Belgium.'

'Small, but not insignificant,' Victoire added.

'When you say "our country", do you mean above or below ground?' Monsieur D'Haricot asked.

'They are one and the same,' Victoire answered cryptically.

'Fraumy is below ground,' Otocey admitted.

Monsieur D'Haricot was finding it a strain to divert his attention between Victoire and Otocey as the conversation ping-ponged. He felt he was watching a seaside Punch and Judy show, but couldn't decide if he was the policeman, the crocodile or the hapless baby.

'Where does this Juan fellow fit in?' he asked, addressing Victoire. She in turn looked towards Otocey, who had developed a sudden interest in sniffing the dregs in his coffee cup.

'Juan is a Libran,' Victoire said.

'Is that supposed to mean something?' Monsieur D'Haricot said. Realising he would get no sense from the pair, he stood up. Victoire rose to stand beside him.

'Please don't go,' she said in a smooth voice, sweet enough to drizzle over crepes.

'There is nowhere he can go,' Otocey said. He too got to his feet and stretched his legs.

'I can find somewhere to poke my nose,' Monsieur D'Haricot declared. 'You have rebuilt an entire underground Paris. I rather fancy a trip to the Moulin Rouge.'

'That is not your style, Louis.' Victoire had a hand on his shoulder.

'I don't imagine you have recreated the Eiffel Tower in this subterranean fantasy world.'

Victoire's eyes lit up. 'Would you like to see it?'

'It's a trick of the lights,' Otocey said, reaching in his inside pocket for a teak cigar case. 'We don't have time to act as tour guides.' He removed a cigar and returned the case to his pocket. 'This has been a mistake. We must finish our search before it is too late.' He held the cigar between his teeth while he patted his pockets, searching for a lighter. Not finding one, and not being offered a light by his companions, he removed the cigar from his mouth and placed it in his top pocket. 'I suggest we take the crab and dump D'Haricot in the Seine.'

Chapter Seven

Monsieur D'Haricot's first reaction was to topple the table over and run, but Victoire's grip on his shoulder had tightened and Otocey had produced a small pistol from his pocket.

'You misunderstand, I didn't say I wasn't intrigued,' Monsieur D'Haricot corrected. 'I enjoy a puzzle, as you know. Besides, this Fraumy affair may be of concern to my employers, who are aware of my whereabouts,' he added pointedly.

Otocey gave a snort sounding more like its grounded prey than a fearsome coyote. Victoire glared at him. 'Don't worry about Nicolas,' she told Monsieur D'Haricot. 'He was joking.'

'That's me,' Otocey bared his teeth to show prominent canines. 'Monsieur Coyote, ever the trickster.' He fired the pistol and a cork on a string popped out.

'If you are still interested in meeting Juan, we will take you to see him,' Victoire decided. She glanced at her silver-banded wristwatch. 'We don't have time to wait on the next aquatran. We shall have to catch a train.'

'For a moment I thought you were going to suggest an underground flying machine,' Monsieur D'Haricot tried to lighten the mood.

'If you would prefer—'

'No, no. I do not like trains, but at least I can understand their workings. Which way is it to Saint-Lazare station?'

Victoire called the waitress and paid the bill with coloured stones. She tipped the woman two green gemstones.

'We shall need a carrier bag.'

The waitress returned with the bag. Victoire held the top open for the crab to climb in. She was reluctant, but her complex eye system spotted the pineapple macaron lying at the bottom and flipped inside without further ado. Victoire handed the bag to Monsieur D'Haricot.

Otocey was looking Monsieur D'Haricot up and down.

'Is something the matter?' Monsieur D'Haricot asked.

'You are hardly dressed for railway travel,' he said. 'I appreciate you are an inexperienced rail user, but you seem barely dressed at all. We must find you a jacket and a hat before we reach the station or it is unlikely the clerk will allow you a ticket.'

Monsieur D'Haricot conceded he was underdressed, due to the haste in leaving his cabin, but they were looking for seats in a train compartment not a box at the opera house. He wanted to unburden his indignation, but picking a fight with Otocey in the company of Madame Chapleau was something an uncouth Prussian would attempt, not a Parisian gentleman. 'I left my jacket on the boat,' he replied. 'My wallet was in my jacket pocket.'

'How convenient,' Otocey sneered.

'It is not at all convenient,' Monsieur D'Haricot snapped. 'There were business cards and… other things inside.' He trailed off, not wishing to reveal confidential information to Otocey.

'I have a friend near the station who is a tailor,' Victoire answered. 'He will have a jacket you can try out. You will have to do without a hat until we reach Rouen. Come.'

Victoire's final word was a command, not to be disobeyed. Monsieur D'Haricot and Vicomte Otocey fell in behind her and they marched into the gallery rooms of the museum. Victoire strode towards the opposite side they had entered from.

'What about our cargo?' Otocey asked.

'It can be picked up later,' Victoire threw the answer over her shoulder. They exited by a side door and instead of the cave with the pier, Monsieur D'Haricot found himself in a busy shopping street. It amused him to see the frail-skinned individuals riding their chargeurs with as little skill as he had demonstrated on la répugnant Mathilde. Horns were blown and arms waved. Monsieur D'Haricot understood at once where Madame Chapleau's driving skills came from. The thought brought back the unfortunate memory of his beloved bicycle Clodette.

'Watch out.' Victoire grabbed his arm and pulled him from the edge of the pavement. The driver of a bright yellow chargeur veered from the road and mounted the kerb. The youthful individual, with an apparent Oriental lineage, shouted an apology before the vehicle took off and shot towards the centre of the carriageway.

'They must be a Newcon,' Victoire explained. 'It takes time to learn how to control a chargeur, although Nicolas told me you took to yours like an egg to the flan, or did you say fan, Nicolas?'

'Perhaps we should take a cab, ma chère,' Otocey suggested. 'That is, if you intend us reaching the station with all our limbs attached.'

'Where do we find a cab?' Monsieur D'Haricot asked.

'That is not a problem,' Victoire said. 'We simply use the cab caller. Nicolas, will you do the honours – you know how I hate these recorded messages?'

A hundred metres along the road was a box made from lustrous, obsidian metal the same height as the Vicomte and about the same depth and width. When he reached it Otocey took a silver key from his waistcoat pocket and inserted it into a lock near the top. A door sprung open, hitting Monsieur D'Haricot in the chest and winding him.

'Best to stand on the other side,' Otocey advised.

Inside the box was a board with numbers printed on raised tabs. Otocey pressed the keys in a sequence which Monsieur D'Haricot surreptitiously made note of, while pretending to be doubled up, regaining his breath. An androgynous voice spoke through the machine.

'Which language shall we have today?' Otocey joked.

'English,' Victoire answered. 'I love how they get the sentence order wrong in that plum-sucking accent.'

'I like the Mandarin myself,' Otocey said.

'You don't understand Mandarin. How do you know where to find the cab?'

'That doesn't matter. The voice is so sexy I could listen to it all day.'

'Why not stick with good, proper French?' Monsieur D'Haricot interrupted.

'If you are being like that, you make the call,' Otocey replied. Monsieur D'Haricot glanced at the array of buttons and levers and declined. Otocey pulled a lever marked 'E'.

THE CAB THAT YOU NEED IS AT YOUR DISPOSAL FROM THIS TIME. PLEASE TO INDICATE YOUR CURRENT TIME ZONE.

Otocey pressed the appropriate buttons.

PLEASE TO INDICATE HOW LONG YOU WISH THE CAB TO BE IN YOUR COMMAND.

Otocey looked at Victoire. 'Who is paying?'

'It was your idea,' she said curtly.

'We are helping your friend.'

'Very well. Say twenty minutes.'

'In this traffic?'

Victoire did not usually mind being corrected on minor faults, but Monsieur D'Haricot noted the furrowing of her brows towards Otocey. He pressed the buttons.

PLEASE TO KEY IN YOUR PREFERRED PAYMENT METHOD.

'We could have walked to the station in the time it takes to order,' Victoire commented. She pushed Otocey aside to press in her payment.

YOUR CAB WILL BE WITH YOU IN 5...4...3... PLEASE YOU WOULD LIKE TO SELECT A CUP OF THE COFFEE WHILE YOU WAIT, NO?

'For goodness sake.' Monsieur D'Haricot moved to press the button marked 'F', which he assumed would change the language to French. Before he could duck, a pipe popped out from the top of the machine and spewed a stream of frothy milk towards his face. Victoire tried not to smile as she handed him a handkerchief.

'I have one already,' Monsieur D'Haricot retrieved the handkerchief Victoire had handed him from his pocket. He wiped the milk from his eyes. The letters V C were embroidered in purple thread in one corner of the silk cloth. He was about to hand it back to Madame Chapleau but, deciding he should have it laundered first, he stuck it in his pocket.

'Somebody called for a cab?' The driver in a dark, shabby suit raised his bowler hat at Madame Chapleau. 'Three of you, are there?'

'Is that a problem?' Victoire said.

'No, if you don't mind waiting until I feed a couple more carrots into the engine.'

'Carrots?' Monsieur D'Haricot asked.

'Metaphorical ones,' the man explained. 'You're a stranger here, no?'

'This is my cousin,' Victoire answered. 'He is from... Belgium.'

'N.I.C.E C.O.U.N.T.R.Y,' the man said, in a loud and slow voice, using his hands to demonstrate what he thought a nice country consisted of. He nudged Otocey with his elbow and winked. 'I knew a girl from Belgium once.'

'Indeed,' Victoire said. 'Why don't you get on with refuelling while we make ourselves comfortable?'

'Comfortable?' Monsieur D'Haricot spluttered. 'It may resemble a hansom carriage, but two mechanical horses on wheels make it an automobile, in my book.'

The machine had come to a halt beside the kerb. Otocey swung open the door while the driver attended to his 'horses' by sticking a funnel into the ear of the first one and pouring oil down it. The liquid gargled and a foul-smelling gas was emitted from the back end of the second metal horse. Victoire waited for one of the gentlemen to offer her a hand inside. Neither did, so she gathered up the skirts of her coat and entered with a flick of the material in Monsieur D'Haricot's direction. Monsieur D'Haricot followed her and seated himself opposite. Otocey was the last to get in, slamming the door closed behind him. He looked at the seat beside Victoire, which was half taken over by the folds of the lady's coat, and chose to sit beside Monsieur D'Haricot, filling up more space than was rightfully assigned to him.

Victoire tapped the front of the cab and a partition opened. The cab driver had finished his maintenance and taken his position up front. He stuck his face through the opening.

'Saint-Lazare station,' Victoire said.

'That's the other side of town,' the driver answered. 'We won't make it in fifteen minutes.'

'Twenty,' Victoire countered, her irritation growing 'I did not pay for you to feed your horses and make crude remarks about people you know in Belgium.' She slid the partition shut before the man could reply.

Monsieur D'Haricot heard what sounded like an engine letting off steam. There was a thud and he was jolted forwards into Madame Chapleau.

'Please do not apologise,' she said coldly, interrupting his stammered response. The carriage continued on its way and her mood lightened. She made witty conversation about the latest fashions, the racing results at Longchamp and society news.

'You will never guess who I bumped into yesterday,' she said to both Otocey and Monsieur D'Haricot.

'You haven't trashed the car again?' Otocey answered.

'I bumped into them at a party, silly. Do you want me to tell you?'

'No, I like a puzzle,' Otocey answered, with a glare at Monsieur

D'Haricot. 'Perhaps, though, you should give me a clue.'

Victoire giggled as she thought of clever responses. 'Ask me questions?' she decided.

'A man?' Otocey said.

'No.'

'A dancer?'

'Yes.'

'Ballet?'

'No.'

Monsieur D'Haricot sighed. It was going to be a tedious journey. After twelve more questions and five wrong guesses, despite it being obvious to Monsieur D'Haricot who Victoire was referring to, Otocey came up with the answer.

'Josephine Baker.'

Victoire clapped her hands. 'A Gemini, like me.'

'What did you talk about?' Monsieur D'Haricot asked.

'We didn't speak, except for me to apologise for banging into her,' Victoire said, waving away the details with her hand.

'It hardly seems worth mentioning the meeting if nothing came of it,' Monsieur D'Haricot said.

'It was Josephine Baker,' Victoire repeated, then turned away to look out of the window. A moment later she jumped in her seat and banged on the partition. It didn't open and she banged louder.

'Don't disturb the man when he is driving,' Otocey said.

'He is going the wrong way,' Victoire declared. 'We have just passed Saint-Sulpice church. We are on the wrong side of the river.'

Monsieur D'Haricot had indeed recognised the two towers of Saint-Sulpice, but he hadn't realised the layout of the underground Paris was so similar to his own city.

'Where do you think he is taking us?' Otocey said in a somewhat flippant manner. Victoire glared at him.

'You know what is going on, don't you?' she accused.

'I have an inkling.' Otocey smirked.

'Perhaps you would like to inform the rest of us.' Victoire crossed her arms over her breast.

'I am sorry, but I have my own itinerary. I am not as convinced of D'Haricot's suitability as you are, my dear. No offence, D'Haricot.'

'Have you not tested Louis-Philip sufficiently?' Victoire said.

'Tested me?' Monsieur D'Haricot was finding it difficult to keep up with the conversation.

Victoire and Otocey ignored him and continued their sparring.

'The outcome in Fraumy will have serious ramifications for our world and that of Monsieur D'Haricot's,' Otocey said. 'We must be certain that we are striving towards the same end.'

'There is only one rational solution,' Victoire answered.

'I agree, but not everyone thinks in the same rational manner as we do, my weasel. The duke, for one, feels it is beneath him to use his own brain. He pays too much attention to the fools in his government who advise him.'

'They are not all inept,' Victoire argued.

'No, the intelligent ones are corrupt.'

'That is where Louis-Philip can help us.'

'Perhaps later, but I feel you may be in need of more—'

Monsieur D'Haricot missed the rest of the conversation. While they were discussing him, he realised the tail of Otocey's coat had caught in the cab door as he entered and the door had not closed properly. The vehicle had approached a crossroads and slowed. Monsieur D'Haricot reached for the handle. He pushed it and, with a jerk, the door swung open.

In a rapid string of actions, Monsieur D'Haricot tumbled out, regained his balance, avoided an oncoming chargeur and sprinted down the nearest side alley. It took a minute to realise that the cab had continued on its way, which dented his pride. Otocey and Victoire could at least have pretended he was worth chasing after. He slowed his pace and emerged at the other side of the alley with his clothing, if not his temper, restored to respectability.

It was not an area he knew, even above ground. His intention was to find a way of surfacing and report what had happened to his superior, but he feared his story would sound pie in the sky, or in this case macaron in the earth. Solid evidence would be required to corroborate his account. It was unfortunate that the effects of the readjustment biscuits were wearing off the crab. Perhaps he could buy more, if he had money, or coloured stones.

There was a bar on the opposite side of the street playing welcoming accordion music and in spite of the squabbling hoots from the traffic he thought he recognised the tune. The street was congested, with a queue of vehicles bumping into one another. Monsieur D'Haricot crisscrossed his way between the stationary chargeurs and mechanical cabs to peer in the bar window. An older woman was sitting on a wooden stool playing her instrument and a man was singing. Monsieur D'Haricot could not hear the words, but the man's mouth was opening and closing. His arms were raised and his body swayed to the rhythm.

While Monsieur D'Haricot was standing outside, a man of his own age came out. He dropped a cigarette end on the pavement and ground it into the kerb. 'Why don't you go in? You will hear the music better,' the man said. He was wearing an apron over his shirt and trousers and Monsieur D'Haricot assumed he was a member of staff.

'I'm afraid I do not have my wallet with me,' Monsieur D'Haricot explained. 'In fact, I have lost it. I left it on an aquatran.' He hoped by using the jargon of the underground city that he would not stand out as a stranger, although he suspected his ruddy complexion had already given him away. 'I'm a Newcon,' he added, remembering how Victoire had described the young Oriental chargeur cyclist.

The man's cheerful manner was extinguished. He drew back. 'One of them, are you?'

'I'm sorry, what do you mean? I arrived in the city about an hour ago and I am unaware of your customs.' He followed his words with a small laugh.

The waiter eyed him up and down. 'A stranger, with no money. Next you will tell me you have nowhere to stay.'

'I don't intend staying here,' Monsieur D'Haricot said. From the man's reaction he realised that had not been the right thing to say.

'Is that a crab?' the man asked. Monsieur D'Haricot looked at the bag he was carrying. The crab had manoeuvred its way out and was hanging onto the rim by its pinchers. 'If you want money, I'll buy it from you.'

Monsieur D'Haricot felt the bag tremble. 'She is not for sale,' he replied.

'It won't be of any use to you if you have nowhere to cook it,' the waiter replied.

'My good friend,' Monsieur D'Haricot looked shocked. 'You cannot be suggesting that I would... I am not a cannibal... We are on first name terms.'

The music had stopped playing and Monsieur D'Haricot noticed the accordion player and the singer standing in the doorway, listening to the conversation.

'She is a beautiful crab,' the old woman said. 'What is her name?'

Monsieur D'Haricot hesitated. The waiter tapped his foot. 'It is Marina,' he declared.

'I have a niece called Marina,' the singer said. 'Barman, bring us cognac. We must toast Marina.'

The bag trembled again. Monsieur D'Haricot grabbed hold of the crab and pushed her back inside before finding himself surrounded by bar patrons who hustled him inside. The waiter produced a half-full bottle of vintage cognac with cobwebs obscuring the stained label. The patrons clattered their empty glasses onto the counter and the waiter measured out a mean one-finger measure into each glass. When everyone had taken their drinks, the waiter lifted a glass from the rack above his head and placed it in front of Monsieur D'Haricot. He poured a dribble of cognac into it. The glass was smeared with fingerprints and what looked like lipstick, but it would have been rude not to drink. Monsieur D'Haricot raised the glass.

'To Marina,' the accordion player trilled.

'Marina,' the others repeated in lower keys. They downed their cognac. Monsieur D'Haricot joined in. The alcohol did not taste as bad as he imagined; indeed it left him with a warm tingle flowing from his lips down to the stump of his missing big toe.

'To all crabs,' the singer declared.

The patrons slammed their glasses on the bar counter. Reluctantly, the waiter refilled them and the toast was drunk.

The few drops of cognac were going to Monsieur D'Haricot's head and he vaguely wondered what strength the alcohol was. Pink ladies began to perform the can-can and doves flew overhead.

Not to be outdone, he raised a toast of his own. 'To this wonderful establishment and everyone in it.'

The bar was suddenly crammed with men and women. They crawled from beneath chairs and dangled from ceiling lights. Instead of the measly drops the waiter had delivered before, the glasses were filled to the brim and overflowed onto the wooden tables.

'Exceedingly gentlemanly of you to stand the round,' the singer said.

'No, wait—' Monsieur D'Haricot began. His impecunious state was something of an embarrassment to him. In his current fuzzy-headedness it was not something he could admit to his new friends. He caught the waiter's eye. The man grinned and rolled his eyes towards a back room.

'Have a seat,' the accordion player insisted, nudging the two baccarat players from their chairs in the corner. She unstrapped herself from her instrument and sat down. The singer joined her and Monsieur D'Haricot took the third vacant chair.

'What brings someone like you here?' the old woman said.

In normal circumstances Monsieur D'Haricot would have been circumvent about the answer, but the cognac had loosened his tongue. 'I was kidnapped,' he said. 'I got onto a barge, an aquatran, to take me to Rouen.' He paused to burp. 'The captain tried to drug me, but I wasn't to be fooled into accepting his poisoned drink. I went ashore to investigate what he was up to and voila, I ended up here.'

'We are a kilometre from the river,' the man said.

'I jumped from a hansom cab,' Monsieur D'Haricot explained, assuming his listeners could piece together the intervening events. 'Why don't we have another song? I feel like dancing.'

'Whose side do you think he is on?' Monsieur D'Haricot overheard the man whisper to the woman. She muttered something back and the man got to his feet, with the help of the table edge.

The woman turned to Monsieur D'Haricot. 'Do you have a request, dear?' she asked in a cheerful voice.

'Allons enfants de la Patrie,' Monsieur D'Haricot sang in an acceptable baritone.

The room was instantly silent.

Remembering the pre-revolution history of his new comrades, Monsieur D'Haricot sensed it was time to change the tune. He was not unfamiliar with cabaret acts, but the lyrics of his favourite tunes evaporated from his mind. The only thing he could remember was Victoire's guessing game with Josephine Baker as the answer. 'I have two loves, my country and Paris,' he sang out, in a poor imitation of the popular singer.

The older man joined in, banging his glass on the table to the rhythm and the woman squeezed out a verse on her accordion. Monsieur D'Haricot attempted to dance his way towards the exit, but he was stopped by the waiter who was grasping a full bottle of cognac in a battle-ready pose.

'Send the bill to the General,' Monsieur D'Haricot declared. 'He will attend to the expenses.' It was the General's private secretary Camille who dealt with such mundane items, but even in his befuddled state he knew that asking for a bar bill to be sent to a young lady was not appropriate.

'Which General would that be?' the waiter asked.

It was the first rule of his profession not to give away personal information. The cognac, however, seemed to have a similar effect on his tongue as the experimental truth serums he had read about. In what he believed was a barely audible voice, he gave the name of the General. Half the people in the bar scribbled it down on the cuffs of sleeves, the backs of hands or match boxes.

'Never heard of him,' the waiter said in a manner that suggested the cognac did not assert any truth-telling compunction on him.

'I shall give you an address, if required,' Monsieur D'Haricot answered in a haughty tone. 'I have never previously been asked for one.' He was warming to his act and made a show of reaching to his inside jacket pocket for a pen. Instantly the two baccarat players pulled knives from their belts and a young woman who had been clearing tables aimed an ex-army pistol at his chest.

'That won't be necessary.' A swell gentleman in an evening suit and top hat had stepped out from the room behind the bar while they were speaking and had heard the conversation. He was holding the end of a cigar which he stubbed on the bar counter and handed to the waiter. 'I know of the General. I would not say we are friends, but I trust him to honour any debts accrued.'

The waiter sniggered like a circus clown with a water pistol rather than a cognac bottle in his hand.

'Good, well, I should be going.' Monsieur D'Haricot straightened up and pulled at the lapels of his jacket.

'What is your haste?' the gentleman drawled.

Monsieur D'Haricot noticed the man's hands. He was not surprised that they were slender and fluid, the fingers rippling like water fountains. What astounded him was the signet ring. It was identical to the one worn by his commander, the General. His eyes lingered on the ring a second too long. The gentleman smiled and twisted it to show he had noticed Monsieur D'Haricot's interest. The waiter and the two baccarat players closed in behind Monsieur D'Haricot.

'I think we should talk,' the gentleman said. 'In private.'

Chapter Eight

The effect of the cognac was vanishing faster than a Tour de France competitor freewheeling down the Pyrenees. Monsieur D'Haricot was hustled into a back room and manhandled onto a wooden chair with a low back and high armrests. The gentleman sat opposite him, balancing his backside elegantly on the edge of a table. His minders stood behind Monsieur D'Haricot, one on either side, with the waiter guarding the door.

'Do you smoke?' the gentleman asked, offering a cigarette from a gold case etched with the letters 'EvL'.

'I prefer cigars,' Monsieur D'Haricot answered.

The case was snapped shut and returned to the gentleman's pocket. 'A man of taste,' the gentleman said, 'Which is unusual, considering you work for the General. You are a common spy.'

'I am a security agent,' Monsieur D'Haricot answered.

'What are you doing here? We have no need of security guards.'

The waiter couldn't smother his chuckle in time. The gentleman glowered at him.

'I'm on holiday,' Monsieur D'Haricot said.

One of the minders put a hand on Monsieur D'Haricot's shoulder and said something in a language Monsieur D'Haricot did not understand. The gentleman fiddled with his pencil moustache, straightening the ends before continuing.

'My friend says that you claim to have been kidnapped. Is that true?'

'Yes.'

'Do you know why? Are you rich?'

'No, on both accounts.'

'Can you describe your kidnappers?'

Monsieur D'Haricot felt the grip on his shoulder tighten. It sent a shiver vibrating towards his heart. He was anxious to learn what part the General played in the recent odd occurrences. Moreover, he feared the security of his beloved Paris was at risk and his own life was undoubtedly a key consideration. He would have to play his hand like a professional gambler.

'The man was called Gustav,' he said. 'I believe he is an employee of Vicomte Otocey.'

At the mention of the name, the gentleman jumped to his feet, catching the material of his trousers on a loose splinter of wood. He freed himself and spat across the floor. It may have been a leftover effect from the cognac, but Monsieur D'Haricot was sure the gobbet of saliva formed into a slug and slithered into a crack in the floorboards.

'That treacherous wolf,' the gentleman cursed, pacing up and down the floor like the vulpine in question. 'We had an agreement.' It took a moment before he returned his attention to Monsieur D'Haricot. He leaned over his prisoner and exhaled until Monsieur D'Haricot couldn't breathe from the odour of tobacco. Monsieur D'Haricot put the back of his hand over his mouth. The gentleman stepped away. 'Why is Old Nick interested in you?' he demanded.

'I really can't say,' Monsieur D'Haricot answered.

'Can't or won't?'

'I only met him yesterday,' Monsieur D'Haricot explained. 'I think it was yesterday. I seem to have lost track of time.'

'We're getting nowhere,' the waiter spoke in French. 'He told the musicians he was heading to Rouen.'

'Rouen?' the gentleman queried.

'It is where Juan is posted,' the waiter answered.

'Who is Juan?' The gentleman asked.

'He's the Libran.'

The gentleman made a snort like a pig with its snout in the swill. He turned on Monsieur D'Haricot. 'Do you know this Juan?'

'I have never met the fellow. Do you suppose I could have a glass of water? My throat is dry.' His throat was not the only part of his anatomy experiencing discomfort. He squirmed in the chair to adjust his posterior.

The gentleman paced the room again. 'I don't like this,' he repeated several times. 'I don't like it at all.'

'If you would explain what it is you find disagreeable, perhaps I could be of help,' Monsieur D'Haricot offered, feeling confident that if the gentleman and his bodyguards intended to kill him, they would have done so already. It was time to show a card. 'Does this concern appertain to the situation in Fraumy?' he asked.

'Apper-what? Is he some simpleton who can't speak French?'

'He knows about the plan,' the waiter said.

Monsieur D'Haricot would have refuted the statement, but the waiter grabbed his neck from behind and thrust his head back to place a sharpened razor at his throat.

'His words are nothing but hot air. He can't know the plan because I haven't made one,' the gentleman answered. His voice was brittle. His outline, or what Monsieur D'Haricot could make out of it from his acute angle of vision, was that of a giant arthropod with a sting in its tail. 'It is clear he is a Virgo.' He gave a staccato laugh, 'And therefore superfluous to Nic's grand scheme. Dispense with him. Meet me at the station in twenty minutes and bring a fishing rod.' He hovered over Monsieur D'Haricot and smiled. 'Goodbye, Monsieur. We won't be seeing one another again.'

One of the baccarat minders opened the door for the gentleman, and he left the room. Both baccarat players followed him out. The door was closed, leaving Monsieur D'Haricot to the wiles of the waiter.

During the conversation, no-one had paid attention to Marina, the crab. She did not appreciate this. The carrier bag had been placed on Monsieur D'Haricot's lap, but thanks to his twisting and posturing it had moved. The handle was now at the level of the waiter's belt. Marina had worked her way out and felt it was time to flex her pinchers. The left one latched on to the waiter's thigh while the right one found itself gripping a delicate part of the man's anatomy. He howled and dropped his razor.

Monsieur D'Haricot's reflexes were trained to react with speed. He nosedived from the chair, seized the blade and darted to the door while the waiter danced a jig around the room with the crab attached to his nether regions. Lesser agents might have taken the chance to escape without a thought, but Monsieur D'Haricot was not the type of gentleman to abandon a friend and ally. He retrieved the bag at the same time as the waiter freed himself from the crab's pinchers and dropped Marina to the floor. The two men's eyes met across the room.

'Drop the blade or I crush the crab,' the waiter threatened, lifting a booted foot a few centimetres above the crab's shell.

Monsieur D'Haricot paused, then dropped the blade. The waiter smirked and moved to pick it up. Marina took the moment to dangle on his boot lace, loosening it before using it as a catapult to whisk herself across the room. The waiter caught his foot on the end of the lace and stumbled to the floor, hitting his head against the chair. Monsieur D'Haricot caught Marina as she performed a near-perfect grand jete and pirouetted towards the floor. He stuffed her into the bag.

'A Virgo, indeed,' he sneered, stepping over the waiter. He opened the door and strode out.

The bar appeared to be empty. The accordion was leaning against a side wall and a half-full bottle of cognac was on the bar counter. Monsieur D'Haricot was tempted to confiscate it as payment for the inconvenience he had been put through, but as he wrestled with his conscience a gnarled hand reached up from behind the bar and took hold of the bottle neck. Intrigued, Monsieur D'Haricot approached the counter and peered over. The old singer was slouched against the shelves of beer bottles. The accordion player was the one with a hold on the cognac. She squeezed her eyes half-shut to focus on Monsieur D'Haricot.

'Would you like to join us?' She raised the bottle and looked around the floor for a glass.

'I'm afraid I am in a bit of a hurry,' Monsieur D'Haricot answered. The clattering coming from behind the door told him that the waiter had recovered and was on his tail. A glance at the exit showed him that the door was barred and he felt an uncomfortable tingle in his chest. There would hardly have been time to open it even if his fingers had not been shaking.

Seconds before the waiter barged into the barroom, the singer stirred from his reverie, grabbed Monsieur D'Haricot's lapels with the strength of an ox and yanked him over the counter. He landed on the skirts of the accordion player, who put her finger to her lips. The singer then tossed what appeared to be the discarded baccarat board at the front window. His thrust was strong and Monsieur D'Haricot heard shattering as the glass broke.

Monsieur D'Haricot's position was as uncomfortable to the woman as it was to him, but he dared not move as he heard chairs and tables being thrown across the room. His nose itched from the woollen fabric and he struggled to withhold a sneeze. The front door bolt creaked, then clicked. A moment later, Monsieur D'Haricot heard a slam. He sneezed three times, avoiding the accordion player's face with at least two of them. The singer was the first to get to his feet and scour the room.

'He has gone,' he said.

Monsieur D'Haricot scrambled to free his limbs from the accordion player's skirts. The woman tried to help, but her bicycling movements worked against his twists and it took a moment for them both to regain their composure. The singer had spoken the truth. Monsieur D'Haricot found it difficult to believe the waiter imagined he had escaped through a bolted door and a half-metre hole in the window guarded by jagged shards, but his attacker was not in the room.

The accordion player stuffed the bottle of cognac into a deep pocket in her skirt before setting about straightening the tables. Her companion replaced the chairs that had sufficient legs to balance on.

'Can I help?' Monsieur D'Haricot offered, spying a broom resting in a corner behind the bar. He swept the broken glass, spreading it across the floor. Most of it stuck in the gaps between the boards, transforming the approach to the counter into a lethal booby trap.

'You seem to have annoyed Gori,' the old woman said.

'Gori, is that the waiter?'

The two old people laughed. 'No, he is a backstabbing slug pool of slime that does what he is told,' the man said. 'His master is Prince Edgori van Lüttich.'

'Gori for short,' Monsieur D'Haricot deduced.

'Gori by name and gory by nature,' the woman agreed.

'Who is he?' Monsieur D'Haricot asked. 'We no longer have princes in France. Why is he important?'

'He's not French and he's not important,' the man answered. The woman disagreed.

'He is the heir to the duchy of Fraumy,' she said. 'Fraumy is French by moral rights, if not by political treaties. His mother is the Grand-duke's elder sister and you don't want to mess with her. She's a—'

'Let me guess,' Monsieur D'Haricot said. 'She's a Scorpio.'

'Oh no, Gori is the Scorpio. His mother is Aries – a proper firedragon.'

'In sheep's clothing,' the man finished.

The phrase sounded like one Otocey would have used, and it aroused Monsieur D'Haricot's suspicions about the pair. He pushed the few pieces of broken glass he had collected into a corner and leant on the handle of the broom, ready to upend it if he were in need of a weapon.

'Until today I had never heard of Fraumy, now I can't stop hearing about it. What exactly is happening there?'

'Nothing,' the man said in a voice too cheery to be believed. 'No-one has heard of Fraumy, because nothing happens there. I wouldn't worry two hoots about it. You need to find a safe channel to the surface. The waiter won't admit he allowed you to escape, but Gori and his henchmen will discover you are still alive before long.'

The couple seemed genuine and Monsieur D'Haricot relaxed his grip on the broom. 'Do you know where there is such a channel?'

The woman shook her head. 'Not in this arrondissement.'

'But in another, perhaps?'

'The best way to the surface is by aquatran,' the man said. 'You need to get back to the river.'

'And ask for Maulise when you get there,' the woman said. 'You will find him painting, if he is not asleep. He knows all the aquatran captains.'

'Can he be trusted?' Monsieur D'Haricot said.

'He is a Capricorn,' the man replied.

'That explains everything.' Monsieur D'Haricot did not hide his sarcasm.

'You may scoff,' the man replied, 'but if I weren't a Taurean I could not pull a man of your physique over a bar counter.'

'And if I weren't a Virgo—' the woman began, but Monsieur D'Haricot raised his hand, thinking it better not to hear.

'Which way to the river?' he asked.

'Henri, the waiter, will have the main routes watched,' the man said. 'What should I do?'

The woman hesitated, then decided. 'You'd better come with us, dear.'

'I don't wish to put you to any trouble.'

The man looked at the clock on the wall. It had only one hand, which appeared to be drawn onto the face at one minute before twelve. 'The bar doesn't open again until twelve,' he said. 'We have plenty of time.'

Monsieur D'Haricot returned the broom to the corner and trod carefully round the spicules of glass sticking up from the floor as he made for the door.

'Not that way,' the woman said, signalling to him to follow her across to the fireplace. Logs of wood were laid ready, but hadn't been lit. Monsieur D'Haricot had wondered what people on the surface made of smoke appearing out of the ground every night, but he imagined the underground folk had invented an elaborate system for expelling it into the river. 'Give me a leg up,' the woman instructed.

Monsieur D'Haricot was about to oblige, but gauging the weight of the woman from her girth, he stood back and allowed her companion to do the honours. The accordion player disappeared up the chimney like Père Noël when he visited England.

'Your turn,' the man said, wiping his hands and then clasping his fingers together to form a pedal. Monsieur D'Haricot put a foot into it. He raised both arms above his head like a platform diver preparing to perform a forward somersault and was propelled up the chimney in a flurry of soot. The woman grabbed his hands from above and pulled him into an alcove. There was barely room for one, and for the second time that afternoon he found himself crushed on top of the woman, wishing she had slacked on the amount of garlic she'd had for lunch. She pulled a lever on the wall and a door slid open behind them. They toppled through and by the time they got to their feet the singer had joined them.

Monsieur D'Haricot found himself in a grand hallway with what was once a plush crimson carpet, now worn in the centre and faded at the edges. Portraits in cracked oil paints lined the walls in rows, scowling at one another across the room. He straightened the crooked frames while he regained his breath. The gentlemen were in summer shirts and shorts, gadding about with butterfly nets or sipping cocktails. The ladies were in stiff military uniforms, complete with medals and braid.

'Are those relatives of yours?' he asked.

The singer pointed to a senior military officer with a scar across her cheek. The lady had drawn her sword and was grinning as she prepared to thrust it downwards. The painting did not show who the hapless victim of her smiling wrath was.

'That is our grandmother,' the man said.

'She strikes a daring pose,' Monsieur D'Haricot complimented.

'Indeed. She fought with Napoleon.'

'I hadn't realised there were female officers at Waterloo.'

'She wasn't at Waterloo. That is why Napoleon lost,' the woman said in a voice reminiscent of Monsieur D'Haricot's headmaster. He thought it wiser to keep further opinions as far from his vocal cords as his little toe.

Two empty suits of armour, one on either side of the doorway, guarded the exit to the hall with their axes forming a cross. The man and woman ducked under, but when Monsieur D'Haricot attempted to do likewise the guards lowered their weapons to bar his way. 'Is there a secret sign or password I should know?' he called to his guides.

The woman looked back, surprised that he had been stopped. 'Are you wearing anything purple?' she asked.

'Do I look the type of gentleman to wear purple?' Monsieur D'Haricot answered.

'What about lilac, maroon or violet?'

'I am wearing grey, although it could pass as green, and a white shirt,' Monsieur D'Haricot argued.

'No mauve or plum?'

'Oh, just let him pass boys,' the old man interrupted.

The armour guards stood to attention with their axes aloft. Monsieur D'Haricot took a deep breath and lunged through the gap, expecting the axes to fall. The guards followed orders and kept their positions.

'They don't like purple,' the woman explained. 'It reminds them of the imperial days.'

'I am not wearing purple,' Monsieur D'Haricot insisted.

'We'll need to get them reprogrammed,' the man said. 'They are usually good at discerning colours.'

'Apart from Hugo,' the woman added. 'That isn't his fault. It has to do with his genes. Colour-blind from birth, the doctors said.'

Monsieur D'Haricot had already ascertained that the two musicians aiding him were not playing from the same score as ordinary folk. He gave a small 'ah' in sympathy with the suit of armour's misfortune and walked the rest of the way in silence.

Their path led through a myriad of attic rooms that were either empty apart from cobwebs and fungi or contained broken wooden furniture. One room had been a nursery and an overstuffed teddy bear with one eye was riding a rocking horse. A doll's house lay on its side and Monsieur D'Haricot was sure he saw the miniature figures inside trying to right their tables and chair. He rubbed his eyes. Fantastic as this underground world was, it wasn't a magical one.

The accordion player spotted his confusion. 'Do you need a swig of cognac?' she asked.

'No thank you. Have we far to go?'

'You want to go to Rouen, don't you?' the woman said.

'Yes, but I thought I was to take an aquatran, not walk the entire way.' They had entered a library with moth-eaten volumes smelling of mildew. The old man had increased the pace and Monsieur D'Haricot struggled to keep up.

'Ha, walk to Rouen, that is funny,' the man said. 'It reminds me of a song I knew once.' He began humming notes, changing keys and rhythms until he hit on one he thought was right. 'Do you know the tune?' he asked.

'I am afraid not.'

'Not everyone has your musical library in their head, Philip,' the woman said.

'Pity you didn't bring your accordion to accompany me, Louise.'

'What would the people below us think if they heard accordion playing in their rafters? They must already believe they are infested with giant rats.'

'Giant rats – ha, that is funny as well,' Philip said.

Monsieur D'Haricot hoped the pair weren't going to continue their comedy act all the way to the river. The next room they entered was an artist's studio. The overpowering smell of linseed oil infused the canvases, pegged together easel, palettes crusted with dried pigments and camelhair brushes paddling in bowls of spirit. The room could have come straight from a painting, although it lacked the self-portrait image of the artist commonly found in such works.

'Maulise's workshop,' Louise, the accordion player, explained.

Monsieur D'Haricot assumed Maulise was out painting until a tarpaulin thrown over a chair in the corner stirred. Four elongated fingers stained with green paint crawled round the edges to pull back the sheet. A dollop of red hair was revealed, beneath which protruded the longest nose Monsieur D'Haricot had seen outwith the pages of an illustrated fairy tale anthology for children.

While the artist was scratching his armpits, wriggling his ears and in other ways getting himself together, Monsieur D'Haricot stepped towards him with his hand extended. 'You must be Monsieur Maulise,' he said.

Maulise rubbed his head, leaving a blob of green on his hair. He pushed his fringe aside to prove that he did indeed have eyes and stared at Monsieur D'Haricot. He sniffed the air three times, then stood up, letting the tarpaulin fall to the floor, and turned to address Louise and Philip. 'Your friend smells Unkylunk.'

Monsieur D'Haricot had no idea what he meant, but 'unkylunk' didn't sound good.

'Indeed,' Louise agreed. 'Monsieur D'Haricot came down this morning, which is the reason we are here. He needs to get to Rouen and wishes to board an aquatran.'

Maulise pulled up his breeches by tugging on a pair of worn braces. He ran his fingers down his shirt, adding green to the multitude of colours already dyed into the fabric. For at least a minute, no-one spoke. To avoid the embarrassment of staring at the dribble of saliva running down Maulise's chin, Monsieur D'Haricot took the opportunity to appreciate a collection of pictures leaning against a wall. The canvases were different sizes, but the picture was the same view of a nondescript bridge. The background was invariably red, but the bridge changed from yellow to green in an ordered manner.

'Don't touch,' Maulise ordered, spotting Monsieur D'Haricot putting out a hand. 'The paint is wet. If you get it on your clothes you'll stink vimficious for a week.'

'I wouldn't want that.' Monsieur D'Haricot stepped away. 'Is there any chance we might find an aquatran prepared to travel to Rouen this afternoon?'

'That depends.'

'Depends on what?'

Maulise moved towards Monsieur D'Haricot brandishing a paintbrush he had pulled from his belt. The hairs were coated with green paint. 'It depends whose side you are on.' He was standing close enough for Monsieur D'Haricot to notice the dash of green paint on Maulise's moustache. The smell was a cross between varnish remover, the Seine downstream from the sewers and stewed apples. *Vimficious indeed.*

'I am a French patriot,' Monsieur D'Haricot declared, puffing out his chest and arching his soles to balance on his toes.

'We are all French patriots,' Maulise answered.

'He can be trusted,' Philip said.

'Gori tried to murder him,' Louise added, as if it were a badge of honour.

Maulise stroked his moustache, transferring the paint back to his fingers. 'Gori has tried to murder his own mother,' he said.

'If I knew what the sides were, I could clarify my position,' Monsieur D'Haricot ventured.

Maulise looked at Philip, who looked at Louise. She in turn stared at Maulise. Monsieur D'Haricot felt like an outsider, which he assumed was the point.

'Shall we start with Victoire Chapleau?' Monsieur D'Haricot suggested. 'I have had the pleasure of meeting the lady, above ground, at what I had assumed were innocent social functions. A few days ago I discovered she works for my boss and today she and her friend Vicomte Otocey tried to kidnap me.' He had gained the attention of the others and continued. 'I have ascertained that this business concerns a place called Fraumy, which in my ignorance I had not known existed until this afternoon. I had no idea there was anything under Paris except sewers, rats and subway trains.'

'There are the catacombs as well,' Louise said.

Monsieur D'Haricot frowned. 'As the lady says, there are the catacombs, which I was also aware of.'

Maulise sniffed, one nostril at a time. He shuffled across the room to find a scrap of paper and a pencil and drew a rough map of France, bordering its neighbours. 'We needn't bother about England,' he remarked. 'This is Fraumy.' He dropped a finger on a tiny area between France and Belgium.

'It is an independent duchy,' Philip explained, 'ruled by the van Lüttich family since its foundation in the fifteenth or seventeenth century. I can never remember if the century number is ahead or behind the year. Traditionally it has been an ally of ours, but that doesn't mean we are friends.'

Monsieur D'Haricot nodded, relieved that Maulise's description was in line with what Victoire and Otocey had told him.

'The Grand-duke is head of the family,' Louise said. 'He has something of a thing for Victoire.'

'He is a fool and he is old,' Maulise said. 'His nephew, Edgori, is the heir and he has ambitions. He would betray our underground world to Germany in exchange for power above ground,' Philip said. 'He has already given them plans for advanced underwater ships.'

'We believe he intends to get rid of his uncle,' Louise said in a hushed voice.

'I assume Madame Chapleau wishes to prevent this,' Monsieur D'Haricot said. 'Where does Juan fit in?'

Monsieur D'Haricot had not mentioned Juan's name to Louise or Philip. He slipped the name in to test the reaction. Maulise stretched his hand across the map of France to thump another finger on Spain. 'Victoire is worried about the political situation in Madrid,' he said. 'She fears the rise in fascism across Europe threatens France.'

'Upper France,' Monsieur D'Haricot said.

'Madame Chapleau is an astute lady,' Louise answered. 'She knows that whatever happens above ground affects us down here. She wishes to offer our technical knowledge and underground transport systems to the French government.'

'That would be altruistic of her.' Monsieur D'Haricot said.

'In exchange for our freedom,' Philip added.

'I hadn't realised you were prisoners.'

'You have no idea what it is like to live underground.' Maulise spat the words out. 'This infernal artificial light plays havoc with the oxide pigments in my paints.'

'It doesn't help my brittle bones either,' Louise agreed.

'It is better than nothing, which may soon be the case,' Philip said. 'Our power relies on coal, which we have dug from deep in the earth for over a century. Now, however, the upper dwellers are extending their mines and stealing from our seams. The supplies are not infinite.'

'Or so our leaders tell us,' Maulise finished. At this, Louise, Philip and Maulise crossed their arms in unison and stared at Monsieur D'Haricot.

'I know nothing of coal mining,' Monsieur D'Haricot said.

'It isn't only coal. There are precious elements deeper in the earth with mystical powers,' Philip said.

'The further down the upper folks' instruments bore, the more chance there is of disturbing the Core Worm,' Louise said with a tremor in her voice. Monsieur D'Haricot failed to hold back his snort.

'You do not believe in that,' he said.

'You know nothing of mining, yet you know everything about the Core Worm,' Louise huffed. 'You say it doesn't exist, but you do not have to listen to its moaning on a winter's evening.'

Monsieur D'Haricot wondered how a worm living at the earth's core could tell the difference between the seasons, but he let it pass. 'My apologies, I didn't mean to offend you. Madame Chapleau mentioned the Core Worm, but perhaps you could tell me more.'

'Some people say there is one worm that coils its tail around the centre of the earth, holding everything in place. Others believe a score of worms burrow tunnels through the earth and one day the world will collapse in on itself.'

'Is this worm a good thing or a bad thing?' Monsieur D'Haricot asked.

'It is neither good nor bad,' Philip answered. 'It is nature.'

'To get back to the matter in hand,' Maulise interrupted. 'You claim Vicomte Otocey tried to kidnap you.'

'Yes.'

'Why would he do that when you had agreed to go to Rouen with them?' Louise asked.

'I didn't think about that,' Monsieur D'Haricot admitted.

'Think now,' Maulise urged.

'The cab driver was supposed to take us to the station, but he headed across the river. Victoire was concerned, but Otocey didn't think it odd.'

'Are you sure it was Victoire Chapleau who was with Otocey?' Louise asked. 'It couldn't have been her twin, Mala Kai? People often mistake one for the other.'

'That is ridiculous,' Monsieur D'Haricot answered. 'Victoire has a splendid complexion, strong cheekbones, lush hair—' He cleared his throat, realising he was becoming a little too intimate in his description of the lady. 'Let us just say that I have met Mala Kai and there is no way I would mistake them.'

'Did you meet Mala Kai above or below ground?' Philip asked.

'At Otocey's house in Paris – above ground.'

'Victoire has been a part of the upper world for some time and has adapted. Mala Kai struggles to find her form there. Below ground they are virtually identical.'

Monsieur D'Haricot rubbed his chin. 'The situation is becoming complicated,' he said. 'Wait, I have a handkerchief she gave me.' Monsieur D'Haricot pulled the item from his pocket.

'I knew you had purple on you,' Louise declared, pointing at the embroidered initials.

'They prove the handkerchief belonged to Victoire,' Monsieur D'Haricot said.

'Do they?' Maulise took the handkerchief and turned it over. The letters M K were embroidered on the back, in the opposite corner.

'I hadn't noticed,' Monsieur D'Haricot admitted.

'If you ask me, Gori will be at the root of it. He is a double-crossing bandit,' Philip said.

'I smell something faldraxial.' Maulise screwed up the map and tossed it across the floor, then turned to Monsieur D'Haricot. 'You are the Sagittarian, aren't you?'

The conversation was beginning to run away from Monsieur D'Haricot. 'I do not believe in astrology. I doubt I am the man you are looking for.' He had made a false move. Maulise reached for a palate knife.

'Not here.' Louise moved to stand between the artist and Monsieur D'Haricot. 'The blood might spurt onto your masterpieces.'

Philip took hold of Monsieur D'Haricot with his strong hands and locked his prisoner's arms in a half nelson. Monsieur D'Haricot tried to utilise his training in self-defence, but he had let his daily exercises slip. Philip hustled him towards a door, which Louise opened. Maulise followed, poking the knife in Monsieur D'Haricot's back. He was shoved towards the unguarded edge of a flight of wooden stairs with planks missing. Only four steps were visible, below them an abyss of darkness.

'I was sure you were the one,' Louise said, by way of a half-hearted apology.

'Au revoir, Monsieur,' Maulise said, giving Monsieur D'Haricot a shove. The creaking boards disintegrated and he fell.

Chapter Nine

'No, no. The crab. We are forgetting about Marina,' Louise shouted.

Monsieur D'Haricot would later describe the experience as being hanged upside down on a gibbet. He was suspended in midair, feet 1.78 metres above his head with the expanse of his body making it difficult for him to breathe. His bag, which he had slung over his neck, was tightening around his windpipe. Philip had grabbed a foot as he plummeted head first and was pulling with his oxen strength. Monsieur D'Haricot's first instinct was to kick out, but realised, as his face turned blue, that this was counter-productive. He hung limp while Philip dragged him back onto the landing. Louise rescued the bag while Monsieur D'Haricot crept onto all fours, gulping air.

'My poor darling, are you injured?' Louise asked, cradling the crab in her arms and stroking it like a puppy.

'We've got the crab, what about him?' Maulise kicked Monsieur D'Haricot's backside and he fell flat against the floorboards.

The blood and oxygen returned to Monsieur D'Haricot's brain and his grey cells clicked into action. 'Did I mention that I speak fluent Spanish?' he said.

'What?'

'The word is "pardon",' Monsieur D'Haricot corrected. He did not intend to be intimidated by an uncouth artist. 'I noticed one of your pieces bore the title "Puente of Rey, Madrid". The "of" should surely be "del", or at least it should be translated as "of the".'

'What is he talking about?' Maulise asked his companions.

'The bridge of the king,' Monsieur D'Haricot answered, growing in confidence.

'A slip of the brush,' Maulise said. 'If you mean I'll need a la-de-da translator, you are mistaken. Juan speaks French like Picasso.'

'Who is also Spanish,' Monsieur D'Haricot said, examining a broken nail. 'Juan may speak French to you, but will you know what messages he is sending to his compatriots in Spain?'

'That is none of our business. It would be spying,' Louise said.

'Spying is my trade, Madam.'

'What secrets about us will you pass on to your paymaster?' Maulise threatened. He turned to Louise and Philip. 'We don't know who he is working for. We've got the crab. I say we kill him.'

'I am no mercenary. I am proud to say that I serve the General. Apart from his taste in German likör, I have never had reason to doubt his integrity.'

'He means the Archduke,' Louise said, giving Philip a nudge.

'He doesn't have to be so uppity about it,' her brother responded.

'He can't be uppity when he is crawling on the floor,' Louise objected.

'Regardless of that, you are discussing killing me. I can be as uppity as I wish.' Monsieur D'Haricot got to his feet and brushed down his clothing.

'Not just a killing. Maulise is an artist. It would be a proper execution,' Louise explained.

'I don't know any prisoner who has been executed by being thrown down a disintegrating staircase,' Monsieur D'Haricot argued.

'There must be some, surely?'

'We are wasting time,' Maulise decided. 'There is no point in us all travelling to Rouen. I'll take him. You two return to the café and find out what Gori is up to.' He reached out a hand. 'Give me the crab.'

Louise held the crustacean to her breast and Marina aimed a pincher at Maulise's fingers. 'She doesn't like you,' Louise said.

'I can't go to Rouen without her.'

'I'll take her,' Monsieur D'Haricot said. 'Pop her back in my bag.'

'You will be fine, darling. Promise mama you will behave.' Louise laid a slobbery kiss on the crab's shell before placing her gently into the bag.

'Me hungry,' Marina said in a pathetic squeak.

'I don't suppose you have any macarons?' Monsieur D'Haricot asked.

'You think we mix with the hoi polloi?' Maulise was scathing.

'What about corporal readjustment accelerator biscuits? She likes those.'

'I have a few, but I'll need them in Rouen. I can't waste them on shellfish.'

'You mean, selfish man,' Louise raged. 'Don't think I'll ever be buying your pathetic pictures again.' She marched past Monsieur D'Haricot into the studio and returned carrying four canvases under her arms. Before Maulise could stop her she tossed them over the edge of the staircase. Monsieur D'Haricot counted twenty seconds before hearing the plop of masterpiece hit water. Maulise stood shaking. He clenched and unclenched his fists.

'Come, ma chérie, I think we should go now.' Philip took hold of his sister's hand and shielded her from Maulise as they sidled past him.

'If it is any consolation,' Monsieur D'Haricot said once the singer and the accordionist had left, 'The pictures weren't actually that good.'

'What do you mean? They took years of my life to create.'

'Really?'

'No, but if you say it enough times, you start to believe it. Wait here until I fetch my coat.'

Maulise vanished into his studio and returned wearing a multicoloured, alpaca wool coat which Monsieur D'Haricot thought effeminate, but he held his tongue.

'It's a disguise,' Maulise said, seeing the look on Monsieur D'Haricot's face. 'It smells woftic, don't you think?'

'Woftic or not, there is no way we will be incognito,' Monsieur D'Haricot answered. He allowed Maulise to lead the way. To the left of the staircase was a door hidden in the shadows, large enough for a medium-sized hound. Maulise opened it and they ventured into a bedchamber. From the smell of oils, paints and varnishes, Monsieur D'Haricot guessed it was Maulise's own room.

'Don't wait up for me, honey,' Maulise said to the rising and falling cover on the bed. A snore or a snort answered from beneath a pillow.

Monsieur D'Haricot averted his gaze from the bed and tiptoed across the carpet after Maulise. The artist opened a side door to reveal a wash room. He stepped inside.

'Do you mind?' he snapped as Monsieur D'Haricot tried to follow him.

'Oh, sorry.'

Monsieur D'Haricot waited until Maulise finished his ablutions, hoping the thing under the bedclothes would not waken and expect him to make conversation with it. Monsieur D'Haricot heard the sound of running water. When it gurgled to a halt, the door was swung open in Monsieur D'Haricot's face.

'Are you still here? I thought you would have gone ahead,' Maulise said.

'Where to?' Monsieur D'Haricot looked around the room. Apart from the bed there was nothing but a rickety chest of drawers and a travelling trunk. Maulise approached the trunk. It was constructed from planks of a dark wood, not ebony, but possibly seasoned mahogany or wenge wood. The original patterned etching had been added to with coloured inlays and carvings, giving clues to where the trunk had been. Actual creatures took on the attributes of the mythological, with rhinoceroses becoming unicorns, lions becoming griffons and eagles transforming into rocs. At the bottom corner a capuchin monkey was in charge of a fruit stall weighed down with exotic goods. The detail was exquisite, and when Monsieur D'Haricot ran the tips of his fingers across the surface he could feel the soft furs, dry scales and smooth feathers. His mouth watered at the thought of pineapple and papaya.

'Where did you get this magnificent trunk?' he asked.

'From a client who couldn't afford to pay for their portrait. I believe it originally came from Elenoceraf – a country hidden in the long grass, south of the Algerian deserts. The carvings were created by elephants using stone tools that they held in their trunks. I suppose that is why it is called a trunk.'

'Elephants are wondrous creatures,' Monsieur D'Haricot agreed.

'Indeed. If elephants formed an army against humans, I would join with the elephants. I don't think I would be the only one.' Maulise paused. 'I'm surprised Otocey hasn't made a pact with them.'

'I don't believe I have ever seen a live elephant,' Monsieur D'Haricot declared.

'Oh, me neither,' Maulise asserted. 'I doubt they even exist.'

'Like manticores,' Monsieur D'Haricot joked. Maulise was showing his amiable side and he wished to take advantage of the fact to learn what he could.

'Tush. I've seen hundreds of those.' Maulise swiped a hand in the air.

'Really?'

'They run up trees in the park and throw nuts at passersby.'

'Those are squirrels,' Monsieur D'Haricot explained.

'Isn't that what you said? You have an atrocious accent. Anyone would think you were from... I don't know where, but not Paris.'

Monsieur D'Haricot was insulted by this slur, but before he could think of a rebuttal, Maulise had opened the lid of the trunk and was squeezing his body inside. A trumpeting noise sounded from the lid.

'Come on,' Maulise urged. 'Or the noise will wake the wife.'

'Are you sure it is safe?' Monsieur D'Haricot asked. 'There is no danger of being trapped inside and suffocated?'

Maulise didn't answer. Monsieur D'Haricot watched as his companion's waist, then chest, and finally his head and neck vanished into the box. He moved to peer inside. The trunk was empty. He could plainly see the wooden base, painted a teal green. Without warning, Maulise's head appeared, rising like Excalibur from the lake. Monsieur D'Haricot put a hand over his heart as he stumbled backwards with an unprintable exclamation. There was a snort and a female head emerged from beneath the bedclothes.

'You've woken Florence,' Maulise scolded.

'Who is Florence?' the woman asked. She took a look at Monsieur D'Haricot. 'And who are you?'

Monsieur D'Haricot looked to Maulise to explain, but the head had submerged into the wood.

'I'm here to treat woodworm,' Monsieur D'Haricot answered. He tapped the chest. 'The blighters get everywhere. Allow me to deal with them.' He took a breath, sat on the rim of the trunk and swivelled his feet inside to rest on the bottom. It felt solid. He massaged the wood with the toe of his shoes. The boards creaked in response, releasing their tension. Picking up his courage he stood up, transferring his weight from the rim to the bottom. The floor of the trunk softened as if he were standing barefoot on a sandy beach. He sank, slowly at first, but when he offered no resistance his downward acceleration increased. As his head was sinking into the floor, he heard the sound of the trunk lid slam shut.

He was surrounded by darkness. There was nothing to touch, nothing to hear and nothing to smell, although he imagined Maulise would come up with a word to describe the odour of 'nothingness'.

'Maulise, are you there?' he asked, but his ears did not pick up his words. 'Where are we? Do we need special biscuits?' He waited for a reply before realising it was unlikely Maulise could hear him.

Perhaps time existed, perhaps it didn't. Perhaps elephants were real and mice ruled the world.

At some point Monsieur D'Haricot felt a solid block against his feet. The relief was unbearable and he feared he was going to cry. He wiped his eyes, becoming aware of a dim, purple light. The effect gave him a sensation of vertigo. He staggered and hit his shoulder against a revolving wheel. Moving away, he hit what could have been the branch of a tree.

The language assaulting his ears was testament that his hearing had returned. The voice was frog-like, reminding Monsieur D'Haricot of the first time he had heard the movie star Jean Arthur in The Return of Fu Manchu, but the vimficious odour confirmed that it was not a tree, but Maulise.

The space around them lightened and Monsieur D'Haricot made out the shape of the artist a few metres away. They were standing, fully clothed, in a shower room.

'Brifalgo, isn't it?' Maulise said, his voice returning to normal.

Monsieur D'Haricot was beginning to understand what Philip meant when he said Maulise was a Capricorn. If he enquired what brifalgo was, or what was brifalgo, the answer would be a series of nonsensical riddles. Maulise decided to elaborate without being coaxed.

'We are in a system that clears our bodies of efraeons.' He smiled, expecting Monsieur D'Haricot to admire the mechanics. 'You do know what efraeons are?' he goaded when Monsieur D'Haricot failed to give the appropriate response.

'No, I don't,' Monsieur D'Haricot replied. 'For all I know, you could have invented the word one second ago.'

'I am not in the habit of making up words,' Maulise huffed. He adjusted the toggles on his coat. They were fastened in the wrong loops, but he didn't correct the fault.

If Maulise could play childish games so could he, Monsieur D'Haricot decided. Ignoring his companion, he tapped randomly on the tiled walls of the room.

'What are you doing?' Maulise asked.

'Checking for toffee lice.'

'Never heard of them. Are they catching? Can they kill you?' Maulise tapped on the wall himself, then drew back and wagged a finger at Monsieur D'Haricot. 'Efraeons are tiny particles,' he explained. 'You can't live down here without picking them up. They are harmless, but you might as well have a large arrow painted on your backside. They allow government agents to keep tabs on your whereabouts.'

'I know little about the machinations of your political system,' Monsieur D'Haricot admitted. 'From what you say, I can't see much difference between it and my own government.'

'We have a Primus, ten senior primites and twenty aides.'

'Primates?' Monsieur D'Haricot suggested. Maulise didn't appreciate his humour.

'The system works, or it did until a year ago. Some form of government was needed to ensure the bins got emptied, but it didn't interfere. The ministers weren't paid, so there was no incentive to change things or invent new laws.'

A government that didn't interfere was surely another of Maulise's fantasies. 'What happened?' Monsieur D'Haricot asked.

'The Primus died. There was no suggestion of foul play; old Marcel was over a hundred, but a new one had to be elected, and that was when the trouble started. The candidates brought ideas of their own.'

'A leader with ideas doesn't sound good,' Monsieur D'Haricot sympathised.

'Now the talk is of returning to the surface—'

'—which is what you said you wanted,' Monsieur D'Haricot interrupted, quick to show he had been listening to Maulise's eulogy on freedom.

'Yes, but like the blurred shadows in crowd paintings that no-one notices. The new government has different ideas. The Primus is raising an invading army.'

'What!' Monsieur D'Haricot forgot his own advice. 'You plan to invade Paris?'

'The whole of France. The plans are well advanced. There are people installed in senior positions above ground, in the government, judiciary, police, universities, beer cellars and the like.'

'Ridiculous. You will never get away with it.'

'There's no need to get shirty with me. I am a part of the Underground.'

'The underground Underground?' Monsieur D'Haricot couldn't resist.

'We are a resistance movement. We are the ones who see the folly of this action. Europe is a mess of grievances. Our government hopes to use this to its advantage, but we see only hardship, bloodshed and war. Our ancestors retreated underground to get away from that. Don't get me wrong; we are not cowards, Monsieur.'

'It takes courage to resist,' Monsieur D'Haricot agreed.

'Government agents discovered our network and have tried to contain our movements. That is why our leader invented this method of cleansing our bodies from efraeons.'

'I see. Brifalgo. Who is your leader?'

'I can't tell you that. You could be a spy. We'd better get going.'

Monsieur D'Haricot followed Maulise towards a doorway. 'Can I ask which side Madame Chapleau is on?' he ventured.

'Madame Chapleau? Why, she is the Primus.'

Chapter Ten

Maulise was holding the shower room door open for him. There seemed little else for Monsieur D'Haricot to do but walk through.

'Going up,' Maulise declared. He had stepped behind Monsieur D'Haricot into an elevator compartment and pressed the green button. It was a tight fit and Monsieur D'Haricot could appreciate the true meaning of vimficious, in all its timbres. The elevator rattled and shook, protesting with clanks of metal and squeaks of compressed air. Maulise kicked the side wall.

'Perhaps you need to be gentle with it,' Monsieur D'Haricot said.

'Pah.'

The elevator jerked into action. Maulise was clearly used to the elevator and appeared unperturbed, but Monsieur D'Haricot's innards felt like dice being shaken by a professional. The lift juddered to unexpected halts and restarted at the exact moment he decided the mechanism was finally kaput and he was trapped with a foul-smelling, mood-swinging troglodyte.

'F... ir... st... F... loo... r.' A childlike voice from the side of the elevator announced in a drawl.

'What floor do we want?' Monsieur D'Haricot asked, trying not to sound exasperated.

'Twenty-seven,' Maulise replied.

'Perhaps you could wake me when we get to twenty-six.'

'Ha, you are making me walk,' Maulise replied.

'I'm sorry?'

'Is that not what you say on the surface?'

'No, the phrase is "pulling my leg",' Monsieur D'Haricot replied.

'Which would make me walk, n'est pas?'

'Go… ing dow… n.' The elevator voice said.

'We'd better hurry.'

The elevator shuddered. Maulise reached for the door handle and opened it. He bundled Monsieur D'Haricot forwards and leapt out before the door slammed shut.

'What do we do now?' Monsieur D'Haricot said. 'Wait on the lift returning or find the stairs?'

'The lift voice programme only has one level,' Maulise explained. 'First floor, twenty-seventh floor, a hundred and fifth – it will always tell you it is the first floor. We have arrived. This is where we want to be.'

Monsieur D'Haricot looked around. It would take a bottle of fine champagne to persuade him this was where *he* wanted to be. They were in a giant warehouse, surrounded by wooden crates and cardboard postal boxes. A giant thermometer on the wall declared the temperature to be colder than Monsieur D'Haricot imagined the North Pole to be. A layer of frost covered the ground. It was no wonder Maulise had thought it smart to put on his woollen overcoat. Monsieur D'Haricot was somewhat peeved that he had not shared this foresight.

'Will we be here long?' he asked, his teeth chattering.

Maulise consulted his watch. 'There should be a consignment due in fifteen minutes.'

'A consignment of what?'

'I've no idea. It isn't important. This is a cold storage unit for perishable supplies. Aquatrans bring them in, then return to the surface. We should be able to hitch a lift.'

'If a consignment is due, why aren't there people around waiting to unload it?'

'There are, but you don't think they are going to hang around in the cold.'

'Why are we?' Monsieur D'Haricot hugged his chest to keep warm. His breath formed ethereal patterns in the chill air.

'We don't want to be seen. Gori will have agents among the workers, as will Otocey and Madame Chapleau.'

'If that is the case, can we trust the aquatran captain?'

'No, but have you any other suggestions?'

Monsieur D'Haricot was unwilling to admit that he hadn't and decided attack was the best form of defence. 'What do we pay the captain with? I have no money, as Louise and Philip will have told you.'

Maulise tapped the bag which held the crab.

'No, never.' Monsieur D'Haricot drew it closer.

'In that case, I hope you are good at washing dishes.'

Fifteen minutes dragged. Maulise spent the time filling a pipe with purple leaves and pressing them into shape. He didn't light the pipe and appeared to have no desire to smoke the leaves. Monsieur D'Haricot hopped from one frozen foot to another. His toes were numb and he feared losing another. The bleating of 'me still hungry' rose periodically from his bag.

The shuffling of approaching footsteps and the sound of voices heralded the imminent arrival of an aquatran. Maulise ducked behind one of the crates near the mooring site. Monsieur D'Haricot was hard on his heels.

A watertight door slid open and the aquatran glided silently into the dock from a sealed chamber.

'I see, the two door system protects the warehouse from the depth of the river,' Monsieur D'Haricot said.

'With the advantage that the glass is kraken-proof,' Maulise added.

'I can't imagine you have had trouble with those in the Seine.' Monsieur D'Haricot suspected Maulise was in need of medication.

'Not since '25. That's when the doors were put in.'

Monsieur D'Haricot turned his attention to the aquatran. It was a similar design to Gustav's boat. A gangplank was connected to allow the goods to be carried off.

'Wait here,' Maulise instructed. 'I'll speak with the captain.'

Monsieur D'Haricot was too cold to reply. His teeth were glued together with icicles. When Maulise returned, he had to take hold of an arm and pull his travelling companion from the spot. Monsieur D'Haricot's legs would not move and the captain of the aquatran came out to assist, armed with a pickaxe.

'Monsieur D'Haricot,' the captain declared. 'I did not think we would meet again so soon.'

'You know one another?' Maulise was surprised. Monsieur D'Haricot was equally amazed to see Gustav. The closeness of the two bodies thawed his jaw.

'Were you not travelling to Rouen?' he asked.

'I told you Suzie was fast.' Gustav grinned. 'No, there was a change of plan. I have a crate to collect here before I can leave.'

He spoke for several more sentences, but Monsieur D'Haricot's frozen mind did not take in everything Gustav said. He only hoped the captain would not associate the theft of the crab from the galley with his disappearance, although having a crab in his bag did appear to be incriminating evidence. Nothing was said of the incident as he was carried by Maulise and Gustav to the aquatran. The ice soldering his feet together melted by the time they negotiated the narrow steps and he was able to make his way to his previous cabin.

His personal possessions, including his wallet, were where he had left them, apparently untouched. Although there were two bunks, Maulise did not share the cabin, which was a relief. The artist left with Gustav, discussing the likelihood of them seeing a giant nonopus that he could paint for an author requiring a book cover.

Once he was alone, Monsieur D'Haricot put down his bag, removed his shoes and socks, wrapped the blanket from the top bunk round his feet and lay on the bed. His mind was foggy, but it occurred to him that the elaborate process to remove efraeons was pointless, since Gustav was clearly working with Otocey and Madame Chapleau. Were efraeons a concoction to convince Maulise of the government's evil intentions? Or was Gustav a double agent? Whatever the truth was, he decided it was best to warn Maulise about the captain. Rising quickly, he banged his head on the top bunk and was out cold by the time his head fell onto the pillow.

The scenery through northern France, above ground, is some of the country's finest. Despite the aquatran having surfaced north of Giverny, Monsieur D'Haricot did not see any of the surrounding flower meadows, farms and neatly painted villages. He woke with a start to find himself on the floor of the cabin. Maulise was standing over him.

'Ha, that did the trick,' Maulise said. The blanket Monsieur D'Haricot had been lying on was beside him on the floor and he realised that Maulise had pulled it from under him. His feet were still swaddled in the second blanket.

'Have we arrived?' He untangled his toes, got to his feet and ran a hand through his hair, pulling out several strands.

'Don't worry, you haven't missed breakfast,' Maulise answered.

Monsieur D'Haricot sat on the bunk to put on his shoes and socks. When he had managed to get his shoes on the right feet, he reached for his bag.

'You won't need that at breakfast,' Maulise said.

'I was thinking of Marina – the crab.' He felt in the bag, but his fingers touched the bottom and sides without being pinched. He looked inside, then turned it outside in. 'Where is she?' he demanded.

'Don't ask me. Are you coming to breakfast or not?'

The thought of strong coffee and fresh rolls started Monsieur D'Haricot's stomach rumbling. He did not want to miss out on the opportunity while he searched the cabin for the crab. He put the bag down and followed Maulise into the corridor and along to the galley. The chef eyed him suspiciously as he entered.

'Fine morning,' Monsieur D'Haricot said. The portholes were covered, giving him no indication of what the weather was like.

The galley was empty apart from the chef, Maulise and himself. Maulise took a chair at a table and perused the menu. Monsieur D'Haricot sat next to him. It took Maulise an age to choose and Monsieur D'Haricot tried to read the menu over his shoulder.

'I shall have the mackerel,' Maulise said, slapping the menu on the table.

'The mackerel is off,' the chef replied.

Monsieur D'Haricot had been about to take the menu, but Maulise snatched it up again. 'The ham omelette,' he decided.

'The omelette is off.'

'It would be faster if you told us what we can order,' Monsieur D'Haricot said to the chef.

'Crab pate,' the chef said, eyeing Monsieur D'Haricot. 'No, wait – that has gone off as well.'

'I do not like your tone,' Monsieur D'Haricot said, putting his palms flat on the table and pressing down. 'If you do not bring my friend and I hot coffee and croissants in five minutes, I shall make sure Madame Chapleau hears of your insubordination.' The chef glowered at Monsieur D'Haricot. He attempted to outstare him, but Monsieur D'Haricot had practised with his neighbour's Siamese cat. Although he never won, he reckoned he could put up a good showing against any non-feline rival. The chef shrugged and turned away. 'And a macaron for my friend Marina,' Monsieur D'Haricot called after him, spotting the tip of a pincher poke out from the side of the drinks cabinet.

'That told him,' Maulise declared, setting down the menu. 'I would have asked for champagne rather than coffee.' He paused for a second.

'Were you bluffing about Madame Chapleau? How did you know the man worked for her?'

Maulise clearly had learned nothing from his conversation with Gustav. Monsieur D'Haricot let the question hang in the air. 'Ah, here is breakfast now.' He sniffed in appreciation.

'Delisooky,' Maulise agreed.

The chef set the coffee and croissants on the table. When he finished, he shook the left sleeve of his jacket and an almond macaron slid into his palm. He laid it on a plate, positioning it with artistic flair, and placed the plate in front of an empty chair. Before he had finished, Marina came scrambling from her hiding place and sidestepped towards the table. The chef stooped to pick her up and make her comfortable on the chair, providing a cushion so that she could be at the right height. There was something slimy about his attitude that Monsieur D'Haricot didn't like. Maulise was of the same opinion.

'Wait,' Maulise said, as Marina reached for the macaron. 'I think you should share a crumb with this nice man.'

'I am afraid I am allergic to the sugar,' the chef said hurriedly.

'But not to the cyanide?' Maulise said.

'What do you mean?' The chef's face turned purple.

'I recognise the smell. It is nezmarising.'

'You are mistaken, Monsieur.' The chef reached to snatch the offending confectionary, but Maulise seized a fork and slammed the prongs into the table, millimetres from the chef's hand. The chef drew his hand away. Maulise got to his feet.

'I wouldn't eat the croissants either,' he informed Monsieur D'Haricot. 'I suggest we take breakfast in the city.'

'Do not fear, Marina, you shall have your macarons,' Monsieur D'Haricot assured the crab as he lifted her away from the chef. He and Maulise left the galley together.

'This way,' Maulise instructed.

'I have things to collect from my cabin.'

'We have to go now. I heard that poisoning traitor listening to a German radio broadcast. He will have used the interlocutor to tell tales on us to Gori.'

'We must warn Gustav.'

'He could be a double-crossing cur too.'

'We can't go that way. It leads down to the cargo room,' Monsieur D'Haricot said. 'Unless the crew are loading or unloading goods, we will be trapped.'

'Oh.' Maulise rubbed his chin, pretending to think.

'Leave this to me,' Monsieur D'Haricot said. 'I have a plan.'

Monsieur D'Haricot's father had played a game with him, which involved objects being laid on a tabletop. His father instructed him to view them for thirty seconds before they were covered with his mother's tea towel and he had to recite a list of the objects. There was no prize for remembering everything, but a whack on the knuckles if he missed even one teaspoon. The author Rudyard Kipling was familiar with the game and had described it in a novel as part of his character Kim's training as a spy. It served Monsieur D'Haricot well for his future career, and in the current circumstance he was confident that two steps to the right of Maulise's left shoulder there was a broom cupboard that held three mops, a bucket, two cloths, a bar of soap, an apron and a banana skin.

'Grab a mop and swab the decks,' he instructed.

'I am not a skivvy. Besides, the captain will realise we are not crew members,' Maulise answered. 'Couldn't we simply hide in the cupboard until the way is clear?'

'Yes, I suppose that would be possible,' Monsieur D'Haricot admitted. He had enjoyed using the phrase 'swab the decks' in a pirate's voice.

There was barely room in the cupboard for the mops and bucket, let alone two well-fed gentlemen. By folding and interlocking arms and legs in what resembled reef knots, they managed to contort their bodies to fit.

'I can't close the door,' Monsieur D'Haricot said. 'Can you reach the handle?'

Maulise's attempt succeeded in knocking one of the mops against the side with a clatter. 'They won't have heard that,' he said, unconvincingly.

'You are standing on my hand,' Monsieur D'Haricot complained.

'And I have a crab pincher attached to my backside.'

While they were arguing, the cupboard door was swung open to reveal Gustav and the chef.

'I told you they were mad men,' the chef said to Gustav. 'It would not surprise me if they had English blood.'

'We can explain,' Maulise began, stepping out of the cupboard and dragging Monsieur D'Haricot with him. Gustav waited, but no explanation came. Maulise looked to Monsieur D'Haricot.

'We are health inspectors,' Monsieur D'Haricot said. 'I have my identification here.' He fumbled in his pocket. 'I must have left it in my cabin.'

'In your bag, perhaps?' Gustav produced the empty bag from behind his back and turned it inside out. Monsieur D'Haricot snatched it from him.

'In my travelling case,' he answered.

'Along with your other spying equipment,' the chef accused.

Monsieur D'Haricot wagged a finger in the air three times while he decided on his next move. It came to him in a flash.

'Run,' he shouted to Maulise, pushing past the startled chef.

Chapter Eleven

Monsieur D'Haricot scurried along the corridor towards the stairs with Maulise clipping his heels. Marina had scrambled into the bag, which he slung around his neck. It occurred to him that they could still be underwater, but the thought had to contend with the vision of him forgetting to lock the front door of his apartment. Neither seemed important when chased by two armed and angry enemy agents.

Maulise had had the sense to upset the contents of the mop cupboard, slowing Gustav and the chef as they tried to disentangle themselves. The banana skin was a star. The chef was the first to slip, grapping hold of Gustav's waist, hauling the captain to the floor beside him.

Monsieur D'Haricot struggled up the steps, Maulise close behind. He slid the door open with a strong push. In his haste to leave the vessel, his foot slipped and caught Maulise in the face. The boat was moored against a landing platform and Monsieur D'Haricot jumped ashore, eager to be off. Maulise emerged on deck and closed the hatch door after him. He stood on top of it grasping his jaw.

'I tink I've swallowed a toof,' he moaned.

Monsieur D'Haricot looked at his companion and gasped. One small, accidental kick could hardly have constituted such a change. Maulise's hair was dropping to the deck in clumps, his ruddy complexion was washed out, his eyes were dangling on stalks, his nose was dribbling down his upper lip and his ears appeared to have been erased leaving a grubby smudge. If he remained there a minute longer his entire being would be reduced to a slimy mess on the wooden boards.

'Whatever is the matter?' Monsieur D'Haricot asked, after several unprintable exclamations learned from his grandmother.

'Bithcut...' The word came from the vague direction of Maulise's head. A slippery hand patted his pocket before a finger dropped off.

Monsieur D'Haricot was not in the habit of putting his hand in gentlemen's pockets, but there was no alternative. He returned to the deck and slipped his fingers, as adept as a pickpocket, between the fabrics of the pocket and trouser lining until he found a readjustment biscuit. He held it between his thumb and forefinger for Maulise to take. His companion was in no state to do so and Monsieur D'Haricot was faced with the gruesome task of forcing the biscuit into the gaping, bloodstained hole in Maulise's head. The biscuit balanced on his molten tongue, threatening to drop to the deck. Monsieur D'Haricot poked it further down with a finger, rubbing it against the side of the ship afterwards to remove the drool.

A thumping sound rose from the hatch beneath Maulise's feet. The door juddered as the chef and Gustav used their force to dislodge Maulise. A crate was positioned next to the hatch and Monsieur D'Haricot moved to slide it across the top. There were conveniently placed holes for fingers to grasp, but one shove made him reconsider. It would take both his weight and Maulise's to achieve the desired effect. The artist was beginning to regain his form. His eyes swung back into their sockets and his nose was once more able to differentiate what was faldraxial and what simply woftic, but he would be useless to help.

'We have to go... NOW.' Monsieur D'Haricot echoed Maulise's words. He was loath to take hold of Maulise in case his arm tore off like a hunk of bread, but it had to be done. Grabbing his sleeve, he pulled him onto the landing platform. Maulise's feet were becoming substantial flesh and bones inside his shoes and he was able to step onto the paved path running parallel to the river.

It was a fine morning and there were townsfolk promenading. Monsieur D'Haricot caught sight of a group of rowers carrying their craft to the river. The boat was balanced on the athletic young men's shoulders, hiding the faces of the rowers on the far side from view. He signalled his plan to Maulise with a tap of his nose and a finger pointing to the boat. They fell into line behind the lead oarsman. The chef and Gustav surfaced, glanced along the riverbank and set off in the opposite direction.

'I thought you were used to being on the surface,' Monsieur

D'Haricot said once they were out of immediate danger, had abandoned the boat crew and were making their way into the centre of town.

'Never been above the tenth floor in my life, and if this is what sunlight is like, I don't want to stay. My head is splitting.'

'What about the famous bridges you have painted?'

'Copied from postcards and magazines. I did tell you I needed the biscuits.'

'How long do they last?' Monsieur D'Haricot asked, hoping he wouldn't have to explain to his fellow citizens why his companion was melting into the sewers.

'One is usually sufficient for a short sojourn above ground, according to Caprice's eldest lad. He does casual work on the surface now and again.'

'Who is Caprice?'

'My wife. You met her.'

'The lady in the bed,' Monsieur clarified.

'Who else would be in my bed?'

'I thought you said her name was Florence?'

'Florence was last month. Keep up.'

Monsieur D'Haricot had no desire to discuss the marital life of his companion. 'How long is a short sojourn?' he asked instead.

'It varies between individuals. Once our bodies get used to the surface dirt, one biscuit a year is sufficient, sometimes less. I believe Vicomte Otocey has not needed to take a biscuit for over five years. Lucky him – they taste disgusting.'

'If you don't like them, I can eat them,' a voice piped up from Monsieur D'Haricot's bag. Marina poked her beady eyes and the rim of her shell above the surface. A crumb of biscuit was attached to her mouth.

'You had better not speak while we are here,' Monsieur D'Haricot warned. 'The people will think it odd.'

'I'm odd? What about him?' Marina pointed indignantly at Maulise.

'Let's find Juan,' Monsieur D'Haricot said before Maulise and Marina came to blows. 'Otocey mentioned a performance in Le Crochet on Friday. What day is it today?'

Maulise swiped a newspaper from a pile on a cart that a young lad was selling. He doffed the boy on the head when he objected. 'It is Thursday,' he answered. 'We have a day in hand.'

'We could find the club,' Monsieur D'Haricot suggested. 'Be

prepared.'

'Or we could visit Juan's place of business.'

'You know where that is?'

'Would I have mentioned it if I didn't?'

Monsieur D'Haricot assumed the question was rhetorical, although he didn't agree with the predicted answer. 'You said you had never been above ground before.'

'I also told you that my stepson has.'

Monsieur D'Haricot wondered what his stepson was doing in Rouen, but he gave his head a slight tilt to show he was willing to accept Maulise's reply. They were on the left bank of the river. A stone spire dominated that part of town and they set off towards it. When they came to a magnificent, mediaeval abbey Maulise sniffed the air three times.

'Can you smell something rotten?' he asked.

Monsieur D'Haricot breathed in the air. Apart from fallen leaves, there was no hint of decay.

'Garjier,' Maulise said with distaste.

'I'm sorry, I have difficulty understanding your descriptions of smells,' Monsieur D'Haricot admitted.

'You know where we are, don't you?'

Monsieur D'Haricot looked around at the row of wooden beamed houses overlooking the abbey, pushing each other to get a better view of the street. A notice declared the building to be the monastic church of Saint Ouen. 'This is a house of God, a Benedictine monastery,' he answered.

'I can pick up vibes and lingering smells. There is an evil that has remained here for centuries. Garjier.'

Monsieur D'Haricot tried to recall his history lessons from school. He snapped his finger and thumb together. 'Joan of Arc was martyred in Rouen,' he said.

Maulise nodded sombrely. 'The lady was tied to a stake in the cemetery here, but recanted. She was burned a week later elsewhere in the town, but the smell remains.'

Monsieur D'Haricot would have removed his hat, had he been wearing one, but somehow in his adventures his headwear had been mislaid. 'I think we should move on,' he said.

They took a path along a narrow alley towards the city's grand cathedral of Notre Dame, passing shop windows with tantalising breads and pastries. Monsieur D'Haricot's stomach rumbled and he regretted his haste in upsetting the aquatran's chef. When they drew near the window of a shop selling pastries in the shades of the French tricolour for the third time, Monsieur D'Haricot realised Maulise was as lost as an elephant on an iceberg.

'We should ask one of the good citizens where Juan has his business,' he suggested. 'What is his family name?'

'Santos, when he is in Madrid, but his mother is English. I have been told he uses an Anglicised version at work.'

'Here, in Normandy?' Monsieur D'Haricot gave a laugh, but Maulise did not appreciate his humour. He changed the laugh to a cough and pretended he had been clearing his throat. 'What line of business is Juan in?'

'Bookmaking.'

'I am not sure I can approve of that,' Monsieur D'Haricot said.

'You read, don't you? Someone has to make the books.'

'You mean a bookbinder,' Monsieur D'Haricot said. 'A bookmaker is something different.'

Maulise was unconcerned about the pedantry. He had already stopped a young lady to ask directions. The mademoiselle was confused by his question and Monsieur D'Haricot felt he should step in.

'We are seeking the business of the bookbinder, Juan Santos, or possibly he goes by the name of John Saint,' Monsieur D'Haricot said.

The woman stared at them with a look of panic. She had her fist tight around her bag, ready to swing it. Monsieur D'Haricot realised they were inadvertently blocking her way in a menacing manner. He stepped to the side. The woman walked on a few steps, then turned. 'Do you mean Saint John?'

'You know him?' Monsieur D'Haricot said.

'I know of the bookbinder Saint John Saint Clair. He has a shop up the hill. My mother and I laugh when we pass his sign. He explained that in England they pronounce it Sinjon Sinclair.'

'Thank you.' Again Monsieur D'Haricot tried to lift his non-existent hat. The young lady giggled and walked on.

The hill was an imposing feature of the city. Monsieur D'Haricot prided himself on his fitness thanks to his bicycle riding, but Maulise declared that he would never make it to the top. Despite cajoling from Monsieur D'Haricot, he refused to attempt the climb.

'I'll find something to do here until you finish talking to Juan,' he suggested. Monsieur D'Haricot made to walk off. Maulise gave a cough. 'A few francs would come in handy.'

Monsieur D'Haricot gave him the money and as they parted he saw Maulise make his way to a tobacconist.

Juan's business establishment was as easy to find as Ville d'Ys, that mythical city in Brittany swallowed by the ocean. His search wasn't helped by being given contrasting directions from the three people he asked. If one of them hadn't been a police officer and another a priest, Monsieur D'Haricot would have believed they were trying to confuse him on purpose.

'No, no, you are heading the wrong way,' insisted a warty hag with a basket of poodle puppies slung over her forearm. A scrawny dog with bald patches kept close to her ankles. 'The only bookbinder in this district is beside Latry, the vintner.'

'Where would I find Monsieur Latry?'

'Madame Latry is a widow.'

'My condolences.' Monsieur D'Haricot regretted his lack of a hat for the third time and resolved to purchase one before leaving the city.

The woman rattled off a list of directions, ending with the phrase 'Use your nose.' Monsieur D'Haricot assured her that he would. The woman smelt of dog, garlic and rotten eggs and he decided not to take her advice until he was at the far end of the alleyway and she was at the other corner. He thanked her and offered her a coin, which the woman mistakenly assumed was payment for a puppy. She picked out a small, black dog and held it round the chest, with its hind legs dangling. The puppy gave a yap and tried to bite her crooked nose.

'I am afraid I am unable to look after a puppy,' Monsieur D'Haricot said.

'They are delicious with fried potatoes and haricot beans.' The old woman smiled, showing her broken teeth. Her bottom canine wobbled.

Monsieur D'Haricot was horrified. He had avoided eating dog in the trenches during the war and was certainly not going to start now. The other pups had started to cry and he noted that their fur was scruffy and their tummies pinched. 'I will take them all,' he declared. 'And also your bitch.'

The woman was reluctant to part with her breeding dog, but Monsieur D'Haricot opened his wallet and handed her three notes. He beheld her chortling like an English witch as she hurried off, leaving him with the basket of puppies. The string round the dog's neck was loose and the animal slipped free and ran after its mistress. Watching it run, Monsieur D'Haricot realised that it couldn't be the pups' mother. Not only was it a male, but it bore more than a fleeting resemblance to a charging ram.

Monsieur D'Haricot exhaled deeply. No-one in his family had ever owned a dog, let alone four puppies. He had nowhere to keep them and no milk or dog food. And he still hadn't found Juan. The yapping from the puppy basket grew louder and the looks from the bystanders were those of concern, even aggression. Monsieur D'Haricot increased his gait and slipped down a side street to avoid a party of middle-aged temperance ladies, armed with parasols. The buildings were residential, but the windows were shuttered and the doors closed.

The hope of finding Juan was fading. Monsieur D'Haricot considered whether to abandon his search. Indeed, above ground with his fellow citizens, his recent experiences seemed unreal – a figment of his overworked imagination. No-one in Paris would believe his tale. He should find a butcher to provide bones for his new pets, then make arrangements to return to Paris. One of his acquaintances there, an affluent matriarch, was fond of dogs and could be relied upon to look after the animals until homes could be found for them.

He turned into an unlit alleyway and was surprised to see a young, well-dressed lady walking towards him unaccompanied. She looked familiar, but she had her head in a book and he couldn't make out her features. She was walking at speed and he had to squeeze into a doorway to avoid a collision. The lady brushed against the basket and the jolt stirred the puppies into further song. Aware that she was not alone, the lady became apologetic.

'I have upset your puppies, the poor darlings,' she said.

'I am looking for homes for them,' Monsieur D'Haricot admitted. 'I cannot care for four poodles.'

'Perhaps I can help,' the lady smiled. She handed Monsieur D'Haricot her book and drew back the cover. Instantly she gave a yelp and pulled her hand away. Two of her fingers were bleeding.

'I am sorry. I didn't realise they bit,' Monsieur D'Haricot reached for his handkerchief and offered it to her. She refused.

'These are not poodle pups,' the lady said in a grave voice. 'They are were-fangs.'

Monsieur D'Haricot had not heard of the breed. 'How large do they grow?' he asked tentatively.

'I'm afraid they do not make good pets,' the lady answered. She replaced the cover with a quick flick of her wrist and mumbled some words in what sounded like an ancient tongue, but she could have been clearing her throat. Even ladies had to do that on occasions. 'My book, please.'

Monsieur D'Haricot caught a glimpse of the title as he handed it to her. 'Advanced Electromechanics for Girls'.

'I hope it has a happy ending,' he said blithely. 'I know you ladies like at least one white wedding.'

The lady smiled at him the way his mother had when he recited his alphabet for the first time, with only two or three mistakes. He beamed back and watched as she went on her way, followed by what appeared to be a wolflike shadow

After the initial wailing, the puppy sounds quietened and Monsieur D'Haricot feared he had done something wrong. He looked into the basket and his heart missed a beat. The pups were lying motionless in a bundle at the bottom of the basket. He shook the handle, but the animals did not stir. He poked the nearest one. It felt cold and insubstantial. While he looked around for somewhere to dump the basket and walk off unseen, a gentleman in a dark frock coat, top hat and cane came towards him from the far end of the alley. He tried to hide the basket behind his back as the gentleman passed him, but the man stopped.

'Quite extraordinary,' he said in an English accent. 'I haven't seen the like for years.'

'They aren't mine.' Monsieur D'Haricot felt his cheeks heat up as he spoke.

'Who do they belong to?'

'An old woman. I'm looking after them for her. I mean I'm looking after the basket, there is nothing important inside.' The man glared at him knowingly and Monsieur D'Haricot tailed off. 'I can explain.'

'There's no need, I'm not a police officer.' The man winked. 'I wouldn't try selling them here, though.' He indicated the darkened houses. 'You will get a better price in town.' The man tapped the brim of his hat with the tip of his walking cane and walked off. A few steps along the road he paused, sniffed the air and turned back. His face had lost its smile.

'Does that basket belong to Dauphine van Lüttich?' he asked sharply.

'I didn't catch the lady's name.'

'She may have a title, but Dauphine is no lady,' the gentleman asserted.

Monsieur D'Haricot could not disguise his look of confusion.

'Look closely inside,' the man instructed. Monsieur D'Haricot did as he was bidden. 'What do you see?'

'Pup... pets.' Monsieur D'Haricot's mouth dropped as he lifted one of the woollen toys. 'I don't understand.'

'I don't mean those.' The gentleman put a gloved hand into the basket and brought out an object Monsieur D'Haricot had not seen the like of before. It was a container, the size of a snuff box and as elegantly etched and painted, but when the lid was open it revealed tiny cogs and wheels moving a stretched rubber tape in a circular motion. 'What it is?' Monsieur D'Haricot asked.

The gentleman examined the box. He shook it beside his ear. 'It is a highly sophisticated instrument. I can't be sure, but I suspect it has uses that I am unaware of.'

'I think, from what you have said, we can be certain on that point,' Monsieur D'Haricot answered. 'Are you are a friend of Madame van Lüttich?' He remembered where he had heard the name and wished he had some way of communicating with Maulise.

The gentleman sneered. 'No-one admits to being a friend of Dauphine – not even her son. Her brother would rather have his tongue cut out.' He dropped the box on the ground and stamped his foot down hard on it. Monsieur D'Haricot heard the sound of metal scraping against stone and then what he imagined was a shriek of human pain.

'Someone was listening to our conversation,' the gentleman said.

'With such a miniscule device and no wires?' Monsieur D'Haricot was envious.

'I have seen more advanced apparatus. Who are you and why are you in Rouen?'

Monsieur D'Haricot wanted to invent a false name and respond that his business was his own, but he had the feeling that wasn't true. 'My name is D'Haricot. I am visiting an associate,' he answered.

'Did Nicolas send you here?'

'I do not know a Nicolas.' Monsieur D'Haricot pinched his fingers so as not to give away the fact that he was lying.

'Madame Chapleau, then? Ah, I see you know her, but which one?'

'Surely there is only one Victoire Chapleau?'

'Indeed. The lady is unmarried, although she takes the title of Madame – as does her sister Mala Kai.'

Two Madame Chapleaus was inconceivable, but Monsieur D'Haricot kept his voice even. 'Which Madame Chapleau is the Prime Minister?'

'The Prime Minister of where?' The gentleman regarded Monsieur D'Haricot's reaction and smiled wryly. 'If you mean the Primus, before I answer that, I need to know your credentials. Who sent you here?'

'Nobody sent me. I am here on my own volition. If you would excuse me, I have business to attend to.'

'You wouldn't be looking for Juan Santos, would you?' the man asked.

'As a matter of fact, I am.'

'Then allow me to accompany you to his shop,' the man offered. 'It is no inconvenience. I am going there myself.'

'That seems somewhat coincidental,' Monsieur D'Haricot ventured.

'You think so?' The gentleman pulled a book from his coat pocket that had no right to fit into such a confined space. The spine was peeling, revealing torn threads 'Truth is stranger than fiction, as someone said in a book.'

'It was the American, Mark Twain,' Monsieur D'Haricot answered, proud of his literary knowledge.

'You know the book?' the gentleman asked.

'A travel journal, I believe. "Following the Equator: A Journey Around the World".'

'The title and genre are unimportant. I meant, what was the binding like?'

'I have no idea, I am afraid.'

The gentleman gave a snort, which Monsieur D'Haricot translated as "useless". While they conversed, they made their way down the hill towards the cathedral and the river. From the previous directions he had been given, Monsieur D'Haricot was beginning to mistrust the gentleman. He turned down a side street and came to a rickety row of coloured houses and shops straight out of a nursery rhyme.

'This is it.' The gentleman rapped on the door of a blue plastered building, so narrow that there was barely space for the doorframe. They waited for a minute. There was no sound from inside. Monsieur D'Haricot could see an upstairs window, but the room was dark.

'Seems like there is no-one home,' the gentleman said.

'Are you sure this is the right place? I don't see a sign,' Monsieur D'Haricot said.

'Are you blind? It is there in bold lettering.' The gentleman pointed above the door. '"St John St Clair, Bookbinder Extraordinaire".' Monsieur D'Haricot saw nothing, but didn't admit it.

'Since Señor St Clair is not here, I think I should find my companion,' Monsieur D'Haricot said, taking a step away from the gentleman.

'He will be in a hostelry drinking away the francs you gave him with a pretty girl, or gambling at cards with naïve foreigners who are afraid to double-deal. It would be better if you waited inside.' With that the man turned the handle and swung the door open. 'It is never locked – bound, but not sealed.'

Instinct warned Monsieur D'Haricot against entering. It was a trap. The strange gentleman knew too much about him, Otocey and Dauphine van Lüttich, not to be an enemy. Monsieur D'Haricot hesitated. In that moment of uncertainty, he was drawn inside by an unknown force tugging invisible cords on his jacket. He was met by a musky smell that suggested the rustling from the corner was a family of rats preparing dinner. The gentleman struck a match and lit an oil lamp, which shone but a few metres in front of him. He wiped a layer of dust from the shop counter with his handkerchief, then fluttered it in the air before returning it to his pocket. Monsieur D'Haricot imagined he saw the forms of alphabet letters dance among the dust particles.

The shop was narrower inside than Monsieur D'Haricot imagined. There was only space for a counter running along the breadth of the room and a margin of half a metre for any customer to squeeze in front.

The gentleman, with the aid of a powerful corset, squashed into position behind the counter. He placed the lamp in front of him. 'I am St. John St. Clair Bart., bookbinder extraordinaire,' he declared.

Monsieur D'Haricot had suspected as much, although he hadn't realised the man was a member of the lower order of the English nobility. He spotted a paring knife with a carved antler handle on the counter and reached to pick it up. The gentleman grabbed it from his reach.

'Careful,' he warned. 'These tools are not toys. Many a finger has been lost through misuse.'

'Of course,' Monsieur D'Haricot was chastened. 'These must be the binding threads.'

'Do not touch them. They are more deadly than a boa constrictor. It has been known for a coil to wind itself round a wrist and act as a tourniquet. I heard of one man, in my youth, whose hand turned black and shrivelled to nothing before the string could be cut.'

Monsieur D'Haricot screwed up his nose at the thought and gave the string a wide berth. 'Ah, inks. I have always had a fascination for those,' he said, eying the colourful glass bottles on the shelf above the counter.

'Were you training to be a poisoner?' Mr. St. Clair accused. 'These dyes contain mercury and lead in sufficient quantities to kill a battalion.'

'Book binding is a lethal profession,' Monsieur D'Haricot said. 'Why, next you will be telling me that the parchment paper is primed to explode.'

St. John St. Clair jerked his back rigid like a jackknife. 'There is no need to be frivolous,' he said haughtily. 'I suggest you give me your message and leave.'

'As I told you, I have no message,' Monsieur D'Haricot answered.

'Are you not the Sagittarian, the messenger of the zodiac?' Mr. St. Clair opened a drawer beneath the counter and took out a pince-nez which he positioned in place over his left eye. 'You look like a Sagittarian, but yet...'

Monsieur D'Haricot's brain was working fast. 'I work for the General,' he said. To make his point he banged a fist on the counter. 'I was informed that you would have a message for me to take back to him.'

'Indeed.' St. Clair was unmoved by Monsieur D'Haricot's show of impetuousness. 'You will need to speak with Juan Santos.'

'But I thought you were Juan. I was told...'

'By whom?'

For a second Monsieur D'Haricot couldn't remember, but the events of the morning trickled back. 'By a young lady, who passes your shop with her mother on a regular basis.'

'If they pass my shop, I won't know them. If they came through my door, it would be a different matter.'

'She seemed convinced that you were Juan.'

'Young ladies can be mistaken. That is Juan.' He twisted to point above him and Monsieur D'Haricot noticed a small photograph in a broken frame hanging at an angle on the wall. It was a picture of a young man with a drooping moustache standing beside a chair with one foot on the seat. He was wearing an over-large sombrero and balanced a guitar on the knee of the leg that was on the chair. The sombrero had been coloured over in pink chalk. 'Does that look like me?'

Monsieur D'Haricot was not close enough to say whether it did or didn't. 'If you cannot help me, I shall leave and find the Juan I am looking for,' he answered.

'You won't find him today,' St. Clair advised.

'Why not?'

'He won't be here until tomorrow evening.'

'Where will he be until then?'

St. Clair's neck moved back several centimetres without taking his head with it. Monsieur D'Haricot had once seen an aged tortoise do something the same. The gentleman removed his top hat and placed it on a hook behind him. 'You see,' he said.

'No, I do not.'

'It is impossible for Juan and myself to be here at the same time.' Having spoken, he retrieved his hat, smoothed down the few hairs on his pate and placed the hat back on his head.

Monsieur D'Haricot watched in silence. There was nothing to be said. He bade the gentleman a good day and walked to the door with as much dignity as he could while squashing past boxes of unbound manuscripts.

'Be careful the glue doesn't spill on your breeches,' St. Clair warned. 'Being stuck inside a book can be fatal. Even a nose in a book can lose you a good two days of your life.'

Monsieur D'Haricot did not answer. He closed the door shut behind him and glanced at the top of the door. The sign which Mr. St. Clair was so proud of, and the young lady and her mother found so amusing, was still invisible to him.

Chapter Twelve

Monsieur D'Haricot hoped that having a spot of lunch would settle his system and enable him to figure out what was going on. Most pressing was whose side everyone he had met was on. Who wanted his help and who wanted him dead? He found a restaurant near the abbey and ordered a side of ham with croquette potatoes, carrots and a white sauce, accompanied by a glass of Chardonnay. The waiter also obliged him with a sheet of paper from his order book and a pencil with a chewed end. Between forkfuls of food, he scribbled a list of names with arrows between those he believed to be of a similar disposition. Between sips of wine he scored out lines and redrew others.

'If I were you, I would put Maulise in with Otocey rather than Victoire,' a voice piped up. He had forgotten about Marina and felt ashamed that he had not ordered food for her. He called the waiter over to remedy the situation.

'Is there something wrong with the ham?' the waiter queried.

'No, tell the chef it is delicious.' Monsieur D'Haricot had no wish to fall out with another cook. 'I would like a fillet of cod to go with it. On a separate plate. A plain fillet, with no sauce or seasoning, if you please.'

Whether the waiter pleased or objected, he presented his customer with the plate of fish. Monsieur D'Haricot waited until Marina was tucking into her cod before querying her observation on Maulise and Otocey.

'It was his stepson who attacked you before you alighted the aquatran, wasn't it?' she said through munches.

'Of course. Maulise said his wife was called Caprice. I had forgotten about the incident,' Monsieur D'Haricot declared. 'How did you know about it?'

'News travels on board ship.'

'It was Otocey who directed me to the aquatran. He knew where I would be, but aren't Victoire and Otocey on the same side?'

'Otocey is consumed with his plan to gather his assembly of zodiac characters. He has use for the lady who bought me the macarons, but that was not Victoire Chapleau.'

'Nonsense. I would recognise Victoire in a photographer's dark room.' Monsieur D'Haricot had raised his voice and was receiving odd looks from his fellow diners, who believed he was talking either to himself, or worse, a bag. He lowered his tone to a whisper. 'It must be Mala Kai Chapleau who is the Primus though. Victoire could never think of invading Paris. What of Maulise? He claimed to be rebelling against the invasion plan.'

'Maulise is not the brightest paint on the palette,' Marina answered. 'Even with the delicious readjustment biscuits. Otocey has fooled him into believing he is the leader of a resistance movement in order to gain his support.'

'Yes, well, I was about to work that out.' Monsieur D'Haricot scribbled another line on his paper. 'Why did the boat chef try to kill me?'

'He is a madman, exposed to too much heat in the kitchen.'

Monsieur D'Haricot wasn't convinced by Marina's answer, but he moved on. 'We know that Gori van Lüttich and his mother are enemies.'

'That depends which side you are on,' Marina said, spitting out a piece of bone.

'I am on the side of the General. I wish I knew where Juan fitted in.'

'He is a Libran – he doesn't fit neatly in any hole. He is either too large or too small.'

'What exactly is all this zodiac sign rubbish about?' Monsieur D'Haricot hit the ends of his knife and fork on the table in frustration and Marina was bounced into the middle of her plate.

'I didn't know they served crab bisque here,' the diner at the next table remarked to his companion.

Marina crawled back to her place. 'Maybe you aren't who you say you are,' she grumbled, snatching the last crumb of fish and heading into the bag with a burp. 'Are we having a dessert?'

Monsieur D'Haricot had the feeling it was a test of his devotion. He called the waiter to enquire what was on the menu. The only dessert available was crepe suzette and he ordered a potion.

'With or without the orange liqueur sauce?' the waiter asked somewhat impertinently.

'Without – no, with. Actually, could you ask the chef to prepare half with sauce and half without?'

'You see, you are showing Libran qualities,' Marina observed.

The waiter returned with the sweet as Maulise entered the restaurant. He waved across to Monsieur D'Haricot, approached the table and sat on the chair opposite.

'Wonderful,' he exclaimed. 'Crepe suzette is my favourite dish.' He moved the plate towards him, picked up the spoon and began swallowing mouthfuls. Monsieur D'Haricot managed to tear a piece from the edge, which he slipped into the bag for Marina, but he did not have the pleasure of enjoying the dessert himself.

'Did you find old Juan?' Maulise asked when the plate was empty and the sauce licked clean.

'I found St. John St. Clair Bart. Apparently he suffers from a form of split personality. He won't be "Juan" until tomorrow, and he refuses to tell me anything until then.'

'He is a Libran,' Maulise said. 'He represents both sides of the scales.'

'So Marina has been explaining to me.' Monsieur D'Haricot brought out his wallet and called the waiter over to pay.

'He has to decide which side Spain will take in events, if they decide to take a side at all,' Maulise answered.

'He is a bookbinder and cabaret entertainer. What has he to do with the decisions of the Spanish government?'

The waiter had slouched over and was calculating the bill.

'Aren't we having brandy?' Maulise said.

'I can recommend the house cognac,' the waiter answered. 'Shall that be two glasses?'

'No,' Monsieur D'Haricot said firmly.

'Just the one – very good sir.'

The waiter scurried off before Monsieur D'Haricot could explain that he didn't want any. When the waiter returned with the glass of cognac he made sure he swiped it from Maulise's grasp and took a gulp.

He wiped his lips with the back of his hand. The cognac warmed his throat and gullet. 'What events are you referring to?' he asked Maulise.

'Sorry?'

'You said Spain had to decide which side it will take in events. Are we talking about events above ground or below?'

'I meant the Extermination. It's what everyone is talking about.'

Monsieur D'Haricot had taken a large sip of the brandy and splashes of the drink spurted from his nose. 'What Extermination?' he spluttered.

'*The* Extermination. How many would you like? Madame Chapleau and her followers prefer to call it the Liberation, and Gori and his foul mother call it Pest Control, but it is all the same.'

'What does the General, I mean the Grand Duke, call it?' Monsieur D'Haricot asked. He had released his grip on the brandy glass and Maulise took the chance to seize it and finish the cognac in one gulp.

'The Grand Duke does not call it anything. He either doesn't know about it or doesn't wish to believe it is happening. If certain parties have their way, he won't be around to see it,' Maulise said. 'It is no great loss. There are other Pisceans in the sea.' He gave a coarse chuckle. 'The Extermination will go ahead, with or without the Grand Duke's input, unless Otocey can stop it.'

He set the glass down on the table and Monsieur D'Haricot noticed that his fingers were translucent. The veins and nerves were dancing below the skin. A small pool of liquid was gathering beside the glass.

'I think you are in need of another readjustment biscuit,' Monsieur D'Haricot said. 'The last one does not seem to have lasted long.'

Maulise snatched his hand out of sight. He reached in a pocket for a biscuit.

'The Extermination, or whatever you call it, will not be successful if your armies start melting every few hours,' Monsieur D'Haricot smirked.

'Mala Kai is working on a new formula. She has a secret laboratory offshore.'

'If it is secret, how do you know about it?'

'Nicolas told me. I haven't to tell anyone about it.' Maulise's face turned a pale pink.

'Aha.' Monsieur D'Haricot pointed a finger in the air, winning a point from Maulise. 'What does Otocey know about this laboratory? You may as well confide everything to me now.'

'There are such things as principles.'

Monsieur D'Haricot opened his wallet and fingered a note.

'But they are for rich folk, or fools,' Maulise continued. 'You could say I am a mercenary.'

'I would say you were a goat,' Monsieur D'Haricot answered.

'Flattery will get you everywhere,' Maulise said, swiping the note from Monsieur D'Haricot's wallet. He put a hand against the side of his mouth to shield his words. 'People disappear to this laboratory and don't return.'

'What sort of people?'

'Mainly 'P's – political opponents. Mala Kai has developed a brain machine that can alter thoughts. Our resistance movement intends to blow it up.'

'Who, apart from Otocey and yourself, is in this resistance group?'

'The movement hasn't been going for long.'

'You mean it is just you.'

'Told you so,' Marina called up from the bag.

'Enough of this chattering.' Maulise stood up. 'We should find a hole for the night, then go out and enjoy the town.'

'If by 'hole' you mean hotel, I shall need to find a bank to make a withdrawal. I am assuming you have no means of supporting yourself.'

'That is where you are mistaken,' Maulise gloated. 'With the francs you gave me I purchased canvas and watercolours and spent the morning painting bridges. Several Rouen ladies admired my artwork and persuaded their partners to purchase a picture.' Maulise reached in his pocket to bring out a handful of notes.

'Then you can honour the bill,' Monsieur D'Haricot declared, removing his napkin from his shirt front and placing it on the table.

They found a guest house kept by a respectable, middle-aged couple. The husband was absent and the lady of the house was pleased to have a male presence in her home, particularly that of two respectable French gentlemen. The room was at the end of a creaky corridor. It was sparsely furnished, but the lady kept it clean and Monsieur D'Haricot was relieved to find two separate beds. He declined the offer of a night on the town with Maulise, but encouraged his companion to go and enjoy himself. Once Maulise had departed, Monsieur D'Haricot returned to the sitting room to quiz his hostess.

The lady was flustered by his attention and the bottle of port she was handling slipped from her hand. Despite her arthritic fingers she niftily caught the bottle before any of the alcohol spilt. Monsieur D'Haricot took over and poured them both a generous helping.

'Are there many guests?' he enquired.

'Have no worries, you won't be bothered by mad orgies. There is only you and your friend.' The lady paused, then asked. 'What is your companion doing?'

Monsieur D'Haricot thought the question somewhat abrupt, but he answered amiably. 'He has gone to enjoy a show at the theatre.'

The lady tittered. 'I wasn't referring to the gentleman. I meant the crustacean.'

The lady's finger directed him to the door. Monsieur D'Haricot had thought Marina was asleep in the bag, which he had left in the bedroom, but she was hanging by a pincher from the door handle.

'I'm sorry, I assumed you took pets,' Monsieur D'Haricot said, 'I should have ascertained if that was the case.'

'My husband does not like dogs, and sadly cat hair brings me out in pestilent boils, but I see no reason why you can't have a crab in your room. I'm afraid we do not have access to salt water in the bathroom.'

'Port will be more than sufficient,' Marina answered. She swung her body and released her pincher at the top of the arc, flying through the air to land on the sofa. 'Forget a girl in every port and give me a port in every girl.'

The lady giggled again and quickly finished her glass of port. Monsieur D'Haricot refilled her glass and poured a glass for Marina. He served the drinks, then took a seat beside Marina on the settee while his hostess sat in an armchair opposite.

'I need to ask you for a favour,' Monsieur D'Haricot began.

The lady put down her port glass. 'I am afraid we do not give credit.'

'No, no, money is not a problem. I have to get a message to my employer in Paris, but I do not trust the telegram or postal services. I would not usually prevail on the goodwill of someone who barely knows me, but the situation is desperate and I can tell that you are a lady of fine moral standing.'

'Oh?' The lady straightened her hair. 'How can I assist?'

'I wondered if you knew a neighbour, relative or friend who would be willing to deliver a letter in person to the recipient. They would have to be trustworthy, but I shall make it worth their while.' Monsieur D'Haricot gave a smile that stretched mischievously across his face.

The lady did not answer. She lifted her glass and took a sip.

'A faithful hound even?' Marina suggested in a voice that left Monsieur D'Haricot in no doubt that crabs were capable of sarcasm.

'It is of national importance,' Monsieur D'Haricot affirmed. 'I work for a government department.' He reached in his pocket for his wallet and showed his identification documents. The lady examined them and also the bank notes poking from the leather compartment.

'Of national importance,' she repeated. 'A government agency. Worth my while?' She emphasised the final question.

Monsieur D'Haricot laid a bunch of bank notes on the table.

'You know, I have thought about visiting Paris myself.' The lady reached to retrieve the money. 'I have a first cousin in Montmartre.'

'Splendid. When can you set off?'

The lady finished her drink, put down her glass, then stood up. She screwed her eyes at the mantel clock until they bulged like a bush baby's and Monsieur D'Haricot feared for a second she was about to leap onto the mantelpiece and knock the clock flying. 'If I pack a portmanteau at once, I should be able to make the late train to Paris,' she declared.

'Splendid. I had better write my letter,' Monsieur D'Haricot answered, smacking his knees. 'Do you have paper, pen and ink?'

Marina finished the port while the landlady packed an overnight bag and Monsieur D'Haricot wrote his missive. He regretted that he had not brought his code book with him on the trip. The General did not have the gumption to work out how to decipher a new code, but some attempt at concealment was necessary.

'You could intersperse the word 'crab' into the letter,' Marina suggested. 'Anyone reading it would think it was nonsense.'

'As would the General,' Monsieur D'Haricot lamented. It struck him that 'interspersed' was an intricate word for a crab to use. 'Have you taken one of Maulise's readjustment biscuits?' he asked.

'No,' Marina answered sharply. 'I have eaten two.'

Monsieur D'Haricot would have reprimanded her, but the landlady chose the moment to return to the room.

'I should let my cousin know I am arriving,' she said. 'I don't have a telephone, but my neighbour does.'

'No, no,' Monsieur D'Haricot prevented her. 'This is a hush-hush mission.'

'It isn't illegal, is it?' The lady raised her voice as her excitement grew.

'Quite the contrary,' Monsieur D'Haricot asserted. 'But there are enemies everywhere.'

'Not here in Rouen, surely?'

'They are everywhere,' Monsieur D'Haricot repeated. 'The walls have eyes.'

'O... o... oh.'

Monsieur D'Haricot was beginning to regret asking the lady to help, but he saw no alternative. Whereas he had nothing against underground refugees making their homes in Paris, the term Extermination made his nails grow an extra centimetre. The General needed to be warned. The lady gathered up her bits and bobs from the sitting room. Monsieur D'Haricot helped her on with her overcoat and handed her the sealed envelope with instructions and money for her train fare.

'You will look after Nautilus while I am away?' the lady asked.

There was a splash of water behind him and Monsieur D'Haricot looked to see Marina balancing on the rim of a fish tank with one pincher reaching into the water towards a goldfish.

'Yes, of course.' Monsieur D'Haricot hurried to remove Marina before she hooked the curious fish. 'Now off you go. You don't want to miss the train.' He tried to smile, but an angry Marina was pinching his fingers.

The landlady left. She didn't return that night, so Monsieur D'Haricot assumed she had caught her train. He imagined it speeding through the countryside to arrive in St. Lazare station. From there, he had instructed the lady to take a metro train to Montmartre. While he was picturing her journey, he saw a pale, watery figure follow her from the station. He pushed it out of his head and retired to bed with a book he borrowed from one of her shelves. It belonged to her husband, he guessed, as he couldn't imagine the lady being interested in the intricate complexities of medieval torture. The illustrations were magnificently drawn and coloured in gruesome detail. He was asleep before Maulise returned.

Monsieur D'Haricot was the first to rise. As he washed and shaved, he was disappointed not to smell breakfast breads and pastries being prepared until he remembered that they were alone in the house. He made a check to ensure Nautilus was swimming the right way up in its tank and fed it a pinch of fish food. When Maulise failed to materialise in the breakfast room, he made a check to ensure his companion had not soaked into the bedclothes overnight.

'Is it morning?' Maulise's croaky voice sounded from beneath the covers.

'It is almost midday,' Monsieur D'Haricot answered.

'Wake me when it is evening and time for Juan's performance.'

Pulling on the blankets did nothing to rouse Maulise and Monsieur D'Haricot accepted he would have the day to himself. It had been some time since he last had a weekday free and the idea did not rest easily with him. Being removed from his office, he could not catch up on paperwork, but he could garner information.

Rouen was a major port on the Seine, with access to Paris. The fantastical business of underground cities had diverted his attention from the real matter of French foreign policy. He would be asked to write an extensive report on his activities while he was, technically, absent without leave. He required something tangible to put in it and he decided to pay the docks a visit.

He was not, however, properly dressed for the business, and feared sticking out like a donkey at Longchamp lining up for the Arc de Triomphe. The photograph the landlady kept on her coffee table suggested that her husband was a similar size and shape to himself. He deliberated whether to borrow a shirt and jacket over a cup of black coffee, but when he came to examine the gentleman's wardrobe he realised he needn't have bothered. The landlady's husband had put on several centimetres round the waist and hips since what he now saw was a wedding photograph.

Marina was also a problem. He couldn't leave her in the house with the fish, but taking her to the dock would present its own dangers. He found her in the kitchen clasping hold of a tablespoon and a teacup.

'Are we going to the seaside?' she said happily.

'I am heading to the docks. I don't think there is any sand there.'

Marina's face fell. 'You promised,' she said in a whining voice.

'I don't believe that I did,' Monsieur D'Haricot answered. One look at her downcast eyes and what seemed to be a trembling lip and he knew he was beaten. 'We can take a train to the coast, but we must be back by eight this evening.' He paused. 'Unless you intend to go out to sea in search of your family.'

Marina was too excited to answer. She danced across the kitchen table, knocking over a sugar bowl and ripping the tablecloth. Monsieur D'Haricot thought he heard her hum the word 'scallops' before he bundled her into his bag.

'No talking on the train,' he instructed.

'I won't if you don't,' Marina answered cockily. Monsieur D'Haricot suspected the day trip was not going to go well.

The train to the coast was busy and Monsieur D'Haricot was squashed against the window by a portly gentleman and his comfortably sized wife. Although the day promised to be sunny, they were both smothered in furs. The carriage had steamed up before they were ten kilometres from Rouen. The lady refused to allow Monsieur D'Haricot to open the window and he was reluctant to go against her wishes, fearing if he stood up to accomplish the task, she and her husband would expand their girths to take over his seat as well as their own.

'If you placed your bag in the overhead compartment, there would be room to breathe,' the lady said.

'It contains a valuable and fragile object,' Monsieur D'Haricot replied in an equally didactic voice.

'Object? I am not an object,' Marina complained. Monsieur D'Haricot cleared his throat to drown out her words, but the gentleman stared at the bag with a knowing glance.

'Are you by any chance a Piscean?' he asked.

'No, I am from Paris,' Monsieur D'Haricot said bluntly.

The lady whispered something to her husband and they both laughed. The gentleman produced a newspaper and the lady a magazine and they began reading. With the exception of a few disbelieving comments, Monsieur D'Haricot was not troubled by them for the remainder of the journey. The man's question bothered him though. The couple looked substantial and were ruddy in appearance – but why the need for winter coats on a sunny day?

'Dieppe. This is Dieppe. Everyone please alight, thank you.' The guard's call roused Monsieur D'Haricot, who had dozed off with his head drooping against the man's fur collar.

'I am terribly sorry,' he apologised, until he realised that the coat was not being worn. The man and his wife were not in the carriage. Neither was his bag.

Chapter Twelve B (certain characters in the story are superstitious about Thirteen)

Monsieur D'Haricot jumped from his seat, slid the carriage door open and rushed down the corridor. He pushed aside a gentleman and leapt out of the train. The platform was emptying and he saw no sign of the couple. He grabbed hold of a porter by the elbow.

'Did you see a middle-aged, portly couple leave the train?'

'The train was full. I saw a good number of couples alight. Some were slim, some were better fed. Most were neither fat nor thin.'

'They were in that compartment.' Monsieur D'Haricot pointed to the coach he had exited. 'The man had a beard and a walking cane.'

The porter removed his cap to scratch his head. He let the hat fall so that it appeared like an offering bowl and shook it under Monsieur D'Haricot's head.

'I see.' Monsieur D'Haricot reached in his pocket for coins and slipped them into the hat. 'This is important. They have taken my bag.'

'You wish to report a theft, sir?'

'They may have lifted it in mistake for one of their own.' Monsieur D'Haricot had no wish for the authorities to become involved.

'What did the bag look like?'

Monsieur D'Haricot realised he was wasting time. The couple could be well on their way before the porter remembered anything useful. They may have changed onto another train and be speeding away from the town as they spoke. He thanked the man and headed towards the exit.

'I did see a man with a talking bag. I thought he must be a

ventriloquist. They say they get into the habit of speaking to their dummies. He was with another man, not a woman,' the porter said. 'I remember, because the gentleman he was with had pale skin. I thought he must be Nordic. We don't see many Norwegians or Icelanders here.'

'It is of no matter where they are from; they are not the couple I am looking for.'

'Suit yourself.' The porter took umbrage at Monsieur D'Haricot's tone and shuffled off, studiously ignoring the waves of an elderly lady on the platform with three heavy cases.

'Excuse me, young man, could you possibly assist me?' The lady rounded on Monsieur D'Haricot.

He wanted to refuse, insisting he was on a life or death mission, but his parents had taught him never to abandon a lady in distress, and particularly not a senior French citizen. A cab was procured and her luggage transferred into the carriage. The lady fussed and fretted and by the time the task was completed the station was deserted.

'Can I drop you off anywhere?' The lady offered him a seat in the taxi.

'I do not know where I am going,' Monsieur D'Haricot admitted. 'I have mislaid my travelling companion.'

'A gentleman or a lady?'

'A lady.'

'Is the lady familiar with Dieppe?'

'I don't think so, although I believe she has family in the neighbourhood,' Monsieur D'Haricot answered.

'Then she will be fine. You must come with me,' the lady decided. 'We shall take tea in a sweet café I know beside the beach.'

'I do not drink tea,' Monsieur D'Haricot said.

'Tea is the answer to all of life's problems,' the lady insisted, and Monsieur D'Haricot suspected that despite her elegant dress and perfect French, the lady may actually be English. Nonetheless, he climbed into the cab and sat opposite her. The lady was glad of a companion and talked throughout the journey. Monsieur D'Haricot was not at all interested in her late husband, children and grandchildren, or even her pet Pekingese who couldn't make the trip because of a bad knee – nothing serious of course. He was relieved when they arrived at their destination, but not so happy when the lady walked into the café, leaving him to unload her luggage and pay the cab driver.

The cases were bulkier than Monsieur D'Haricot believed decent and smelt of almonds. He left them on the kerb and entered the café. The lady had chosen a table beside the window and he approached to ask her what should be done about her luggage which was blocking the pavement.

'I am staying in the hotel two doors down,' the lady said. 'Would you be a dear and have a porter take them to my suite?'

Monsieur D'Haricot did not recall seeing a hotel on the street, but he didn't admit this. 'What name should I say?' He asked.

The lady laughed. 'Why, don't you recognise me? I am the Duchess of …' Monsieur D'Haricot was unable to make out the place and he sensed the lady had mumbled the word deliberately. He hoped the mention of her title would be sufficient for the hotel staff.

The hotel was not what he expected in a coastal town. Monsieur D'Haricot could not believe he had overlooked it. A mole with two glass eyes could have seen it, although it was easier to imagine it had sprung up on the lady's command rather than having existed since the date carved above the door. The authentic marble pillars, gold-threaded Persian carpets and vulgar chandeliers made it decadent even for the nobility, and he feared the young gentleman standing to attention at the reception desk would have a list of duchesses on his register. He slicked back his hair and marched to the desk.

'The Duchess of gobbledegook would like her cases taken to her suite. They are outside the café 'Chat Rouge'.

'Certainly, sir.' The receptionist lifted a finger and wiggled it at one of the bellboys.

'You will need assistance,' Monsieur D'Haricot advised. 'The duchess has three heavy cases.'

The boy looked affronted that Monsieur D'Haricot should doubt his ability to carry the cases. He straightened his hat and marched out of the door with Monsieur D'Haricot following him.

'Where did you say the cases were?' the boy asked. Unable to see them, he lifted the lid of a litter bin to peek inside.

'They were here one minute ago,' Monsieur D'Haricot had the cold feeling of déjà vu, but either his sixth sense or a snigger from the promenade across the street made him look across. 'There, that gentleman is carrying them.'

The gentleman in question was struggling under the weight of the cases and had abandoned one beside a stall selling ice cream. Monsieur D'Haricot suspected from his portly appearance that it was the same man as on the train. His companion was not with him and he could not see his own bag.

'Stop, thief!' he called, rushing across the street. The gentleman decided it was wiser to abort his mission and abandon the cases. He made off at a sprint.

Monsieur D'Haricot was held up by a lady on a bicycle, who swerved in the same direction as he did and fell off her bicycle trying to avoid him. Naturally Monsieur D'Haricot had to stop to assist her to her feet as the bike chain had become entangled in her skirts. The lady's language was far from genteel. The activity attracted a small crowd and when Monsieur D'Haricot finally succeeded in extricating the lady from her bicycle, he was awarded with a round of applause and even an "encore" from the onlookers. The lady made a huffing sound before remounting her bicycle and pedalling off.

'Wait, your crank arm is wobbly and your down tube is twisted,' Monsieur D'Haricot called after her, only to receive further laughter from his audience. The lady raised an arm with fingers raised, but didn't stop.

Meanwhile the duchess, having observed the events from the tea shop window, had come out to investigate. She hailed a passing police officer with her parasol and sent him scurrying after the thief, whistle in mouth.

'I believe you are in need of your cup of tea,' the duchess said, once Monsieur D'Haricot rejoined her.

'That man, I'm sure he was the one on the train who stole my bag. It is imperative that I get it back as soon as possible.'

'You won't catch him now. Leave it to the police.'

Much as the duchess tried to entice him, Monsieur D'Haricot was reluctant to return to the café. He did not trust the police, worthy officers that they were, to understand his concern for Marina.

'Can I ask what is in your bag that makes it attractive to the gentleman who took it?' the duchess said.

'What is in your cases that he would risk falling foul of the law?' Monsieur D'Haricot countered.

'Touché!' the duchess clapped her hands in glee. 'There are things we should talk about. Would you like to know about the zodiac prophecy?'

Monsieur D'Haricot stared at her. He considered whether he had met her before, above ground or below, but there were no recognisable features.

'Aren't you curious to know why Vicomte Otocey is interested in everybody's astrological sign?' the duchess asked.

'You know Vicomte Otocey?'

'Everyone knows Old Nick.' The duchess laughed in a coarse manner before putting a gloved hand over her mouth and clearing her throat. 'My apologies, I recently had my adenoids removed. We should go inside.'

Monsieur D'Haricot followed her into the café and took a seat at the table. He waited until the duchess had ordered green tea and biscuits and a waitress had brought it before enquiring what she had meant by the zodiac prophecy.

'It goes back four hundred years,' the duchess began, but was interrupted by a snort from Monsieur D'Haricot.

'The forefathers of Vicomte Otocey and his kind went underground during the Revolution. How can a four hundred year old prophecy apply to them?'

'The nature of prophecies is to foresee the future. If the future was known, it wouldn't be a prophecy,' the duchess replied. 'You are correct about Otocey though. He is from younger stock. My family was forced to flee in the seventeenth century. Huguenots terrorised by Louis XIV's rule, on my father's side. They founded the duchy we now rule over. There have been refugees living beneath our country for nearly a thousand years. Persecution is not new.'

Monsieur D'Haricot had suspected the duchess was involved in the underground world, but it was satisfying to get confirmation. 'What about the prophecy?' he asked. The duchess took a sip of tea and wiped her lips before answering.

'Have you heard of Nostradamus?'

'Yes. Is this one of his prophecies?'

'It has been claimed that his second wife Anne Ponsarde was the true seer.'

'Claimed by whom?' Monsieur D'Haricot asked.

'By me, for one.' The duchess smiled. 'She couldn't make the fact known, fearing that because she was a woman she would be declared a witch. She was a rich widow before she married Nostradamus and you know how people talk. I understand how she felt. My mother's family descended from an unfortunate lady seeking asylum from the witch trials. The zodiac prophecy was found written in a secret diary discovered in the cellar of Anne's house in Salon-de-Provence. Nicolas borrowed money from me to buy it at auction before the war. If I had known why he wanted the loan, I would not have given it to him.'

'You did not approve of the purchase?'

'I would have bought it myself – and bargained a better price – but that is no matter. If you will allow me, I shall continue my story.' Monsieur D'Haricot nodded. 'Our underground homes were meant to be temporary until the time was right for our return. As the decades turned into centuries, it became increasingly more difficult for us to leave our burrows, but I think you already know that.' The duchess paused to wet her mouth with the tea. 'This prophecy was written in archaic symbols which few can interpret. Nicolas has been striving to do so for years. The gist of it is that when all the zodiac signs come together at an exact spot, at a given time when the planets are aligned, we will succeed in returning to the surface in full health and as overlords.' The duchess's eyes sparkled and Monsieur D'Haricot saw reflected in them millions of stars.

'I see.' He took a gulp of his tea. The liquid scalded his palate. 'And now is the time for the fulfilment of the prophecy?'

The Duchess took a bite from a biscuit before answering. 'It may be, it may not be. There have been many false alarms. Nicolas would be the man to ask.'

'Why are you telling me this?'

'Because, unknown to Nicolas, I borrowed the parchment and had a copy of the prophecy made. I have studied the symbols. I do not read into them the same as Nicolas does. Yes, many of the signs are coming together, working towards a common goal in their different ways, but from my understanding, it is the water signs alone that can truly affect an outcome.'

'And these are... what? You will have to excuse me, but I am not familiar with magical hocus pocus.'

'Do not play games with me.' The duchess's mood changed. She stood up, shoving the table towards the window and upsetting Monsieur D'Haricot's cup. 'You had a crab in the bag that was stolen from you, did you not?'

The two ladies at the next table hid their faces in their cups as they controlled their amused response. 'The Grand Duke, my brother, is a Piscean. I have tried to fathom his thoughts, but they are too deep to be worth bothering about. My son Edgori is a Scorpio. He is a cog, but the crab is the key. According to the prophecy, the crab will be the reason for the fulfilment or the destruction of our dream.'

Monsieur D'Haricot was horrified. He had been drinking tea with Dauphine van Lüttich. He felt a tightening of his throat. Had she tried to poison him? It was fortunate he hated tea and had dribbled the contents into the nearest ornamental plant pot. He was mortified that fancy clothes, real jewellery and expensive make-up had fooled him. A veil had been lifted and he could see the warty skin and crooked nose of the puppy seller. His training allowed him to hide his emotions.

'Perhaps the nice police officer will apprehend the thief and bring the crab to you,' he said. 'I doubt it, because I intend to rescue her first.'

He was out of the café, with the waiter close on his tail waving the bill, when he heard Dauphine van Lüttich's voice behind him.

'You are heading in the wrong direction,' she remarked. 'Nicolas will have taken a shark to Sark.'

'Thank you.' Monsieur D'Haricot changed direction and strode along the pavement. He may have mistaken Dauphine van Lüttich for a kindly old lady, but she could not fool him into believing the portly gentleman thief was Otocey. If he were, his partner would have been… Mala Kai Chapleau. He began to see the couple in a new light, or rather, in a lack of it.

What on earth had Dauphine van Lüttich meant by a shark to Sark?

He was well aware that Sark was one of the smaller islands in La Manche, in what the British called the Channel Islands. It did not surprise him that such lunacy as underground countries and nobles fighting one another for control should involve Britain. He would not have batted an eyelid if he heard that Brits had begun the whole shenanigans.

It complicated matters though. It would be impossible to take a boat to Sark and return to Rouen by eight that evening. He could either rescue Marina or speak with Juan, but not both.

The choice was not difficult. He doubted Juan had anything important to say, otherwise Otocey would be in Rouen, whereas, if he believed the duchess, Marina was the crux of the plan to takeover France. He doubted that as well, but he would not have it etched on his tombstone that Louis-Philip D'Haricot abandoned a friend in the soup.

When he arrived at the harbour, he was disappointed by the fleet of fishing boats lined up against the wall. The names were freshly painted and the ropes oiled, but it was unlikely even 'Daughter of the Waves' was speedy enough to reach Sark before sundown. Whatever Otocey intended to do with Marina on the island, he would have done it before 'The Maiden of Dieppe' or 'Sweet Suzette' had rounded the Cotentin Peninsula.

A salty fellow in a striped jersey was chewing on a plug of tobacco. He spat the unwanted juices out before speaking. 'Grand day for a foofaraw.'

'Indeed. I am looking for a boat to take me to Sark,' Monsieur D'Haricot did not have time for pleasantries.

'Shark hunting, eh? I used to do a bit of that as a boy. None of these wrecks will be up for that.'

'Not shark, Sark. I need to go to the Channel Islands. Do you know a captain who could take me?'

'A wood snake free? Where is it?' The sea dog produced a knife for gutting fish and twisted with the speed of a pup.

'Never mind.' Monsieur D'Haricot's attention had been drawn to a gang of youths gathering on the beach. They were whooping and cheering, and he was sure the word "crab" was shouted above the kerfuffle. He quickened his pace as he saw pebbles being thrown.

'Move aside lads.' Despite protests, Monsieur D'Haricot pushed his way to the front.

'Watch your feet, Monsieur,' a girl cried as he was about to crunch down on top of a tiny crab. He managed to swirl out of the way, but there was nowhere to put his foot down. The edge of the beach, about a metre from the water, was alive with crabs, ranging in size from pin heads to dinner plates, covering the tide line in greens, browns and reds. The crusty animals had formed rows and were marching from the promenade towards the sea.

'Allons enfants,' a familiar voice blared.

Monsieur D'Haricot raised a hand to his forehead. 'Marina, where are you? What are you doing?'

'Liberte! Equalite! Fraternite! Macarons for all crabs.'

The crabs continued their advance, circling their way around him. It was difficult to remain upright on one leg, which was sinking into the wet beach, especially with a number of the crabs, annoyed at the detour, clipping his ankles with their pinchers. The children on the shore were singing La Marseillaise and the adult passersby had stopped to enjoy the show.

'My crabs!' An irate voice rang out. A stallholder from the

promenade ran at Monsieur D'Haricot wielding a cleaver. The sand slowed his progress and the children were able to get in his way. Monsieur D'Haricot finally caught sight of Marina. Most of the crabs had managed to attain the freedom of the sea and he was able to dance round the stragglers to reach her. He whisked her into his arms before the crab seller could free himself from the tangle of children.

'Liberte!' Marina rallied.

'We shall talk about this later,' Monsieur D'Haricot answered, hurrying in the opposite direction from the commotion. He crossed the street and darted down a side alley, not stopping until he was sure the crab seller wasn't behind him.

'I see you found your family,' he said to Marina. 'I suppose that means you will be going to join them.'

'Non. I have decided to become a freedom fighter,' Marina replied. 'There are crabs, not only in France, but throughout the world in need of help.'

'I understand. I shall take you to a quiet spot on the beach and let you go.' For a moment he felt emotional and his voice cracked.

Marina peered up at Monsieur D'Haricot. Her pinprick eyes were bright and her whiskers twitched. 'You could join the movement. We can do this together.'

'I'm afraid I have to get back to Rouen this evening.'

'I can come with you. There will be crabs in Rouen in need of our help,' Marina said.

Monsieur D'Haricot swallowed the saliva in his throat. 'Don't you think the skull and crossbones shell tattoo is going a bit far?'

'It isn't permanent,' Marina answered. 'And the rim rings are clip on.'

Monsieur D'Haricot hadn't noticed the decorative beer bottle tops attached to her shell.

'Freedom fighting is hungry work,' Marina said. 'What do you say to something to eat?'

'An excellent idea,' Monsieur D'Haricot agreed. 'While we eat, you can tell me how you managed to escape from Otocey.'

Chapter Fourteen

Marina managed to spin her tale out over four courses. As she slurped fish soup, she described how she had been resting her eyes when Otocey unravelled the bag from around Monsieur D'Haricot's fingers, otherwise the Vicomte would now be without several digits. Between bites of prawn cocktail, she enhanced the exploits of her escape, drawing blood from a disintegrating Mala Kai, who had been put in charge of the bag while Otocey was engaged in pilfering Dauphine's cases. Her shell was expanding like a child's balloon as she shovelled slices of citron tart into her mouth and recounted how she had toppled into a bucketful of distant relatives.

'I bounced to and fro until the bucket fell over, then I nipped the stallholder's ankles while my comrades charged to the sea,' she declared.

'Magnifique. Now if you have finished I shall purchase a new bag and we shall return to the railway station,' Monsieur D'Haricot said.

'You are forgetting the Camembert is still to come.' Marina was in no hurry to stir. Monsieur D'Haricot feared, with the amount she had consumed, that such an exertion would be impossible. He tapped his fingers on the table. 'You haven't heard the important piece of information I overheard.' Marina dangled the titbit like a banana before a monkey.

'What is it?'

'The Camembert first.'

The waiter was hovering with a plate of cheese and crackers in his hand. Monsieur D'Haricot nodded and the plate was laid on the table.

'Will you want coffee?' the waiter asked.

'A cognac would go down nicely,' Marina replied. She had kept herself hidden beneath the tablecloth whenever the waiter appeared and the man was surprised at the sudden feminine quality to his customer's voice. Monsieur D'Haricot cleared his throat and lowered his voice to a bass.

'Yes, a cognac, if you please – and a straw.'

Monsieur D'Haricot watched Marina suck her cognac for several minutes before his impatience got the better of him. 'You said you had important information.'

'Otocey has taken a shark to Sark.'

'I knew that,' Monsieur D'Haricot kicked the leg of the table. 'Who told you?'

'The duchess.'

'You are in league with Dauphine van Lüttich?' Marina screeched. She released the straw, allowing cognac to spout from the top.

'Don't be silly,' Monsieur D'Haricot wiped the spillage with a napkin. 'What exactly is a shark?'

'It is an enormous, evil fish with no brain and a crazy tail.'

'Why would Otocey take one of those to Sark?'

'Oh, you mean the other kind of shark,' Marina finished the last crumb of cheese and wiped her mouth on the edge of the tablecloth. 'It is a submarine hovercraft aeroplane racing kayak. It is one of Otocey's inventions. It looks like a mechanical shark – the evil fish variety – but as well as swimming underwater, it can travel on land with the speed of a hound and through the air faster than an albatross.'

'Did you find out why he has gone to Sark?' Monsieur D'Haricot asked.

'That is where the secret laboratory Maulise told us about is. Mala Kai has gone with him. They are keeping Madame Victoire Chapleau there against her will to carry out experiments on her. Otocey wants to transfer Victoire's ability to cope above ground to Mala Kai. He connected their heads with coloured wires and had some success, but they need to do it again.'

'What?' Monsieur D'Haricot could not believe Marina had waited almost an hour guzzling delicacies before telling him that Victoire had been kidnapped and was in danger.

'You knew she had been abducted,' Marina said. 'You told the Taurean and Virgo as much in the bar.'

'If Otocey has already tried his experiment once, Victoire must have been taken before my cab journey.' Monsieur D'Haricot banged on the table. 'Otocey was trying to fool me and I fell for his trick. The woman in the museum and the taxi was Mala Kai.'

'I told you that,' Marina mumbled through stuffed cheeks.

'I have to rescue Victoire.'

'That is what Otocey intends,' Marina said. 'He has gathered his pack of zodiac heroes and villains. He is short of a Cancer and a Sagittarian, but he knows you will come after him, and I shall be with you.'

'Maulise and Juan are in Rouen. Louise and Philip I assume are under Paris. Dauphine is here. Gustav could be anywhere on the river and Gori will go where his mother tells him.' Monsieur counted the people, including himself, Marina, Otocey, Mala Kai and Victoire. 'I am missing a sign.'

'A Piscean,' Marina answered.

'The General.'

'Exactly, and where will he be?'

'He should be in his office, in Montmartre. I have sent him a letter warning him of events.'

'I wouldn't rely on that,' Marina said. 'Look behind you.'

Monsieur D'Haricot did as he was instructed. There was a lone male diner at a table in the corner reading a newspaper. The edge of the paper was smouldering thanks to the proximity of his pipe.

'Should I warn him?' Monsieur D'Haricot asked.

'I am not talking about the private detective,' Marina said.

'How do you know he is a private investigator?'

'He looks and smells like one, but that is unimportant. Look above his head.' It was clear Monsieur D'Haricot was not going to understand, even with clues. 'The calendar,' Marina said.

'I can only see a picture of a bridge.' Monsieur D'Haricot looked closer. In one corner was a tiny tag with months and numbers.

'There is a date circled in red,' Marina explained.

'It looks like three days from now.' Monsieur D'Haricot said. 'I don't see the significance.'

'That is the day of the celebration marking the anniversary of Fraumy becoming a dukedom.'

'For a crab, you know an awful lot about the goings on underground,' Monsieur D'Haricot accused.

'It must be these biscuits,' Marina answered. 'My dream is that one day all crabs will have access to them.'

'That sounds more like a nightmare,' Monsieur D'Haricot muttered, glad that crabs did not have particularly large ears. 'What do these celebrations involve?'

'Bands and marches, dancing, fireworks…'

'Underground?'

'Of course. Please do not ask a question and then interrupt when I am answering. It is extremely rude.' Monsieur D'Haricot apologised. 'Fireworks, champagne, good food, sweets, singing, games, assassination…'

'Assassination?'

'You have done it again. What is the point of apologising if you don't mean it?'

'This needs clarification,' Monsieur D'Haricot protested. His voice was raised and had attracted the attention of the private investigator in the corner. The man put his paper on the table and got to his feet, only to realise that the tablecloth was smouldering. A corner burst into flames. He flapped at them with his hat, spreading tongues of fire towards the wooden chairs. A waiter rushed across holding a vase of flowers. He tossed the contents onto the table from a distance and the water landed on his patron's arm.

'I think we should leave,' Monsieur D'Haricot said. For once Marina agreed. He left sufficient coins on the table to cover the meal, grabbed the crab, then strode out the door.

'Where are we going?' Marina asked, once they were safely along the street.

'To Sark, to rescue Victoire. I appreciate your warning, but I am of the opinion that the Vicomte underestimates my prowess. He may have oodles of money and technological know-how at his disposal, but when it comes to intellect I have him on the ropes.'

'How do you intend getting to Sark?' Marina asked.

'Give me a moment and I shall find a way.'

'Do we have time for an ice cream?' Marina asked.

'If by "we" you mean "you", the answer is no. You have eaten enough for one day.'

'Shan't tell you my plan then,' Marina huffed.

A girl of nine or ten with plaited, dark hair was standing at the street corner trying to hand out leaflets. The passersby were avoiding her and Monsieur D'Haricot suspected she must be part of a religious or political cult.

'Please take a leaflet, Monsieur.' She pressed the paper into Monsieur D'Haricot's hand. He was about to crumple it and throw it in the litter bin when the message caught his eye.

SHARKS FOR HIRE - 2 francs an hour.

The girl had moved down the street and Monsieur D'Haricot saw that she walked with a severe limp. There was no need to increase his speed to catch up with her.

'Where can I find these sharks?' he asked.

The girl coughed up a mouthful of green phlegm before replying. She directed him towards a disused pier at the far end of the promenade. The boards were rotten and there were large gaps between them. Monsieur D'Haricot slid several times on the green algae marking the walkway. A fisherman was sitting on a deckchair at the end of the pier smoking a pipe. The man had only one eye, which seemed, in the absence of a partner, to have moved across his face to occupy a more central position. An eye patch covered the space between it and the man's right ear. Monsieur D'Haricot was not surprised to see blue smoke rise from the pipe, obscuring the man's nose. He waved the leaflet in front of the fisherman.

'I am interested in hiring a shark,' he said in a tone that implied he was familiar with the machines.

The fisherman sucked on his pipe. Monsieur D'Haricot was about to ask again in a louder voice when the man struggled to his feet.

'You're in luck; there's one free. How long do you want it for?'

Monsieur D'Haricot made a swift calculation. He didn't know the speed of the craft and had to rely on an optimistic guess, but Sark was a small island. Above or below ground, it wouldn't take him more than twenty minutes to find and rescue Victoire. 'Two hours will be sufficient,' he answered, handing over his four francs.

The fisherman pocketed the money and gestured Monsieur D'Haricot to follow him to the top of a metal ladder. The shark was bobbing in the water below. The craft resembled a children's fairground ride, painted a garish sky blue with red stripes. The roof had been lifted to allow access to a cabin, large enough for one person of slender disposition. The fisherman saw his look of unease.

'The control panel shifts to give leg room,' he said helpfully.

Monsieur D'Haricot made his way down the rickety ladder, taking care not to dirty his clothing. One of the uprights had become detached from the holding bracket and the ladder swung as he descended. The craft bobbed as he stuck a foot towards it.

'A little to your left,' the fisherman called.

Monsieur D'Haricot moved his foot to the right and dropped into the cabin of the shark. As he sat down, he struggled to fit his feet into the box in front of him and remained with his knees poking against his chin.

'You are squashing me,' Marina complained.

'I don't know how Otocey managed to fit into one of these,' Monsieur D'Haricot grumbled.

'He has a great white at his disposal,' Marina said. 'This is little more than a dogfish.'

The fisherman was watching from the pier. 'Do you know how to drive it?' he called down once Monsieur D'Haricot was settled.

Monsieur D'Haricot examined the control panel. 'I have ridden a bicycle since I was a boy and I am adept at driving a chargeur. This cannot be any harder than that.'

'As you will,' the fisherman replied, gripping his pipe in his teeth to prevent it falling overboard. 'The blue button takes you down, the green one brings you up. Don't touch the yellow one.'

'Why not?'

The fisherman chuckled. 'If I had an extra franc for every time someone asked me that—'

'It was a leading remark.' Monsieur D'Haricot smarted. It took a moment for him to realise that the man expected another franc before answering. He tossed the coin towards him. A hand reached out to retrieve it with the alacrity of a mechanical cuckoo marking the hour and indeed, as it did, a clock sounded from the direction of the town hall.

'The yellow button on this model activates the flight mode. Normally it can be used when the vehicle is on land, but that one is broken.' The fisherman waited until the chimes from the town hall clock finished. 'Two hours,' he reminded Monsieur D'Haricot, saluted and swaggered off.

Monsieur D'Haricot reached for the blue button.

'You should close the roof first,' Marina said. 'Not that you ever listen to me, but I believe humans find breathing underwater awkward.'

Monsieur D'Haricot pulled the roof closed and listened for the hiss as the watertight seal engaged. Two portholes the size of apples placed either end of the front panel gave a skewed view ahead of him. He pushed the blue button before Marina could give further advice. The shark sank at once. Monsieur D'Haricot felt his ears pop. His chest tightened and his head swam. The craft bumped against the bottom of the seabed, sending a jolt up his spine. Monsieur D'Haricot pushed the pink button marked with a forward arrow, which was next to the blue one. There was a grinding noise as the bottom of the boat scraped against the rocks and came to a halt. No manner of pulling levers and thumping buttons would entice it to move further.

'We're stuck,' Marina said.

Monsieur D'Haricot pushed the buttons in a different sequence with no success.

'We can surface and try again,' he said.

He pressed the green button three times. There was a screeching sound and the smell of welded metal. A red light flashed at the bottom of the control panel, but the shark did not budge. Monsieur D'Haricot was unable to see his feet, but he sensed they were getting wet. A cold dampness worked its way up his socks and trouser legs.

'I think we have a leak,' he said to Marina.

'I'm too young to die,' Marina screamed, grabbing hold of his jacket sleeve.

'Crabs don't drown,' Monsieur D'Haricot assured her.

'I know. I wanted to add drama to the scene.'

'It would be better if you could try looking for the hole so that we can plug it. I can't move.'

Marina let go of his arm and crawled beneath the seat. She appeared a minute later.

'The hole is too large to plug,' she said. 'I would say there is more hole than bottom to this shark.'

Monsieur D'Haricot had deduced that himself from the water lapping at his thighs. 'I'll open the roof and we can swim to the surface.'

He was unable to locate a lever or button to raise the roof automatically and reached up to give the metal a shove. Nothing happened. 'Is there a flare we can dispatch for help?' he asked.

'I doubt anyone will see it,' Marina answered.

'Are you always so optimistic?'

'You are the Sagittarian,' Marina argued. 'I am a Cancer and, as such, have a highly developed sixth sense. It tells me that Edgori van Lüttich would have ensured he selected the most out-of-the-way spot for his shark hire business.'

'Am I missing something? What has Gori to do with this?'

'I told you sharks were EvL.' Marina waited for Monsieur D'Haricot to appreciate her humour. She gave a huff when there was no response. 'I also have a highly developed sense of smell, and can detect a van Lüttich from twenty boat lengths away. The fisherman was Gori and the girl who gave you the leaflet was his mother.'

Monsieur D'Haricot wanted to demand why she hadn't warned him of this before, but the water was now up to his chin and if he spoke he would be in danger of swallowing enough to risk salt poisoning.

'If I were you, since Gori told you not to, I would press the yellow button,' Marina advised.

Monsieur D'Haricot was not in the habit of ignoring direct warnings, but Marina's logic made sense in a sidestepping, crablike way. He reached for the yellow button.

Chapter Fifteen

There was the thumping of a tent door flapping open and the plop of a suction cap being pulled. The water level began to fall and Monsieur D'Haricot knew by the descent of blood to his toes that the shark was rising. Within seconds the surface of the water was visible from the tiny portholes that served as eyes.

'We need to open the roof,' Monsieur D'Haricot said. 'If only I had my skeleton lock picker.'

Marina had worked her way to where the roof was attached to the body of the vessel and was working at the mechanism with her pinchers. There was a click and the hinges sprung open.

'Grab the open end,' Marina said.

'Shouldn't we wait for the hydraulic device to do its job?' Monsieur D'Haricot objected. 'I wouldn't want to be responsible for breaking it.'

Marina stared at him with her beady eyes.

'I suppose we can't do much more damage,' he admitted.

The roof was raised and Monsieur D'Haricot wriggled his way out of the machine. His clothing was drenched and puddles formed as he stood on the quay examining the stricken shark. What appeared to be a giant yellow balloon, attached by ropes to the sides of the vessel, was deflating on the surface of the water, sending bubbles towards England. A starfish crawled from his pocket, dropped to the ground and dragged its body back to the water.

'I shall demand my money back,' Monsieur D'Haricot said, feeling he should show he was in command of the situation.

'You will have to find Edgori first,' Marina answered.

'First,' Monsieur D'Haricot emphasised the word, 'I have to rescue Victoire. I trust you have not forgotten about her.'

While Monsieur D'Haricot shook his trouser legs and shirt front to dry them out, Marina convinced him that a trip to the Channel Islands was unnecessary. It was noble of him to desire to rescue Victoire Chapleau from her laboratory cage, but Otocey's journey to Sark was to collect his prisoner for the final stage of his plan. He would round up Juan and Maulise from Rouen, then head to Fraumy.

Monsieur D'Haricot snapped his fingers. They were still wet and little noise was heard. 'We need to return to Rouen tout suite,' he declared, claiming the idea for his own.

'First,' Marina reminded him, not to be outdone in the use of the pre-eminent, 'we need a bag for me. I feel exposed on land.'

The assistant in the department store looked Monsieur D'Haricot up and down, wishing he had the authority to ban half-drowned customers from the shop. He did a magnificent job of remaining professional while Monsieur D'Haricot spoke to his inside pocket. When a voice from the pocket asked for a silk lining, the assistant answered, without a moment's hesitation, that all their cases were lined with durable Eri silk.

'I shall also need a hat,' Monsieur D'Haricot said, once a suitable case was found.

'And perhaps an umbrella, monsieur?' the assistant asked with only the slightest hint of a grin.

Fifteen minutes later, Monsieur D'Haricot was sitting on a bench on the station platform, homburg hat on head, case open to allow Marina to observe the goings on and waiting for a train to Rouen. He had contemplated bypassing Rouen and heading directly to Fraumy, but short of finding a trustworthy guide, he had no way of reaching the territory. Marina was no help, claiming she could swim there in a matter of weeks, assuming she wasn't eaten along the way.

'Maulise is expecting me. I shall meet him as arranged,' Monsieur D'Haricot said to the contents of his case, receiving looks from the only other passenger on the platform. 'I still don't like the idea of leaving Victoire in the hands of Otocey,' he grumbled.

'Although lacking a good set of pinchers, she is not defenceless,' Marina argued. 'She is four times as clever as he is, or has eaten four times as many crab biscuits. Either way, I have no doubt she is using the time well.'

Monsieur D'Haricot scratched behind his ear. 'How many crab biscuits have you eaten? Your intelligence seems to have quadrupled. Plus you are getting a good deal heavier to carry.'

The second passenger moved across to stand next to him. Monsieur D'Haricot closed his case, leaving a gap for air.

'Heading to Paris?' the stranger asked in a jovial manner.

Monsieur D'Haricot was about to answer 'Rouen' when it occurred to him that the train arriving at that platform did not go to Paris. The man sensed Monsieur D'Haricot's suspicions and added, 'All roads lead to Paris.'

'I thought that was Rome? I take it you are travelling to Paris,' Monsieur D'Haricot said.

The traveller made a grumbling noise which could have signified anything. He wiped the bench seat with a handkerchief before sitting at the opposite end from Monsieur D'Haricot and searching in his briefcase for his newspaper. The Prime Minister was in the headlines. Monsieur D'Haricot expected the picture beneath to be a grainy image of Léon Blum, the recently elected Prime Minister of what he now had to consider as being Upper France. Instead a flattering photograph of Madame Chapleau glared back at him. When the man spread the newspaper out Monsieur D'Haricot saw to his dismay that the bottom edge was burnt. He had not paid specific attention to the facial features of the private investigator in the cafe, but he feared it was the same man. Part of him was curious to know why he was being followed, but his overriding feeling was to flee.

'Excuse me, when is the train due?' he asked the guard who had sauntered onto the platform carrying a red and a green flag in one hand and a bottle of cognac in the other.

The guard positioned his flags under his elbow and held them there while he consulted his pocket watch. 'Forty-two seconds sir... forty-one... forty...'

'Thank you.' There had been little need to ask, because by the time the guard had answered he could hear the engine trudging towards the station. It slowed and hissed a steam of air that misted over the platform. Monsieur D'Haricot approached the carriage door and allowed three young ladies to descend the small step, giving a hand to their older chaperone.

'After you,' he said to his fellow traveller, standing back until the man had entered the train. He delayed his own entry by pretending to tie a loose shoelace, giving time for the investigator to move along the corridor.

'All aboard,' the guard called.

The engine let out another puff and as it did Monsieur D'Haricot ducked unseen behind a porter with a barrow load of cases belonging to the young ladies. The guard made sure the doors were closed, then took a swig from his cognac. He stuffed the bottle in his jacket pocket and brought out a whistle, which he blew. As the note died, he raised his green flag. The train creaked out of the station. Monsieur D'Haricot stood on the platform and waved at the window where the investigator was standing, peering back at him.

'I suppose he could have been on our side,' Marina commented.

'That is impossible,' Monsieur D'Haricot answered. 'I don't know which side I am on.'

'I am on the side of freedom,' Marina declared. She was ogling the guard's flags.

'Freedom for crabs,' Monsieur D'Haricot clarified.

'Why should crabs be less important than anything else?'

'I didn't mean to imply that they aren't. I too am on the side of freedom,' Monsieur D'Haricot said, pondering what the word meant. 'Freedom for the underworlders may mean a loss of rights for my own people. To gain democracy for the people of Fraumy rather than living under the rule of an autocrat could involve supporting Dauphine van Lüttich and her son, which would condemn the Grand-duke, who is technically my boss.'

'Mmm,' Marina thought for a moment. 'I suppose it is easier for crabs.'

'And I suppose we should find another way of returning to Rouen,' Monsieur D'Haricot said. 'I see from the timetable that the next train stops at the same stations as the last one. Our friend will be waiting for us further down the line.'

'Your "friend" is waiting for you here.' Monsieur D'Haricot turned to see the gentleman from the train wiping dust from his jacket.

'But how…?'

'I jumped,' the man said. 'Let me introduce myself, I am Agent Delanoir, your replacement.' Monsieur D'Haricot mouthed the final word as Agent Delanoir continued. 'I received a telegram from the General this morning. I have it here.' Delanoir retrieved the paper from his top pocket and read.

'Message from weird woman. In danger. D'Haricot involved. Replace him at once. Kisses to your mother. The General.'

He folded the telegram and replaced it in his pocket before Monsieur D'Haricot could confirm that what Delanoir spoke was what the General had written.

'Why have you not destroyed the message?' Monsieur D'Haricot demanded. 'One of the first rules of our trade is to swallow missives from above.'

'I have a touch of indigestion this morning and my mother will wish to see the kisses herself.'

'This is who I am to be replaced by,' Monsieur D'Haricot huffed.

'Who were you talking to a moment ago?' Delanoir asked.

'That is none of your business,' Monsieur D'Haricot replied. 'Now that I am relieved of my duties, I bid you farewell.'

'Not so fast. I have orders to escort you to Paris, where you will explain your conduct to the General.'

'The telegram said nothing of that.'

Delanoir shuffled from one foot to the other.

'You aren't a real agent at all,' Monsieur D'Haricot declared.

'Am so,' Delanoir protested.

'You are not even French.' Monsieur D'Haricot felt he was gaining the upper hand and wanted to press home his advantage. Delanoir did not deny the accusation.

'I am German and proud of it,' he averred. 'God save the King.'

Monsieur D'Haricot did not have the ability to raise one eyebrow independently of the other, but if he had, he most certainly would have used it. Instead he muttered a brief 'hmm'.

'I may not be one of the General's agents, but the General won't be in charge for much longer,' Delanoir said. 'You thought you were clever sending an ordinary housewife with an important message – except the woman you picked isn't your average housewife and her cousin isn't a silly nobody without a name. She is my mother. We have royal blood.' Delanoir paused while Monsieur D'Haricot tried to work out what he was saying. Was the landlady his mother, or was her cousin his mother? It hardly mattered.

'Explain yourself, or I shall have you arrested for treason,' Monsieur D'Haricot said.

'Ha,' Delanoir forced a laugh. 'I am the one with the gun.' As he spoke he whipped a revolver from a holster beneath the flap of his jacket. 'Hände hoch.'

'The porter and guard are watching,' Monsieur D'Haricot reminded him.

Delanoir partially covered the body of the revolver with the sleeve of his jacket. 'Move,' he ordered.

'Where to?' Monsieur D'Haricot stood his ground.

'I would suggest the waiting room,' Marina said. Delanoir's eyes popped. His neck jerked towards the case. It was clear he was not aware of Marina or the fact that she was no ordinary crab. Monsieur D'Haricot deduced he wasn't one of Otocey's thugs.

'You are working for Edgori van Lüttich,' Monsieur D'Haricot stated.

'What makes you think van Lüttich isn't working for me?'

'We are getting nowhere,' Monsieur D'Haricot said. Delanoir was green when it came to the espionage game and Monsieur D'Haricot suspected that he had no intention of using the gun, if indeed he had any idea of how to. It was time to play a straight. 'Tell your master, if he messes with me, he messes with Vicomte Otocey.'

'That joker couldn't frighten a mouse.' The words were brave, but the pistol wavered as the sleeve of Delanoir's jacket shook.

'Hurry along, gentlemen, or you'll miss the train.' The guard broke into their conversation. Unnoticed and unheard, the next train had glided into the station. The strangeness of this fact was not lost on Monsieur D'Haricot; nonetheless, when he looked round, he expected to see a familiar engine and carriages. He did not expect to see a piece of advanced engineering hovering over the platform, a cross between a mechanical fire dragon and an extraordinarily active electric eel.

Monsieur D'Haricot rubbed his eyes. When he removed his hands the train was still waiting.

'All aboard,' the guard said cheerfully. He turned to Delanoir. 'I'm afraid I will need to confiscate your firearm.'

Delanoir refused to hand it over.

'Where is the train going?' Monsieur D'Haricot asked.

'Does that matter? I can smell fresh pastries and… mmm… pistachio macarons.' Marina was about to swoon.

Monsieur D'Haricot felt faint himself, although it was more nausea brought about by the blue smoke circling around the train, obscuring the fabulous engineering. Within a minute the only part of the train in sight was the funnel. The guard was becoming more animate in his urgings that they should board and Marina was drooling. She had popped her head from the bag and the saliva was creeping down his sleeve. There was nothing for it but to get onto the train, which he would have done if he could see the door. The guard came to his rescue with a pair of peach-tinted spectacles. Delanoir was not offered a pair.

With the glasses fitting snugly on his nose, Monsieur D'Haricot was able to see the train in detail. He moved away from his companion and opened the nearest carriage door. He too could smell the pastries that Marina was keen to get her claws on and reckoned they must be near the restaurant carriage. He stepped into the compartment and slammed the door behind him, fearing Delanoir was clinging to the tail of his jacket. He heard the sound of a lock clicking.

'Welcome aboard.' A man in a salmon pink uniform with mauve trim bowed. He accepted the spectacles back from Monsieur D'Haricot and in return offered him a menu. 'Will you require lunch?'

'We've eaten,' Monsieur D'Haricot replied. A gentle nip from Marina made him add, 'Afternoon coffee and pastries would be welcome though.'

'This way, please.'

The train compartment was like none Monsieur D'Haricot had seen before. He had read that in Britain the king used royal coaches and he imagined they were suitably grand, but he doubted they reached the height of Gallic luxury he had entered. A carpeted corridor led to a marble staircase, more in keeping with the atrium of an opera house than a locomotive. A quartet of musicians played jazz tunes on the landing. At the top of the stairs was a hallway. The uniformed maître d' indicated a room directly ahead.

'The dining car, monsieur. The window tables are reserved. We use a rotational system for frequent travellers. Otherwise you may choose whichever one you prefer.'

The tables were laid out in preparation for a magnificent banquet, with sufficient cutlery to confuse the most experienced master of etiquette. Monsieur D'Haricot counted six different glasses and three China cups. The carriage was empty apart from one other diner, a lady, who sat at a window table looking out. Monsieur D'Haricot could not see her face, but he recognised the perfume. His surprise made him forget his manners.

'Victoire,' he exclaimed.

Madame Chapleau turned slowly. There were lines of worry across her face and she did not break into her usual smile when she engaged with him. 'Monsieur D'Haricot, how good to see you,' she responded in a monotone without opening her mouth.

'Is something wrong?' Monsieur D'Haricot asked, moving towards the table. It was rare for her to use his title when they were alone.

Madame Chapleau forced her lips into something resembling a smile. 'I am feeling a teensy touch of travel sickness,' she said.

'Was it the sea journey?'

'I'm sorry?'

'I was told you were on Sark,' Monsieur D'Haricot explained.

'Was I?'

'You have been drugged. You must try to regain your senses.' Monsieur D'Haricot sat down beside her without asking permission. 'You are in need of strong refreshment,' he advised. 'What are you drinking?' He examined the liquid in her cup. It smelt like coffee.

'I am tired,' Madame Chapleau answered. 'My head hurts.'

Monsieur D'Haricot took hold of her hand and rubbed her fingers. For a moment he had feared he was talking to Mala Kai rather than Victoire, but the fingers were warm and solid. 'There is nothing to worry about now that I am here.'

The train entered a tunnel and the carriage was lit by the artificial light he remembered from the underground city. Madame Chapleau's skin glowed a luminous green. He let her hand slip free. The tunnel extended a significant distance. He didn't remember it from his journey to Dieppe.

'Do you know where this train is heading?' he asked.

'After a brief stop in Rouen, we are going to Fraumy,' a voice answered from the doorway. Monsieur D'Haricot had been looking out the window at the darkness. He turned to see an exact copy of Madame Chapleau leaning an arm against the doorframe. The lady was dressed in identical clothes, but was holding a lacquered ebony cigarette holder with a smoking cigarette.

'Madame Chapleau.' Monsieur D'Haricot rose and gave a bow.

'No need to be so formal, Louis,' the lady replied. She glided towards him. 'It has been ages since I last saw you. Why don't we make use of the journey to catch up on old times?'

'Old times?'

The second Madame Chapleau smiled broadly, keeping her lips

145

shut tight. She took a seat at the table and glanced at the menu. 'Waiter,' she called. The man appeared immediately. 'A plate of pastries and macarons for my friend, please. I shall have the quiche and bring a basket of bread. Where is the wine list?' The waiter produced it from under his arm. 'Would you prefer red or white?' she asked Monsieur D'Haricot, ignoring the first Madame Chapleau.

'Red,' Monsieur D'Haricot answered. 'What is your preference?' he asked the first Madame Chapleau.

'I never touch that filth,' she answered weakly.

The second Madame Chapleau smiled again. Her smile had actually not faded from when she sat down, but it appeared to be refreshed. 'Mala Kai is allergic to grapes,' she answered.

'Our drinking won't affect you, will it, Madame?' Monsieur D'Haricot asked out of politeness rather than concern.

'There is no point speaking to her when she is like this,' Victoire said. 'You might as well be talking to a duck.'

'That is rather uncharitable,' Monsieur D'Haricot answered. He did not wish to admit he had been unaware which sister was which and, despite confirmation, something niggled. 'When did you start smoking cigarettes? I thought you preferred cigarillos.'

'Oh, this? It is some filth Nicolas gave me.' She stressed the word 'filth' in the same manner her sister had, such that Monsieur D'Haricot experienced the odd sensation of hearing it from the mouth of the other woman. Victoire handed the cigarette holder to the waiter. 'Bring a bottle of Beaujolais. Make it a Magnum.'

The waiter left and there was silence until he returned with the pastries, quiche and bread. Another man, similarly well-groomed in a matching pink uniform, brought the wine for Victoire to taste.

She wafted the aroma towards her nose, swirled the wine in the glass and sipped. 'Perfect. You can leave us now,' she instructed before the waiter could pour Monsieur D'Haricot's drink.

'Will I be permitted to leave the train at Rouen?' Monsieur D'Haricot asked. Outside the train window it remained dark and he suspected they were travelling underground.

'Why would you wish to do that?' Victoire asked. 'We have everything you need on the train, except we don't call it that. This is a trans reality interface connector.'

'I prefer to call it a train,' Monsieur D'Haricot answered.

'Whatever you call it, it has bedrooms, cinemas, restaurants, reading rooms, billiard rooms, a swimming pool, tennis courts, dance halls, music rooms. This TRIC has two grand pianos and a pipe organ.'

'I have arranged to meet someone in Rouen,' Monsieur D'Haricot said.

'If you mean Juan or Maulise, they will both be joining us on the TRIC,' Victoire assured him.

'Will they? I can't imagine Juan or even St John acceding to that command, but it is not my cause for concern. I fear Maulise is in danger.'

'We do not intend harming him.'

'I am not speaking of Otocey's objective. The guest house he is staying in is run by a relation of a German noble working for Edgori van Lüttich.'

Victoire laughed. 'Wolfie Schwarz? He is no more of a nobleman, or a German, than that waiter.'

'Which makes him no less of a danger,' Monsieur D'Haricot countered. 'I don't know how fast this train can go, but if Delanoir, or Schwarz as you call him, telephones a colleague in Rouen, I would bet my new hat they can reach Maulise before you can.'

Victoire's smile shrank. 'How do you know this?'

'It is my profession to know things,' Monsieur D'Haricot smirked but, feeling foolish, he added, 'He was on the station platform. He tried to kill me.'

'What do you suggest we do?' Victoire said gravely.

Monsieur D'Haricot's brain was clicking. 'You must have the technology to contact Maulise,' he said. 'What about that machine I saw in your case at The Red Duck?'

'What red duck?' Victoire looked puzzled. She cast a swift glance at Mala Kai, who had slumped against the window.

'The Café de Canard Rouge,' Monsieur D'Haricot prompted her. It seemed a lifetime since his beloved bicycle had been destroyed by Victoire although it was only a week ago.

Mala Kai stirred. 'He means the signal communicator,' she croaked. Colour had returned to her cheeks and she seemed more vibrant now that the TRIC was underground.

'That is an experimental instrument,' Victoire regained her poise. 'It requires the person receiving the transmissions to be in possession of a linked aerial. Although I believe Maulise may have one. Nicolas—' she glanced at Monsieur D'Haricot, considering whether to speak out in his presence, but decided to continue. 'Nicolas planted aerials on all his zodiacs.'

'You mean… how?' Monsieur D'Haricot surreptitiously patted his arms and chest, feeling for a hidden aerial.

Victoire didn't answer. Mala Kai was staring back out of the window at the darkness.

'We are wasting time,' Monsieur D'Haricot said. 'Where is the transmitter on this train?'

'In the communication room,' Victoire answered.

Monsieur D'Haricot got to his feet. He reached for Marina, who had crawled from the case, but was prevented from lifting her by a sharp nip from her pinchers.

'I'll stay here,' she said, her mouth full of macaron crumbs.

Monsieur D'Haricot looked at Mala Kai. She gave no indication of being interested in the crab, but given past experiences he didn't intend taking risks.

'No you won't,' he said, popping her back in the case along with the last two pastries and a macaron.

Chapter Sixteen

Victoire and Monsieur D'Haricot had reached the door of the carriage when Mala Kai decided to join them. Victoire did not complain. The communication room was down a back staircase and along a corridor. It was a fifth of the size and lacked the luxury of the dining car, but Monsieur D'Haricot could tell that no expense had been spared on the equipment. An officer in a grey uniform sat at a table pressing keys on a three-layered typewriter. The top keys were as Monsieur D'Haricot expected. The second layer incorporated letters from the Cyrillic, Coptic, Arabic and Chinese alphabets. The third layer was composed of hieroglyphs and runic letters.

The operator rose when Victoire and the others entered. He left the room when she waved a hand towards the door. The signal communicator was on a shelf on the far wall. It was a larger, more sophisticated machine than the portable version Victoire had used in the café. She pulled a lever at the door to switch it on. A green light appeared and a bell rang. Victoire lifted the receiver and blew into it. The light changed to amber and flashed three times.

'Are you sure you know how to work this?' Monsieur D'Haricot asked. 'Allow me. I have had extensive training in communications.' He edged Victoire aside and ran his hand across the workings, letting his thumb rest on a purple knob.

'Do not squeeze that,' Mala Kai warned from her position at the door. Monsieur D'Haricot doubted she could see what he was doing, but he paused. She moved to stand beside him. 'Pressing that will alert all controllers to your activity,' she said. 'Is that what you want?'

Monsieur D'Haricot lifted his hands from the machine and allowed Mala Kai to take control. The light reverted to green. 'What is Maulise's identity number?' she asked Victoire. Her sister gave her the digits and she typed them into a keyboard. A noise like a singing robin tweeted from the machine and Mala Kai handed Monsieur D'Haricot the receiver. He put it to his ear.

'What's going on? Who is calling? Where are you?' Maulise's belligerent voice could be heard as a tinny echo.

'It is me, Louis-Philip D'Haricot, where are you?'

'I asked you first.'

'This is no time for foolery. Your life could be in danger. The landlady and her husband are in league with Gori.'

'You woke me at this ungodly hour to tell me that?' Maulise was annoyed.

'It is well into the afternoon and I thought you might think it important,' Monsieur D'Haricot responded, equally as irked.

'I already knew about the landlady,' Maulise replied, giving what sounded like a yawn. 'And while we're at it, that fish you've been feeding isn't alive.'

'How did you know I was feeding…? I didn't kill it.' The two Mesdames were listening to the conversation and Monsieur D'Haricot felt his cheeks redden.

'It is a spy camera,' Maulise affirmed.

Monsieur D'Haricot wanted to reply that he knew it was and had been keeping up the pretence, but he didn't feel his fibbing skills would convince an expert like Maulise. 'Are you in the house now?' he asked.

'No, I am in the Le Crochet – the proper one, this time. Some joker directed me to a ladies' knitting circle.'

Victoire seized the receiver from Monsieur D'Haricot, catching his ear and giving it a tweak. 'Is Juan with you?' she shouted in an un-lady-like manner.

'We are enjoying a Calvados before he begins his act,' Maulise answered. A few strums of guitar music played in the background followed by a deep laugh.

'Hola, señora,' Juan called.

'You both need to get out of there immediately. We will meet you at the railway station in five minutes,' Victoire instructed.

'I haven't performed yet,' Juan protested.

'And I haven't finished this rather exquisite bottle of Calvados,'

Maulise added, putting in a hiccup for good measure.

'Our plans have changed,' Victoire said. 'I told Nicolas not to involve a Sagittarian until we had to. They always feel they can meddle with perfectly good instructions.'

'Excuse me,' Monsieur D'Haricot interrupted. 'I didn't ask to be involved.'

'You stole Mademoiselle Jouet's fan,' Mala Kai said.

'Is that what Otocey told you? I am not a thief. I accidentally lifted it in my rush from Victoire's party. I would have returned it.'

'Enough of this squabbling.' Victoire returned the receiver to its holder and switched the machine off. 'I don't trust those two imbeciles to do anything they are told. We shall have to go to the club to collect them. Come, sister.'

'Can't Nicolas see to it?' Mala Kai asked.

A look from her twin, although suggesting nothing to Monsieur D'Haricot, made Mala Kai shiver. Victoire linked arms with her and the two ladies walked to the door with Victoire in the lead. Monsieur D'Haricot followed them. Victoire turned and raised her hand in his face. 'We are going to our boudoir to change. I suggest you return to your room and do likewise.'

Monsieur D'Haricot watched the two ladies stroll arm in arm along the carriage corridor, wondering where his room was. One of the uniformed attendants was happy to direct him.

'Were you expecting me?' he asked casually as he followed the man along a passage lined with surrealist paintings, including a picture of an enormous green apple taking up an entire room which he believed was painted by Rene Magritte and entitled 'The Listening Room'.

'Oh, yes sir. The Vicomte said you would be joining us in Dieppe. We made the detour especially for you. Here we are.'

At the end of the corridor, and strangely out of place, was a picture he recognised from Maulise's studio, a green bridge set against the red background that was Maulise's signature colour. The man directed him to the room next door with an outstretched arm. A childish picture of a Centaur firing a bow and arrow was garishly painted on the woodwork.

The room was not as spacious or as comfortable as he hoped, but he remembered he was on a train, which, no matter what it was called, had to comply with certain width restrictions. The single bed was sturdy and the oak wardrobe was stocked with an adequate supply of shirts and jackets. He had removed his shirt when an assistant popped his head round the door. Monsieur D'Haricot shielded his pale, hairless chest with his arms.

'The washroom is second on the left,' the man informed him before departing.

Monsieur D'Haricot was relieved to find a solid bolt on the washroom door. He had no wish for Otocey or anyone else to barge in on his bath, although from the lack of luxury he doubted the Vicomte ever set a bare toe in the room. The towels were stained and threadbare and the soap was a block of lye and lard. Having washed, shaved and waxed his moustache, Monsieur D'Haricot returned to his compartment and selected a dark suit. On a whim, he changed the jacket for a crimson one, cut from a velvet material. He spent a moment in front of the mirror adjusting a handkerchief in the top pocket before making his way to the restaurant car, leaving Marina in the bedroom reading his copy of Jules Verne's fantasy book.

He ordered a brandy aperitif while he waited on the ladies. Victoire was the first to appear, dressed in a low cut blue gown which he had seen her wear on a previous occasion. Her cleavage was protected by three strings of pearls and she carried a matching clutch bag. He knew it was Victoire, rather than her sister, because although both sisters had one emerald and one sapphire eye, they were a mirror image of the other. He had also identified a tiny mole on Mala Kai's right earlobe, which was present on Victoire's left.

'Finish your drink and come with me,' she said.

'Shouldn't we wait on Mala Kai?'

'Shouldn't we do this, shouldn't we do that. You are very proper today, Louis.' Victoire gave a high-pitched trill, then covered her mouth.

'I hope I am always "proper", as you call it.'

'I'm afraid you are, darling.' Victoire swung her jewel encrusted bag over her shoulder and swaggered to the door. Monsieur D'Haricot followed. He looked along the corridor in the direction of the ladies' room. 'You won't find her,' Victoire said.

'Has she gone ahead?'

'She is here, silly.' Victoire nudged him with her elbow.

'My mistake. Should I have asked where Victoire is?' Monsieur D'Haricot said.

'She is here too.' Victoire giggled. 'Don't you understand we are one and the same person?'

'I know twins are close,' Monsieur D'Haricot said, 'But there were two of you sitting at that table less than thirty minutes ago.'

'A trick of the lights.' As if to indicate her point, Victoire pointed to the illuminated ceiling. 'Now come along, we don't want to miss Juan's solo performance.'

Monsieur D'Haricot had not believed Marina's tale of a mind melding machine, feeling she was prone to exaggeration and fantasy, but it was becoming evident that something untoward involving Victoire and her twin had indeed been carried out on Sark. He had heard rumours of minds taking over bodies, or vice versa, in less civilised cultures. It seemed preposterous, but Otocey had studied such phenomena, and who knew what machines he had at his disposal? If the swaggering coyote had done anything to harm Victoire, Monsieur D'Haricot swore he would make him pay tenfold for it.

The TRIC had stopped at an underground station, similar to any station above ground apart from the light, which Monsieur D'Haricot considered eerie.

'Is there an escalator, or do we use the stairs?' He feared another elevator like the one he and Maulise had encountered. To offset the possibility, he didn't offer Victoire the option.

'In these heels?' Victoire lifted the folds of her dress to show a stockinged ankle slipping into a shoe with a Spanish heel twice the length of his thumb. 'We'll take a land cabin. It will be faster.'

Monsieur D'Haricot did not hide his dismay. Already that week he had been compelled to use more forms of transport than he had in the past twenty years. He dared not imagine what a land cabin was capable of doing to his systems. He was nostalgic for his bicycling days.

The land cabin was a black box coupled onto six glossy spheres with double axles. Inside, the box was large enough to accommodate three comfortable armchairs around a low table with a plate of biscuits and a decanter of water on it, but it was a box nonetheless. There were no windows and no driver. Monsieur D'Haricot allowed Victoire to enter, then got in behind her. She shielded her fingers as she pressed a series of numbers into a gadget on the wall. A whistle sounded before the door was automatically closed. A gentleman's voice instructed them to familiarise themselves with the safety regulations. Victoire took a seat on one of the armchairs and Monsieur D'Haricot sat opposite her.

'Are we moving?' he asked after a minute.

'We can't until you have signified that you are au fait with the safety precautions,' Victoire answered.

'Where will I find them?'

The table was held steady by a thick tome. Victoire retrieved it from under the nearest leg and handed it to Monsieur D'Haricot. He flicked through the three hundred pages.

'Basically, if anything happens, we die,' Victoire said. 'Are you happy with that?'

'Not particularly,' Monsieur D'Haricot answered.

'We would die in each other's arms,' Victoire said in a husky voice. 'Doesn't that sound divinely romantic?'

'If you put it like that, how could I disagree? How do I comply?'

Victoire leant towards him. She twisted his tie between her fingers and drew him forwards in order to place a kiss on his lips. It lasted a fraction of a second. Monsieur D'Haricot felt a thrill travel down from his mouth to his toes. He felt like he was floating above the armchair until a jolt shook him back to reality. The cabin was in motion.

Once the initial euphoria evaporated, Monsieur D'Haricot wondered what the citizens of Rouen would think when they saw the box emerge in their streets. He refrained from asking Victoire. She had her mouth full of biscuits and was in no position to answer.

The cabin had barely started when a second whistle sounded and the door slid open. Monsieur D'Haricot was the first to step out and was confronted with an outer door. He opened it with a twist of the handle. Immediately his nostrils were bombarded with smoke. He assumed it was the same blue smoke that rendered things invisible, but when it didn't clear he realised it was tobacco smoke from the club. Victoire was waiting to be helped from the cabin. She cleared her throat to get his attention, projecting biscuit crumbs at Monsieur D'Haricot's collar.

'I believe this is Le Crochet,' he said as he offered her a hand.

'There is the proprietor, Monsieur Hector.' Victoire's smile reached every cell of her body. Monsieur D'Haricot looked round to see who the unworthy recipient of it was. Victoire swept across the room, adeptly swinging her hips between close packed tables of patrons. She reached the only empty table, which had a reserved label attached to the vase of red roses in the centre. Next to it was an ice bucket cooling a bottle of champagne. One of the chairs was mysteriously drawn back by invisible hands and Victoire sat down. The champagne was poured by the unseen hand and Victoire took a sip. Looking up she spotted Monsieur D'Haricot standing across the room and waved him over.

'Champagne?' she offered. Wine was poured into a glass for him.

'What trick is this?' Monsieur D'Haricot asked.

'It is no trick. Monsieur Hector trained as a wine waiter in his youth.'

'Did he also train as an illusionist?'

Madame Chapleau looked surprised. 'You can't see Monsieur Hector?'

'I can't see him, hear him, feel him or smell him and I doubt, if I took a bite, I could taste him.'

'I am disappointed,' Victoire said. 'Monsieur Hector is an Ophiuchus, the serpent bearer. It is the thirteenth sign of the zodiac, although many astrologers don't feel it is significant.'

'Most normal people have never heard of it,' Monsieur D'Haricot said.

'I take issue with your word "normal". If a person doesn't believe the sign exists, consequently they don't believe Monsieur Hector exists, but clearly he does.'

Monsieur D'Haricot peered at the empty space around him. He tried to believe, but no, he was fooling himself if he said he saw a finger on the bottle or heard a sniff of the nose. 'Shouldn't we be finding Maulise and Juan?' he asked, to change the subject.

'This is their table,' Victoire said. 'Juan is about to perform.'

Monsieur D'Haricot's eyes were getting used to the smoky environment and he was able to see the stage a few metres in front of them. 'Where is Maulise?' he asked, preparing to sit on the chair beside Victoire.

She put out a hand out to stop him and he noticed the puddle of clear liquid on the seat.

'Poor Maulise,' Victoire said. 'He always was forgetful about eating the biscuits.'

'You don't mean…?' Monsieur D'Haricot's eyes widened. 'Should we get him to the cabin and below ground?' He patted the liquid with his handkerchief.

Victoire tried to stifle a laugh, but failed. 'Oh Louis, you are hilarious. You don't believe in Monsieur Hector, yet you have fallen face first for my little joke.'

Monsieur D'Haricot frowned. He sat down on the chair opposite, checking the seat was clear beforehand. The hall lights dimmed and a beam focused on the side curtain. The chattering hushed. The curtain fluttered to the accompaniment of guitar chords, growing faster and louder. Monsieur D'Haricot felt his heart beat louder and faster in time to the music. When he feared his heart would burst, the music stopped with a dramatic flourish. Juan stepped out from behind the curtain, his guitar strung on a beaded strap round his neck. He made his way to the centre of the stage pulling a donkey by a rope. The crowd cheered.

'Juan and his dancing donkey,' Victoire explained.

Juan bore little resemblance to St. John St Clair. The bookbinder stood erect. His hair was a distinguished grey, swept over his scalp. Juan's shoulders were slouched, with his neck disappearing turtle-like into his poncho. His hair looked like it had been dipped in tar and stuck out at odd angles beneath his pink sombrero. The moustache had been stolen from a Latin American gaucho. He let go of the rope and positioned his guitar for playing.

Despite his lackadaisical appearance, Juan knew how to play his guitar. He slapped the body of the guitar with his palm and began to strum samba music. Everyone's attention was on the donkey. The beast swung a leg to the side and managed to kick Juan on the calf. The audience howled with laughter.

'Madame Chapleau, I haven't seen you here for a while.' A lady in her mid twenties with cropped, dyed platinum hair stopped beside Victoire.

'Estelle, have a seat. Have champagne.'

Monsieur D'Haricot stood and offered her the seat between himself and Victoire.

'I would love to honey, but the doctor told me I wasn't allowed alcohol.' Monsieur D'Haricot noticed the plaster cast on the lady's left leg.

'Whatever happened to you?' Victoire asked.

'I sprained my ankle. It's a complicated story for another time.'

'Since you aren't on stage, who is assisting Juan?' Victoire said.

'I don't know. Someone he met this afternoon. He is no dancer, but the crowd love it.'

Juan was strumming a paso doble and the donkey had managed to twist his back legs around his front ones. The man at the next table to Victoire and Monsieur D'Haricot was on his knees on the floor, doubled up with laughter.

'It isn't that funny,' Victoire said.

'Wait, you mean that isn't a real donkey?' Monsieur D'Haricot was amazed.

156

'Of course not,' Estelle said. 'That would be animal exploitation. I'll see you around, babe.' She swaggered off, thumping her cast on the tiled floor.

'Someone he met this afternoon?' Madame Chapleau leant over to accept a cigarette from the unseen Monsieur Hector. She positioned it in her mouth and allowed him to light it, then blew a circlet of smoke towards Monsieur D'Haricot. 'I'm guessing that is Maulise in the donkey costume,' she said.

Monsieur D'Haricot didn't answer. He tilted his head from left to right, trying to see the dancing donkey as a person. The more he looked, the more it seemed like a real donkey.

Madame Chapleau worked her way through three cigarettes and the bottle of champagne while Juan performed. When he took his bow she rose to shout 'bravo' and drained her glass. She made to refill it, but the bottle was empty.

The room was on its feet and Monsieur D'Haricot felt he should show approval. 'Encore,' he called above the noise.

Madame Chapleau glared angrily at him. 'Nicolas will be expecting us back at the TRIC,' she said.

Juan was more than happy to perform another tune, but the donkey had collapsed in a heap. Juan gave it a kick.

'Ouch.' Monsieur D'Haricot recognised Maulise's voice.

A lady in the front row threw a plate onto the stage, which hit Juan on the foot. The donkey's head drooped and Maulise's head appeared from the neck of the costume. Juan helped Maulise to his feet and he trotted off stage. Juan appealed to the audience, who cheered the departing donkey, then quietened to allow him to play a sombre Spanish concerto.

'You get Maulise. I shall see to Juan,' Victoire instructed. She was already on her way towards the side of the stage and Monsieur D'Haricot followed. The club patrons had made way for Victoire to pass, but they weren't prepared to give ground for Monsieur D'Haricot. He tried to squeeze between a table of card players and a kissing couple, but found his way blocked by a rotund, cigar smoking gambler.

'Excuse me,' Monsieur D'Haricot said. The man eased his belly fat out of the seat and towered over Monsieur D'Haricot. The stench of neat whisky was on his breath and at any moment his cigar ash might cause his face to combust. He put out an arm to push Monsieur D'Haricot in the chest. His friends laughed.

Monsieur D'Haricot was not to be intimidated. 'Be careful, or the ace of spades might fall out of your sleeve,' he warned.

The gambler grabbed at the arm of his shirt. The edge of a card slipped from beneath his cuff. It was the Queen of Diamonds rather than an ace, but the revelation produced the desired outcome. Realising his cheating had been exposed, the man pushed the table over before his fellow poker players could react. Glasses shattered and the patrons at the nearby tables took shelter from the broken shards. Monsieur D'Haricot dashed behind the stage curtain. Maulise was disengaging himself from the donkey costume. One foot was in the air, shaking off the hoofs, when Monsieur D'Haricot barged into him.

'Steady on,' Maulise grumbled.

'We have to go.' Monsieur D'Haricot grabbed the end of the costume and yanked Maulise free.

'Juan promised me a bottle of brandy if I helped him. He didn't say anything about making an ass of myself. That kick hurt. Where is the scoundrel?'

'Victoire is fetching him. He is coming with us. There is plenty of brandy on the train.'

'What train? Where are we heading?'

'Fraumy,' Monsieur D'Haricot answered. 'I thought you knew the plan.'

'You won't get Juan to go to Fraumy. He was booed off the stage in 1920 and vowed never to return. It was a silly misunderstanding. Juan went to the wrong theatre and the audience were expecting The Tempest.'

'I imagine a samba dancing donkey would have kicked up a storm,' Monsieur D'Haricot smirked.

Maulise did not get the joke. 'There wasn't a donkey in the act then. He was going through his "Diablo" phase.'

Monsieur D'Haricot did not have the time or enthusiasm to listen to descriptions of Juan's art. He picked up Maulise's colourful coat, which had been lying on a chair at the side. 'Otocey is waiting for us.'

'You should have said it was Nicolas's brandy. Take me to it.'

Monsieur D'Haricot assumed the land cabin would be waiting where they had left it. His sense of direction, even in a smoke filled room, was excellent. He peered round the curtain to make sure the belligerent card players had moved on.

All the tables except one were overturned or broken, with splinters of wood stuck by gooey cocktails to the smashed bottles on the floor. Two security guards were extinguishing a fire that had broken out from a dropped cigarette and had caught on the far side stage curtain. They ducked as a ceiling beam crashed down beside them. A fire alarm sounded until one of the guards swung a table leg at it to silence the siren. Ladies with black eyes and bruises were supporting gentlemen with ties transformed into nooses round their necks. Shirttails were hanging out and stockings, freed from their garters, were sliding down baby smooth legs.

An invisible hand hoisted the gambler who had caused the problem in the air by the collar of his evening jacket. Monsieur D'Haricot assumed Monsieur Hector was behind the action. Two police officers arrested his companions. Victoire and Juan were seated at the only upright table, talking and drinking as if nothing untoward was going on around them. Estelle had rejoined them and had an arm around Juan's shoulder.

'The coast is clear,' Monsieur D'Haricot said to Maulise.

Maulise had put his coat on and was going through the pockets. 'I almost forgot. This came for you at the guest house this morning.' He handed Monsieur D'Haricot an envelope with an official seal. Monsieur D'Haricot accepted it and slipped it into his inside pocket. 'Shouldn't you read it?' Maulise asked. 'It is marked "urgent".'

'It is also marked "private",' Monsieur D'Haricot answered.

'Nicolas has already steamed it open,' Maulise said.

'You told him about it? Wait, when did you meet him? He has been in Dieppe, Sark and on a train.'

'He's always somewhere,' Maulise answered. He stepped into the room, crunched on a broken bottle and jumped in the air. 'Shoes. I've forgotten my shoes.'

Monsieur D'Haricot did not help him find them. He strode across to the table with Juan and the two ladies. Juan removed Estelle's arm and got to his feet, offering Monsieur D'Haricot his chair. Monsieur D'Haricot accepted and Juan rescued an upturned chair from the next table. He tested its stability, and his own agility, by thumping his right foot on the seat before sitting down back to front, his legs straddling the sides and his head looking over the back. Monsieur D'Haricot sat in a more conventional manner. 'Maulise is finding his shoes,' he said.

'He hasn't found his feet yet,' Juan joked.

'Would you like a drink?' Madame Chapleau offered. 'We have time while we wait on Nicolas.'

'I have a bone to pick with him,' Monsieur D'Haricot complained.

'His funny bone, I hope.' Juan nudged Estelle and she feigned a laugh.

'Here he is now, with Maulise,' Victoire said.

Maulise had failed to find his shoes and was wearing the donkey hoofs from his stage costume. It forced him to walk on his toes and he made his way gingerly, leaning on Otocey for support. Monsieur Hector handed the cheating gambler over to a police officer. Monsieur D'Haricot followed his movement towards Otocey by the shuffling of glass and the replacement of tables and chairs to their rightful place.

There was no conversation, but Otocey removed his wallet and handed over a bundle of notes that disappeared when in Monsieur Hector's possession. After a moment Otocey handed over the entire wallet.

'An expensive evening out,' Otocey complained when he and Maulise arrived at the table. 'We should be leaving.'

Although Otocey's words sounded like a mere suggestion, they were instantly obeyed. Juan was first to rise. He bent to give Estelle a kiss. 'You are superfluous to requirements, dear. We have a Virgo.'

Estelle slapped him on the cheek. 'I am no Virgo.' She walked off with as much dignity as her cast allowed.

'You shouldn't have said that,' Maulise advised. 'You will find it hard to get a new assistant.'

Madame Chapleau tottered to her feet, clasping a quarter full bottle of champagne. Afraid that she might topple over on her heels, Monsieur D'Haricot rose to link arms with her.

'Are you bringing him along, my weasel?' Otocey asked, seemingly surprised.

'You need me, don't you?' Monsieur D'Haricot answered. 'I am your Sagittarian.'

'There are others,' Otocey answered. 'Not that I don't appreciate your sacrifice.'

'My sacrifice?'

Otocey managed to twist his eyebrows towards Monsieur D'Haricot's pocket. It was a peculiar talent which Monsieur D'Haricot had never seen outside of Betty Boop cartoons. 'Haven't you read your letter?' Otocey asked.

'My *private* letter.' Monsieur D'Haricot emphasised the adjective.

Everyone was watching him and Monsieur D'Haricot pulled the letter from his pocket. He picked up a table knife to use as a letter opener and took his time to slice through the envelope with the blunt edge. The message was curt, consisting of two short sentences.

Your absence from duty has been noted. Report to HQ by noon tomorrow or you will be dismissed.

The letter was signed by a secretary on behalf of the General. It was dated that morning.

'Who delivered this letter?' Monsieur D'Haricot turned to ask Maulise.

'No idea. I found it shoved beneath the door when I left the house.'

'It is a fake,' Monsieur D'Haricot declared. 'Someone does not want me to travel to Fraumy.'

'Unless it is a double bluff,' Juan suggested. 'Someone knows you won't give in to intimidation. Or a treble bluff, where you know it is a bluff, the writer knows you know, and you don't go, or maybe you do.' Juan scratched his head, dislodging his hairpiece.

'There doesn't seem any point sending it if it is a bluff or a double bluff or whatever,' Monsieur D'Haricot crumpled the letter into his pocket.

'It must be genuine then,' Madame Chapleau said.

'Enough of this. I am ready to leave,' Monsieur D'Haricot declared, remembering that Marina was still on the train. He dreaded what mischief she could have instigated, inspired by a nautical fiction novel, while he had been gone.

Chapter Seventeen

Miraculously, the three-seater land cabin was able to accommodate all five of them with comfort, having acquired a settee in their absence. The extra weight added a second to the journey time, but they returned to the TRIC without incident. Once they were on board a whistle sounded and the train began its journey. Monsieur D'Haricot had worked out where he thought everyone stood, but now that they were on their way to a showdown in Fraumy he needed to discover the intricacies of their plans. They had congregated in the lounge and he suggested they have a drink together. Maulise, Juan and Madame Chapleau were in favour of this, but Otocey declined, claiming he needed 'sanctuary from madness'.

'Do make yourself at home, D'Haricot,' Otocey offered. 'The rest of you, enjoy the refreshments.' He gave an almost imperceptible signal to Victoire, but Monsieur D'Haricot's sharp eyesight caught her look in return. She plonked herself on a chair, crossed her legs and held out an empty champagne glass which she had removed from Le Crochet. One of the pink suited waiters rushed to fill it. Victoire swallowed half the contents in one gulp. Otocey clicked his heels together in a somewhat Germanic manner and left. Victoire waited until he was at the door of the lounge before bursting into hysterics.

'Sank your army from sadness.' Her slurred syllables died as she slumped in the chair.

'Perhaps you have drunk enough for today, Victoire,' Monsieur D'Haricot reached to rescue her glass. It was in danger of toppling to the floor as Victoire's hand struggled to find the tabletop.

Victoire started. 'I have not touched a drop,' she answered, then hiccupped. 'It is Mala Kai's fault I feel groggy. She can't handle her liquor.' She began beating her breast. 'Stop it! Get out!'

Monsieur D'Haricot was at a loss to know what to do.

'Allow me,' Juan stepped in. 'Music soothes the wildest beast.' He had brought his guitar on board and strummed the strings. Victoire calmed. After a three chord introduction, he sang a doleful ballad involving runaway brides, lovelorn suitors and dead fish. Monsieur D'Haricot feared the night was going to be a tedious one.

'How long will it take to reach Fraumy?' he asked.

'As long as Nicolas wants it to,' Maulise answered.

'It is five hundred kilometres,' Juan explained, incorporating the words into his melody. 'Otocey will decide on the TRIC's velocity.' He somehow managed to rhyme Otocey with velocity and paused, expecting applause.

Monsieur D'Haricot was aware the idea of having a nightcap had been his, but he made his excuses and retired to his room. Marina was tucked up in his bed with her pinchers grabbing hold of the pillow. She appeared to be asleep and Monsieur D'Haricot tried not to waken her as he undressed. She was lying in the middle of the bed and it was difficult for him to squeeze in beside her. She woke when he nudged her shell and gave a scream.

'It is me,' Monsieur D'Haricot assured her.

'Since when has a gentleman thought it permissible to get into bed with a lady friend without her permission?' Marina demanded.

'Em, yes, ah, sorry,' Monsieur D'Haricot stuttered. He retreated from the bed and, having found a spare blanket in the wardrobe, he spent a cramped five hours on the floor, listening to the exaggerated movement of the bogie.

The train continued its journey underground and it was impossible to know when it was dawn. Monsieur D'Haricot was reluctant to switch on the light in case it resulted in Marina's further disapproval. He had decided to risk her wrath when there was a knock on the door.

'We shall reach our destination in forty-three minutes and four point two seconds. Breakfast is currently being served in the restaurant.' Monsieur D'Haricot recognised the voice of the dining car attendant. He got to his feet, stretched and switched on the light. The bed was empty. A thorough search beneath the bed, behind the back of the drawers and under the carpet showed that Marina was not in the room.

Monsieur D'Haricot wondered how she had managed to open the compartment door without him noticing. Wherever she had gone, she had done so of her own volition and he suspected her reasoning involved food. He dressed, made a rapid trip to the washroom, then went in search of breakfast.

It being a new day, Juan had reverted to the persona of St. John St. Clair and was not happy at being "abducted" as he called it. He was arguing with Otocey, backed by a piece of paper outlining the rights of Spanish citizens in France, demanding to be taken back to Rouen.

'You can change TRIC in Fraumy,' Otocey replied nonchalantly. St. John was not to be placated and Otocey turned his attention to Madame Chapleau, who was seated nearby filing her nails. The lady looked unscathed by the previous evening's adventure, whereas Monsieur D'Haricot's head was spinning.

'Is Maulise up?' Otocey asked Madame Chapleau.

'I don't believe he has retired to bed yet,' she answered.

Otocey signalled to one of the waiters to look for him. The man had reached the door when Maulise entered the room with the second Madame Chapleau hanging on his arm. She looked worse than Monsieur D'Haricot felt.

'Are those mushrooms? Take them away before I'm sick.' She let go of Maulise and staggered towards a hostess trolley which held an empty ice bucket. She lifted the bucket and stuck it in front of her mouth.

'Really, Kai.' Otocey showed his disapproval by taking his cigarette case from his pocket, removing a cigarette and tapping the end on the silver case.

Monsieur D'Haricot looked from the second Madame Chapleau to the first. 'Am I seeing double or is this another trick of the lights?'

'Whatever do you mean, darling?' the seated Madame Chapleau answered.

Otocey gave him a jovial thump on the back. 'Mala Kai is a tease. You didn't fall for her 'we're the same person' joke, did you?' He turned to the ill-looking Madame Chapleau. 'So old hat, Kai.'

Monsieur D'Haricot glowered at Mala Kai, who had handed the ice bucket to a waiter and was wiping her mouth on a tablecloth. He would have to devise a more accurate method of distinguishing between the twins before the situation got out of control.

'Shall we have breakfast?' Otocey said. 'Fine champagne will revive the spirits.'

'Top hole,' Maulise answered. He took his seat next to Victoire at the table, which was set for four. Monsieur D'Haricot sat opposite her and Otocey took the remaining chair.

'We'll need a bigger table,' Maulise remarked to Otocey.

'Not on my behalf,' St. John said. 'I am leaving now.' Before Otocey could stop him, he rushed to the window and pulled the emergency cord above it.

There was a screech and the TRIC shuddered.

Otocey pushed his chair back and stood up. 'Fool, you shouldn't have done that,' he shouted. 'The authorities will be alerted to our presence. We need to surface immediately.'

'What authorities? I thought Madame Chapleau was the Prime Minister,' Monsieur D'Haricot said.

Otocey dashed out of the room without replying. The others stared first at one another then at St. John.

'I'll get my luggage,' St. John said. He gave a slight nod of his head towards Victoire, frowned at Mala Kai and ignored Monsieur D'Haricot before leaving.

'He means the Fraumy authorities,' Maulise explained. 'Now, I think I am in the mood for kippers.'

'Kippers?' Victoire queried.

'An English delicacy,' Maulise answered. 'Gutted herring, pickled and cold smoked.'

'And they eat that for breakfast?' Victoire asked.

Mala Kai grabbed the edge of the tablecloth and held it over her mouth. Monsieur D'Haricot tried not to stare as her face changed from white to yellow to lime green. When it reached a perfect shade of emerald, she swiped the cloth from the table. The cutlery, which had been set out for breakfast, was thrown in the air and landed in reverse order on the table. Mala Kai dashed out of the room.

'Kippers sound delicious. I shall join you in those,' Marina's voice came from the door to the kitchen and she appeared with a chef's hat perched on her shell. Monsieur D'Haricot helped her onto the chair vacated by Otocey.

When the kippers were served, Monsieur D'Haricot decided that his constitution was not ready either for eating the dish or for watching Marina claw apart the fish into individual scales. He requested a glass of orange juice and retired with it to the lounge, where he expected to be the only occupant. Otocey was seated in one of the armchairs conversing with a white-haired and bearded gentleman. Monsieur D'Haricot did not recognise the man. Otocey's jovial mood had returned. He rose to address Monsieur D'Haricot.

'D'Haricot, I believe you have met Olivier,' he said.

'We weren't officially introduced,' the strange gentleman replied, getting to his feet with the help of the chair arm.

'Please, no need to get up,' Monsieur D'Haricot assured him. 'I am Louis-Philip D'Haricot from Paris.' He put a stress on the 'H' in his surname and reached over to hold out his hand. Olivier had a frail handshake. Monsieur D'Haricot was drawn to his signet ring, which was a snake with crimson eyes. The snake's body was wound in an intricate Celtic pattern that was as much part of the man's finger as the wrinkled skin covering the sharp bones.

'Olivier Hector,' the man introduced himself. It took a moment for Monsieur D'Haricot to recognise the name.

'Ah, you are the proprietor of Le Crochet.' Monsieur D'Haricot had expected, if not a younger man, then certainly a fitter one. He imagined that being invisible to rational beings was a sufficient advantage in a fight.

'More importantly, Olivier is an Ophiuchus,' Otocey said with an air of self-importance that clogged Monsieur D'Haricot's throat.

'Victoire told me. She seemed unclear as to whether you believed in the sign or not,' he responded.

'As I said, Mala Kai is a tease,' Otocey answered coldly.

'I know who I kissed,' Monsieur D'Haricot answered in an equally impartial voice. 'You should check if your Machiavellian mind melding procedure is functioning as smoothly as you imagine.' He sat down on the chair next to Monsieur Hector before Otocey could object. 'I haven't interrupted a private conversation, have I?'

'Nothing of significance,' Otocey said.

'How to deal with Edgori and Dauphine van Lüttich,' Monsieur Hector explained.

'From my experience of the scoundrel and his diabolical mother, I would say your discussions are of the utmost importance,' Monsieur D'Haricot responded, leaning back and testing the armrests of the chair.

'Thanks to St. John we have lost the edge of surprise. They will know exactly where we are,' Otocey said.

'I imagine the gruesome twosome would already have had the train bugged. Delanoir, or Schwarz, saw me get on,' Monsieur D'Haricot pointed out.

'Why didn't you tell me this before?' Otocey demanded.

'I told Victoire, or it may have been Mala Kai. Besides, don't you require Van Lüttich and his mother for your zodiac prophecy?'

Olivier Hector leant across to whisper in Otocey's ear. Monsieur D'Haricot did not hear what he said, but Otocey's facial muscles relaxed.

'You know it is rude to whisper,' Monsieur D'Haricot said.

'You have inadvertently done us a favour,' Monsieur Hector replied. 'If Schwarz is on the case, he will no doubt detain St. Clair when he alights, and take him to his master.'

'In Fraumy,' Otocey added, in case Monsieur D'Haricot failed to grasp the point.

Monsieur D'Haricot finished his orange juice. He set the glass on the table and turned it so that the crystal caught the artificial light and reflected the rays in colourful patterns. 'Where are we and what do you intend doing?' he asked.

Hector looked to Otocey, who circled the inside of his cheek with his tongue.

'If I am not to be trusted with confidential information, then I am afraid I cannot agree to be part of your plan and neither can my travelling companion. Once she has finished her fish, we shall leave the train.' Monsieur D'Haricot stood up and gave a curt bow to Olivier Hector.

'Wait,' Otocey called. Monsieur D'Haricot paused on his way to the door. Otocey consulted his wristwatch. 'We are twenty kilometres from the Fraumy border. What we do next depends on you.'

'Me?'

'I have been hearing of your inimitable skills.' Olivier Hector flattered Monsieur D'Haricot.

'Let me explain,' Otocey continued. 'I would prefer to continue to Fraumy this morning, giving me time to set my plan in motion and prevent Edgori from assassinating the Arch-duke in two days time. Olivier thinks differently.' Monsieur D'Haricot could sense the friction in the Vicomte's voice.

'Not about preventing the assassination, I hope,' Monsieur D'Haricot said.

'Indeed no. I believe the Arch-duke should be prevented from attending the celebrations,' Monsieur Hector replied. 'That would confound Gori and his plan.'

'The Arch-duke will not be easily dissuaded,' Otocey said. 'His family have overseen the celebrations for centuries.'

'I regret that some underhand method may be required.'

'You wish to kidnap the General?' Monsieur D'Haricot accused. 'I will never allow that.'

'You would rather he was murdered?' Olivier Hector spoke softly.

'That is not what I said.'

'I myself would prefer if the Archduke—' Otocey began.

'—your Piscean,' Olivier interrupted.

'The Archduke,' Otocey repeated, 'joined us willingly.'

'He will never do that,' Olivier declared. 'You know how superior Fraumians feel towards Ecnarf. They believe they are in charge of their own destinies.' He gave a laugh to show what he thought of that opinion.

'Nonsense, I know, but that being the case it would be wiser if the Arch-duke remained in a safe house for the next week,' Otocey conceded, rubbing his chin in an unconvincing manner. 'You, Louis, could help us. You could speak with the Archduke. The letter you received did ask that you report before noon today.'

Monsieur D'Haricot had already forfeited his bicycle, the beautiful Clodette, to this mad fantasy. If the letter he received was genuine, he did not wish to lose his job as well. Yet being addressed as Louis by someone he barely knew and liked even less set his teeth on auto-grind. Neither was he blind to the sly look that passed between Otocey and Hector.

'You said we were twenty kilometres from Fraumy. How far is that from Paris?' Monsieur D'Haricot asked.

'You agree to persuade the Arch-duke to stay out of the public eye?' Otocey asked. Monsieur D'Haricot tilted his head in an ambiguous manner. Otocey rose and slapped him cheerfully on the shoulder. 'Good, I'm glad you've seen sense. I shall reset the TRIC co-ordinates for Paris. Enjoy the brandy while I am gone.'

Monsieur D'Haricot did not fancy brandy for breakfast, but wishing to speak with Monsieur Hector, he moved to sit on the chair Otocey vacated. The arms wrapped themselves around his body in a motherly hug releasing a soothing fragrance. He felt a gentle amiability

168

seep through his veins and looked across at Monsieur Hector. He was dismayed to find the gentleman fading before his eyes. 'Please stay,' he beseeched.

'I am going nowhere,' Monsieur Hector answered in a weak voice. 'If you cannot see or hear me, it is because you do not believe.'

'I saw you a moment ago. You were as solid as the Arc de Triomphe.'

'You saw me because Otocey's belief is strong enough for a room full of sceptics.'

Monsieur D'Haricot tried his hardest to believe the rising of Venus or the crossing of Saturn had the greatest significance to events in the world, but in less than a minute Olivier Hector was gone. Monsieur D'Haricot lifted his empty glass and left to have it refilled.

It took thirty-four minutes and thirty-two seconds, according to Monsieur D'Haricot's pocket watch for the train to reach Paris. He spent most of it waiting for Maulise to finish using the washroom facilities, only to be informed there were several other washrooms, more suited for genteel guests, further along the corridor. When he was ready he made his way to the exit doors. Otocey was waiting for him.

'We are at the Gare du Nord,' Otocey informed him. 'My watch makes it three minutes past eleven. You have time for a round of Pétanque and still reach your headquarters before noon. Do you wish me to ask one of the stewards to telephone the secretary and advise the General of your arrival?'

'Yes, no, yes,' Monsieur D'Haricot dithered before deciding on the affirmative.

He didn't wait for a response from the General's office. He had mislaid the homburg hat he bought in Dieppe, and rather thought Marina had been using it for sanitary purposes, but he had found a boater in the bedroom. He had it in his hand and it was time to put it on. Otocey opened the train door and he stepped out with trepidation. To his surprise, it was drawn up at the platform edge as any normal train would be. A second glance made him aware of the blue smoke hiding it from the view of normal commuters. Passing an inspector, he hoped he would not be asked to show a ticket. The man tapped his hat respectfully and allowed Monsieur D'Haricot to pass through the barrier.

There was a delicious aroma of coffee wafting through the station, tempting Monsieur D'Haricot to linger, but no. The decadence on board Otocey's train had turned his head and he gave it a shake, partly as a symbolic act to rid himself of the effects and partly to make sure he was fully awake. He was Louis-Philip D'Haricot, Agent Charon, and he was on a case of the utmost gravity. A matter of life or death.

Chapter Eighteen

Outside the station, he breathed in the Parisian air. He was surrounded by his fellow citizens going about their business as they had done a week ago. Car horns hooted, strangers increased or decreased their pace to avoid contact with other citizens, waiters carried trays to street tables where coffee swallowers talked of changing the world and cognac sippers lamented the passing of the good old days. Nothing was different, yet Monsieur D'Haricot was on edge. At any moment a chargeur could crash through a traffic signal and he would be called upon to rescue an unsuspecting damsel or a manhole cover would shake as the elusive Core Worm twisted in its sleep.

'Are you going to stand there blocking the pavement until the earth falls away from under your feet?' a nanny with twins in a pram demanded. Monsieur D'Haricot stepped aside, casting a glance at the babies to make sure they were flesh and blood.

Otocey was optimistic in his assessment of the time it took to negotiate Parisian traffic. Despite his dislike of automobiles, Monsieur D'Haricot hailed a cab to take him to headquarters, grateful that the car had a driver who spoke French. They reached the Sacre Coeur to find the traffic was at a standstill, thanks to an accident involving an overturned apple truck and a window cleaner's ladder. Monsieur D'Haricot stuck his head out of the window to see what was going on. An elderly Romany lady was bent double, grabbing the bruised fruit that was running free along the street. When she looked up his heart missed a beat.

Dauphine van Lüttich.

A second look showed he was being paranoid. The lady had grey hair, but her nose was snubbed, her earlobes were rounded rather than pointed and her eyes lacked the burning desire of the duchess.

'Is there a shortcut you can take?' Monsieur D'Haricot asked the driver. 'I have an urgent appointment.'

'If there was one, do you think these ten cars in front of us would be waiting here?' the man answered brusquely.

The police did not seem capable of diverting the traffic around the truck in an orderly manner. Monsieur D'Haricot paid the cab driver half the agreed fare and got out to walk the remaining kilometre. He arrived outside the headquarters at five minutes before twelve and hurried up the stairs and into the building. The General's office was on the tenth floor. Monsieur D'Haricot did not wait on the elevator. He was struggling for breath when he reached the reception. The secretary stared at him as if he had been chased by a pack of wild dogs. It was not Camille, but a young gentleman.

'I believe I am expected,' he said, removing his hat.

The secretary examined the diary. 'There is nothing in the appointment book. What is the name?'

'It is me, Monsieur Louis-Philip D'Haricot – Agent Charon.' The secretary had been in the job for over two months. He had seen Monsieur D'Haricot speak with the General on numerous occasions including the previous week when, as if by foresight, the General had wished him a safe journey.

The man ran his forefinger down the page, licked it and flicked over to the following day.

'I have a letter from the General,' Monsieur D'Haricot said. The secretary held out his hand, expecting to be handed the brief. Monsieur D'Haricot was reluctant to give it to him. The clock on the wall struck the first note of the hour. 'Is the General in his office?' Monsieur D'Haricot asked.

The secretary dilly-dallied over the answer, which should have been a simple yes or no. The clock reached nine chimes. Monsieur D'Haricot had seen Fred Astaire glide across a dance floor many times in the movies. He had performed the steps in his bedroom until he felt they were perfected. Now was the opportunity to put his skill to the test and reach the General's office before the secretary could prevent him. Unfortunately he did not have the grace of the American, tripped on his feet and fell against the door, which swung open. Monsieur

D'Haricot picked himself up and stepped inside. He closed the door behind him.

The General was reclining on a chaise longue. Next to him, and closer than was professionally acceptable, was Victoire Chapleau. They both stared at Monsieur D'Haricot, the General with a scowl and Victoire with a grin.

'What are you doing here, man?' the General demanded.

'I was requested to attend before noon today.' On cue the clock finished announcing the hour.

'Cutting it fine,' the General answered, getting to his feet and straightening his tie. He stiffened his back to walk to his desk in a military manner. 'You have been absent from your post for three days. Senior officers have received worrying reports of your activities. You were spotted in a Rouen nightclub of disrepute.'

'It was in the line of duty,' Monsieur D'Haricot explained. 'And the establishment is hardly one of disrepute. The proprietor is an acquaintance of Vicomte Otocey.'

'What were you doing in Rouen?'

'I am glad you asked,' Monsieur D'Haricot answered. He had been trying to think of a way to broach the subject of Fraumy. He hadn't anticipated Victoire being present. 'I was meeting Juan Santos.'

'Is that supposed to mean something?'

'I am not sure how much you know of Vicomte Otocey's plan, but I have met your sister Dauphine van Lüttich and your nephew Edgori. You would be wise to be wary of them.'

'What are you blabbing about?' The General opened a carved box on his desk and took out a Havana cigar. He didn't offer one to Monsieur D'Haricot. 'You are a good man, Dupois,' he said, sniffing the tobacco.

'It's D'Haricot.'

'Yes, well, you are still a good man, but you are spouting nonsense, or should I say "sprouting".' He looked to Victoire, who gave a polite laugh. 'It is an occupational hazard,' the General continued. 'It happens to the finest agents. The deuce, it almost happened to me once. I had the sense to keep my mouth shut, though. You need to take a break. Rio de Janeiro is nice at this time of year.'

'I have no intention of travelling to South America. Your nephew intends to assassinate you at the celebrations in Fraumy in two days.'

'Where is Frowmee? What celebrations are we talking about? Who

173

is my nephew? I have a sister, but the lady is unmarried. Have you been drinking? Your breath smells of brandy.'

Monsieur D'Haricot appealed to Victoire for assistance. She was holding a silk handkerchief to her nose, which he suspected she was using to hide her sniggers. 'Perhaps you can convince the General of the danger he is in,' he said.

'Oh Louis, you are a tease. I never know what jokes you are going to play,' she answered.

'I do not regard this as funny.' The General snapped the cigar case shut. 'I do not appreciate jibes at my expense, especially not ones that involve my assassination.'

'It is no tomfoolery, sir. I know you are the Arch-duke of Fraumy. Do not fear, your secret is safe with me, but you have to listen. There is a plot to kill you.'

Victoire stood up. Her mouth had lost its smile. She put a gloved hand on Monsieur D'Haricot's forehead and drew back. 'Louis, you are burning. You have a fever,' she declared. The General had lifted the telephone receiver on his desk and dialled for security.

'What are you playing at, Victoire?' Monsieur D'Haricot asked, swiping away her hand. He rushed to grab the telephone receiver from the General and slammed it on its holder. 'What has Otocey convinced you to do?'

'You keep mentioning Vicomte Otocey. What has that blackguard got to do with anything other than stargazing?' the General asked.

'Otocey is an acquaintance of mine,' Victoire answered. 'He is an amusing party guest, if you want your fortune told. He knows nothing of my work here.' She feigned a laugh. 'Nicolas would never believe a mere woman could be involved in espionage work.'

'What about Mata Hari?' Monsieur D'Haricot muttered.

'Enough of this,' the General said. 'You have lost control of your mind, Dupois.'

'D'Haricot.'

'You are relieved of all duties from ten minutes ago. You will report to Agent X for decommissioning immediately.'

Decommissioning sounded like something that happened to creaking hulks. Monsieur D'Haricot would have preferred the word 'retirement', but this was a fleeting thought. He stood his ground while he considered his move.

What was Victoire doing here? Was it Victoire or her twin?

His first thought was that Otocey did not trust him. His second was that Madame Chapleau, whichever lady it was, was working independently. Otocey was tangled to the neck in his zodiac prophecy. If the lady was Mala Kai, she might fear this was getting in the way of her own plan to invade France. Victoire, on the other hand, would wish to avoid an invasion and an assassination.

He glanced towards the lady in question. She arched an eyebrow in what appeared to be a challenge. Mala Kai's allergy to the biscuits would make it difficult for her to keep a solid form, but she had been exposed to the upper levels for some time. Long enough to have adjusted naturally to conditions, or the bounder Otocey may have succeeded in permanently blending Victoire's genes with her twin's?

'I said you could leave,' the General repeated.

'I believe this agent is a fraud,' Monsieur D'Haricot declared, stabbing the air in front of Madame Chapleau. 'She had been sent to make sure you do not heed my warning and, instead, travel to Fraumy.'

'You're a scream, Louis,' Madame Chapleau reached a hand towards him. Her fist was closed and he wondered if she was attempting to pass him something. The General's face had turned purple.

'I do not appreciate this talk of assassination. If Madame Chapleau wishes to shoot me, why does she not do it now? Why drag me to somewhere no-one has heard of?' Immediately the words were out, the General saw the sense in secrecy and didn't look for an answer. He clipped the end of his cigar, lit it and took a puff. Monsieur D'Haricot half expected blue smoke to be released through his ears.

'I do not believe Madame Chapleau wishes you dead,' Monsieur D'Haricot explained once the General had calmed. 'She wants you to go to Fraumy for a different reason. She and Otocey, her beau, intend to take over Paris with the help of a crazy army of troglodytes. First Paris, then France, finally Europe and the world.' Monsieur D'Haricot imagined he had spoken dramatically and paused for effect. The General was staring wide-eyed while Madame Chapleau was attending to the cuticles of her nails.

'What does the General's presence in some strange city have to do with an invasion of the world?' Madame Chapleau asked, blinking her eyelashes. 'You haven't taken the fantasy book I gave you seriously, have you?'

An image of the words 'Enough, enough' written in Victoire's handwriting flickered into Monsieur D'Haricot's mind. He suspected it was a cryptic message, but one he was not in a position to decipher.

'You should really see a doctor,' the General said. He marched to the door and opened it. 'You man, fetch security,' he commanded his secretary.

Monsieur D'Haricot realised he was getting nowhere. He tugged at his jacket lapel and strode out of the room before the guards arrived to manhandle him down the stairs. Madame Chapleau again reached her hand out to him as he left. This time he could see the scrap of notepaper poking through a gap between her fingers, but he pushed her away.

The feeling of indignity did not leave as he descended the stairs and stepped outside the building. Although he did not shirk the demanding duties of the job, as his colleagues unfairly claimed, he was not suffering from overwork. His mind was as sharp as it had been in the trenches, where a false move would lose a man not only his own life, but that of his comrades. He was not prone to lying and did not have the creative abilities to invent fantasies. If he could find proof… such as the repugnant Mathilde… but he doubted even that would convince the General. He was faced with the choice of returning to his apartment and forgetting about the past few days, or working on his own to solve the mystery and save France.

He had been walking as he thought, and doing so at good speed, without paying heed to the direction of his travel. It came as a surprise when he found himself staring through the window of a familiar bar. The chequered tablecloths covered with melted candle wax told him where he was before he looked at the sign. He was outside 'The Red Duck'. The proprietor, that patriotic, off-key baritone, was a friend of Victoire Chapleau. He was accustomed to her staying there and familiar with her use of the unusual transmitter. Fate, and his feet, had made his decision for him. It was time to ask difficult questions and demand honest answers.

Buoyed by his resolve, Monsieur D'Haricot walked into the bar. A gramophone was playing a folk song and the barman was wiping a clean glass on his filthy apron. He spat onto the glass as Monsieur D'Haricot approached. His eyes flicked towards the only other man in the bar, a red-headed fellow who was drinking ale at the far end of the counter. The man put his drink down and moved to the gramophone to change the record. After a bout of crackling, La Marseillaise began playing. Monsieur D'Haricot sighed and put his hand on his heart. The three men stood to attention.

'Marchons, marchons.'

Monsieur D'Haricot had the sinking feeling of deja vu. His courage was in danger of being court-martialled for desertion. Looking for Dutch reinforcements, he waited until the record droned to its final chord, then ordered a cognac. The barman poured the drink into the glass he had been wiping.

'I would like a room for the evening,' Monsieur D'Haricot said.

'We don't have rooms,' the man answered.

'There is one on the first floor which I understood you rented out. My friend Victoire Chapleau told me about it. She recommended you.'

The drinker appeared at Monsieur D'Haricot's side and put a heavy hand on his shoulder. 'Are you the King of Hearts?' he asked.

'No,' Monsieur D'Haricot answered instinctively. 'I am the Ace of Clubs.'

The man dropped his hand and took a step back. He reached for his belt and Monsieur D'Haricot saw the glimmer of metal.

'Ha,' Monsieur D'Haricot gave a high-pitched laugh, similar to Otocey's, and took a swig of cognac, wiping his mouth with his sleeve before continuing. 'You must be the Knave of Diamonds.'

The man kept his gaze on Monsieur D'Haricot, trying to outstare him. The deadlock was broken by the barman. 'I am the Ace of Clubs,' he said. 'You, my friend, are an impostor.'

'I admit my cover has been blown,' Monsieur D'Haricot said, thinking fast. 'I was sent by the Queen of Diamonds to make sure everything is in order for the big day.'

'The Queen of Diamonds?' The drinker took a step back. His face was pale and he eyed the nearest exit.

'He is feigning,' the barman answered. 'The Queen of Diamonds would not send the likes of this fool.'

'That is what she wants you to think,' Monsieur D'Haricot pressed his advantage, but he was not a card player and had produced his ace too soon.

The barman nodded at the drinker, who swung round to lock the door and turn the sign in the window to 'CLOSED'. When he twisted to face Monsieur D'Haricot, his finger was tickling the trigger of a handgun. Monsieur D'Haricot recognised it as a Luger P08. A German pistol.

'Allons enfants de la Patrie,' Monsieur D'Haricot sang weakly.

The drinker spat on the floor.

'The Queen of Diamonds is a gentleman,' the barman explained.

'Really? I couldn't tell,' Monsieur D'Haricot said.

'Don't be flippant with me,' the barman said.

'What should we do with him?' the drinker asked. 'Shoot him and bury him in the basement?'

'Don't be ridiculous. I keep my best wines there,' the barman answered.

'Shoot him and drop his body in the sewers?'

'That is where I keep my ale.'

'Shoot him and—'

'Hold you tongue,' the barman instructed in German. Monsieur D'Haricot did not speak fluent German, but was familiar with certain uncouth phrases courtesy of his time at the front.

'May I make a suggestion?' he said. 'Why don't you tie me up and keep me in the room on the first floor?'

'Keep you until when?' the drinker asked.

'Until he escapes,' the barman answered. 'He believes because we are not French, we are idiots.'

'Not at all,' Monsieur D'Haricot said. 'I shall come clean. I was sent by Dauphine van Lüttich to make sure you can be trusted.'

The drinker lowered his pistol. 'Why would she send you?' he asked.

'Because she does not trust her son to undertake the task without running someone through with his epee,' Monsieur D'Haricot replied.

The barman furrowed his brows and narrowed his eyes until they began rolling in their sockets. Dirty brown steam spurted from his ears and nostrils.

'Werner, what is the matter?' his friend asked.

'I think he has blown a fuse,' Monsieur D'Haricot said. 'What is he, some sort of automaton?'

'I don't understand.' The drinker rubbed his forehead. 'We have known each other for years.' He moved past Monsieur D'Haricot to the bar counter and put out a hand to touch the sleeve of Werner's shirt. The robot's arm began swinging, then circling, knocking the pistol from the drinker's other hand. Monsieur D'Haricot was quick to retrieve it. He aimed the barrel at its owner. 'Hände hoch!' he ordered. The man raised his hands in the air.

'Who is your leader and what have you done with the real bartender?' Monsieur D'Haricot demanded.

'I thought that was the real Werner,' the drinker protested. 'Honest.'

'Werner is not the real proprietor of this establishment. I met him recently and he was called François. No German could be moved by the La Marseillaise the way François was, the first time I heard him sing it. That thing is an impostor posing as an impostor.'

Monsieur D'Haricot was reminded of Maulise in his donkey suit. He had been convinced it was a real donkey, although he had put his mistake down to the smoke in the club. Apart from the residual whiff of a cigar, the bar was free from smoke. There was nothing to blame except his eyesight for his failure to recognise that Werner wasn't human. As he considered his stupidity, he heard the shuffling of footsteps and recognised the same whiff of toilet water he smelt in the Rouen nightclub. Flicking the pistol to indicate the drinker should take a seat at the nearest table, where he could keep one eye on him, Monsieur D'Haricot faced into the room.

'You may as well show yourself,' he declared. 'I know you are here.'

Chapter Nineteen

Nothing happened.

'I repeat, I *know* you are here.' Monsieur D'Haricot waited. He heard ticking on the wall behind him and hoped it was the bar clock and not Werner counting down to explode. He didn't look round. His eyes flickered between the tables seeking out movement or shadows. The drinker still had his hands in the air, but with one finger he pointed behind Monsieur D'Haricot.

Monsieur D'Haricot did not wish to be fooled by the trickery of a German, but at the same time he heard the creak of a door open. 'Monsieur Hector, it is good of you come,' he said without looking round.

The newcomer laughed. 'I may not have finished my make-up, but I hope I do not look like Monsieur Hector.'

Monsieur D'Haricot swivelled on his heels in a move taken from Juan's stage act. He had seen the lady standing behind the bar before, but he could not recall where.

'I see you do not remember me,' the lady said. 'I, however, remember you, and I should like my fan back.'

'You were at Madame Chapleau's cocktail party?' Monsieur D'Haricot said. It was not from the party that he recalled the face. 'I am afraid I do not have the fan with me. It is in my apartment in Montparnasse. In a safe place,' he added, in case the lady intended sending her heavies to find it.

'I should have spoken more with you in Rouen,' the lady admitted. 'I hadn't thought you knew of our plan. How much has Victoire told you?'

'I am the one with the gun,' Monsieur D'Haricot retorted, trying to place the lady in Rouen. 'I shall ask the questions.'

'You have a tiny pistol which has eight rounds.'

'Three,' the drinker put in. 'I have already spent five of them.'

The lady smiled. 'I have a fully automatic, indestructible, highly trained killing machine.' She clicked her fingers and the automaton reverted to being Werner the barman. He picked up a bottle and smashed it against the counter, threatening Monsieur D'Haricot with the broken end. 'My hand wins, I believe,' the lady said.

'Really?'

'Try shooting him,' she offered.

Monsieur D'Haricot was unwilling to fire a peacetime shot at something that appeared to be flesh and blood, German or not. While he dithered, he heard the clinking of someone turning the outer door handle, trying to open the locked door. After a short pause, a key was turned and the door swung open. Madame Chapleau was the first to enter, followed by three guards. Two of them flanked the General, the third was supporting him from behind, as his feet dragged and his head flopped onto his chest.

'Victoire!' the lady exclaimed at the same time Madame Chapleau called, 'Angelique!'

Monsieur D'Haricot turned his gun towards Victoire's guards. 'General, have they injured you?' he demanded.

While Victoire and Angelique stared at one another and Monsieur D'Haricot gaped at the unconscious man and his handlers, the drinker took the opportunity to scurry out of the bistro. The automaton creaked round and raised a limb to throw the broken bottle at the fleeing man, but was stopped by an order from Angelique. Once the drinker was gone, Victoire relocked the door.

'What is going on?' she demanded of Angelique.

'I could ask you the same?' Angelique countered.

'Ahem, have you forgotten about me?' Monsieur D'Haricot broke in. 'Is the General ill?'

'He has been deactivated,' Victoire answered. 'We needed to move him. It is perfectly safe.'

I am aware that zookeepers use tranquilizers on a regular basis,' Monsieur D'Haricot argued, 'But the General is not a wild beast.'

'You should see him when he is annoyed,' Victoire said.

Angelique shared the joke. She relaxed and moved to the bar to pour three glasses of cognac. She positioned two on the counter and drank from the third. Victoire lifted one of the glasses, wafted it beneath her nose, then drank the contents in one gulp. The two ladies stared at Monsieur D'Haricot, encouraging him to take up the challenge. He moved to the bar, considering, one, how he could get out of drinking the alcohol, and two, how he could rescue the General.

'What about these three gentlemen, do they not get refreshments?' he asked, indicating the men guarding the General.

Angelique laughed. 'It would make their working seize up.'

'You mean these are automatons?' Monsieur D'Haricot said in disbelief.

Victoire slid the full cognac glass along the counter towards him. He stopped it from falling off the edge. Angelique tilted her head in recognition of his pencil-sharp reflexes. He lifted the glass to his nose. The alcohol smelt of peaches and apples dancing a minuet. It was on his lips before he realised he had opened his mouth and tipped the glass. The liquid bubbled on his tongue, bounced off his palate and slithered down his throat. For a second, a film glazed his eyes. When it cleared, he could see plainly that the two men holding the General were no more than chunks of metal with cogs controlling limited movement.

Victoire snapped her fingers and the robots clanked into action, positioning the General with numerous stiff gestures onto the nearest chair. The General's head drooped onto the table. With the bump, he prised an eye open.

'We don't have much time,' Victoire said. 'Is the room ready?'

'I believe so,' Angelique answered.

'Ah, I understand,' Monsieur D'Haricot said. The brandy was having an unexpected effect on his nerves and he could see an emerald green aura round Angelique. 'You will detain the General at this establishment until after the celebrations in Fraumy. That way he will not be assassinated by Edgori van Lüttich or his mother. They will not be able to align Fraumy with Germany, giving the Nazis access to the underground routes into France.' Victoire was about to speak, but with a wave of his hand he indicated he hadn't finished his summary. 'Otocey can't rely on Juan and help from Spain, and he will not have his full complement of zodiac characters, and therefore he will not be able to proceed with his plan to flood France with underground refugees who would take over our government, military and civil offices.'

'Well done,' Angelique said. 'But you are forgetting one little thing.' She was completely encompassed by her emerald light. It was giving Monsieur D'Haricot a headache and he felt faint.

'I have forgotten nothing. I have a memory like a... like a...' Monsieur D'Haricot's knees gave way. He collapsed to the floor and blacked out.

I have forgotten nothing, I have a memory like a...

He came to with the words contorting into weird sentences in his head.

Memory forgotten. I have nothing. Have I an eye?

He was sitting on a wooden chair, with his hands tied together behind its back frame and his ankles bound to its front legs. He seemed to be facing a door, which gradually came into focus. His head was woozy, but he gauged he was less than two metres from the exit. He could bump his way towards it. Monsieur D'Haricot was a natural optimist and although it occurred to him that the door would be locked, he nevertheless thought it worth the while trying. As an intelligence agent, he had practised the manoeuvre on numerous occasions and it did not take long to reach the door and take the handle in his mouth.

To his surprise, the door was not locked. It opened outwards and, as soon as it did so, he bounced out. He had not bargained for the staircase immediately in his path. The legs of the chair fell forwards and the weight of Monsieur D'Haricot ensured that it continued, knocking against the stair posts and round the bend, until it came to rest on the bottom landing. The wood was shattered and fell about him as he lay for a moment in shock.

Realising that he was neither dead nor seriously injured, Monsieur D'Haricot was able to free his feet and hands from the fragments of the chair and stand up. His left elbow was bruised as a result of the fall, but nothing was broken or dislocated. The fact that no-one had appeared to investigate the rumpus led him to believe he was alone and the smell of stale smoke and sour alcohol told him he was still in The Red Duck. He did not know how much time had elapsed since he had been drugged. His pocket watch had been smashed during the journey down the stairs.

He attended to his clothing, making himself presentable for a busy Parisian street. His boater had fallen beneath him and the ribbon was tattered. He reshaped the straw before putting it on his head, then he strode into the public area of the café. As he expected, there was no-one in the room. The automaton guards and the imitation barman had been either dismantled or removed. There were no leftover pieces of wiring or clockwork mechanisms, which relieved Monsieur D'Haricot, as he would not have known what was active and what not. His head smarted from his fall and he was drawn to the bar, where the unfinished bottle of cognac was sitting out, inviting him to drink.

It was a trap, obviously, but the amber liquid was appealing. The slightest of sniffs could do no harm. He approached the counter and heard a groan rising from the floor. Monsieur D'Haricot put his hands on the counter to support his weight as he tried to peer over.

'Philip, what are you doing here?' The Taurean singer was collapsed on the floor, grasping an empty bottle of Scotch whisky. It seemed an age since he had left him in Maulise's apartment.

'Is that you, Louise?' the man slurred.

'No, it is Louis-Philip D'Haricot.'

'You are not Louise, but I am Philip.' He tried to get his inebriated head around the situation.

'We met underground, in a café where you were singing.'

'Underground? You're not a "Purple", are you?'

'A purple what?' Monsieur D'Haricot decided not to wait on an answer. 'You led me to Maulise, remember?'

'Maulise, where is that devil?' Philip struggled to his feet, pulling at the dishtowel on the counter and dragging it onto his head.

Monsieur D'Haricot lifted the flap and walked round behind the bar to help him. When Philip was on his feet, clinging to the handle of a beer tap, Monsieur D'Haricot poured water from the sink tap into a glass and handed it to him.

'You forgot the ice.' Philip pointed a finger at the glass.

Monsieur D'Haricot looked along the bar, but couldn't see an ice bucket. 'You will have to do without. What are you and Louise doing here?' he repeated.

Philip held a finger to his lips. 'We are guarding some busybody in the room upstairs.'

Monsieur D'Haricot lowered his voice. 'Who for?'

'Madame Chapleau, of course.' Philip teetered to and fro, adjusting his eyesight. 'What are you doing here?'

'I came to buy cognac. I was told The Red Duck sold the best cognac in Paris.' He had an idea to take the cognac and have it tested in a laboratory.

'What about him?' Philip gestured to the empty space beside Monsieur D'Haricot.

Monsieur D'Haricot was puzzled for a moment, but suspected Philip was seeing double from the effects of the whisky. 'He is with me,' he answered.

Philip turned round to examine the shelves, searching for a bottle of cognac. 'We seem to be out of cognac,' he said.

'This bottle will do fine.' Monsieur D'Haricot picked up the one on the counter.

'No, no,' Philip snatched it from him. 'That has been opened. Who knows what germs have contaminated it?' He glanced furtively round the room. 'I have heard that Germans drink in this bar.'

'It is not forbidden,' Monsieur D'Haricot said.

'Isn't it? When we take over Paris, all Germans will be sent packing.'

'How do you intend to accomplish that?' Monsieur D'Haricot probed.

'Don't answer him,' Louise said. She was standing at the door to the stairs with a broken chair leg in each hand. Unlike Philip, she had not been drinking. 'I trusted you, monsieur,' she spoke to Monsieur D'Haricot. 'We both did.'

'How have I let you down?'

'The crab. Where is Marina? What have you done with my beloved?'

'She is... I left her... why does it matter?'

'Why does it matter? How can you say that?' Louise thrust one of the pieces of wood towards Monsieur D'Haricot. He ducked out of the way.

'She is on Vicomte Otocey's TRIC enjoying macarons with one of the Mesdames Chapleau,' he answered.

This answer placated Louise. She put the second chair leg on the counter. 'You took your time freeing yourself,' she complained. 'I had to unlock the door, and even then I thought I would have to rescue you myself once I'd finished powdering my nose.'

'I don't understand. Philip said he was guarding me.'

'Only until you escaped. We were told it would be no more than a couple of hours. I wouldn't want to be the one to imply that Victoire had made a mistake, but you don't strike me as being suitable for the task you have been selected for.' It was an effort for Louise to finish her sentence without taking a new breath. She rewarded herself with a swig from the cognac, which she took from Philip.

'I wouldn't…' Monsieur D'Haricot began, but it was too late. She licked the dribbles round her lips with her tongue.

'Pleasant as it is to talk with you both, I should be on my way,' Monsieur D'Haricot said. He moved past Philip and Louise to the door, expecting to be stopped and was disappointed when he wasn't. The door was unlocked. He opened it and tapped his fingers on the panelling. 'I shall be at home, if anyone is looking for me.'

'I don't expect they will be, dear,' Louise answered.

'If you see Madame Victoire Chapleau, could you ask her to give me a call?' Monsieur D'Haricot said.

'Yes, yes.'

Monsieur D'Haricot walked out of the café. He imagined he heard Louise and Philip sniggering as he closed the door behind him. Outside, he was at a loss for what to do. The General had been kidnapped, but how long ago? Louise implied he had been unconscious for some time. There was a chance the danger in Fraumy was over and the General had been returned to his office.

An omnibus slowed and came to a halt at the shelter fifty metres along the pavement. Two people alighted, a middle-aged woman and a girl in her early twenties with the same tight lips and high forehead. Their clothes, although not expensive, were well looked after. The older woman clung onto a faux fur bag.

'Excuse me, ladies.' Monsieur D'Haricot approached them. 'I wondered if you could tell me what time it is.'

The older woman tried to ignore him, but her daughter tucked up her sleeve to show off what looked like a new wristwatch.

'It is twelve,' the young lady said. 'You will hear the church bells in a minute.'

'Thank you.' Noon meant it clearly wasn't still Saturday, but was it Sunday? Monsieur D'Haricot did not wish to look a fool by asking the ladies what day it was. He suspected that if it were Sunday, the two ladies would be inside the church.

The newsagent shop on the corner was open and he entered it as the bells from the Sacre Coeur peeled. The front page of Le Figaro on the display rack told him it was Monday. A peek inside showed his football team had lost to their local rivals and there was the continued threat of workers' strikes in the capital. He had lost almost two days to one small glass of cognac. A look from the newsagent indicated he had dallied too long and it was time to reach in his pocket and pay. He handed over a coin and took one of the papers he hadn't read. He folded it under his arm, left the shop and headed for the nearest underground train station.

Monsieur D'Haricot was not paranoid, but he was attracting more attention on the train than befitted his appearance. A one-eyed war veteran tilted his head to examine him from a ninety degree angle and a nun peered over her Bible to watch him. On his walk home from the station, he imagined that his fellow citizens must be mistaking him for a movie star or sports hero by the looks he was getting. He checked his clothing to make sure his shirt was tucked in and his buttons were fastened. He smoothed down his hair and moustache. He was in need of a shave, but so were several other men. He avoided eye contact with passersby. His apartment was on the avenue that met the street he was on at the next corner. He increased his pace as he overtook a man and a boy, who by his calculations should have been attending school.

'That is the man in the newspaper,' the boy cried out in a high-pitched shriek of fear.

Monsieur D'Haricot could not help but turn to look at the boy. The man with him stared back and rubbed his shaved chin. Monsieur D'Haricot pulled his hat over his forehead and crossed the street. He marched down an alleyway until he was out of sight and waited until he thought it would be safe to return. While he did so he unfolded his newspaper. The alley was empty and there was room to open it out and turn the pages. On page four there was a side column informing the nation that the General had been kidnapped from his office. There were few details of the crime, but beneath the wording was a blurred photograph of him, Louis-Philip D'Haricot, taken when he entered the service. His name was printed in bold beneath it.

Monsieur D'Haricot crumpled the paper and tossed it on the pavement. He exhaled red-hot air from his lungs.

'Me, a criminal? Ridiculous,' he fumed, kicking the nearest brick wall and stubbing his four remaining toes.

It took several minutes for his head to cool and his foot to stop smarting. He could not go home. There would be police officers guarding his house, waiting to arrest him. He could hardly explain to detectives that the General had been taken to an underground duchy, either to be assassinated by German robots or to be used as a cog in an intricate plan to take over Paris. The only way he could prove his innocence was by rescuing and returning the General.

He did not doubt his ability to complete such a textbook task. Had he not recaptured a whole village in 1915 with the help of a servant girl and her pet cat? According to the Saint Sulpice clock, he had several hours to do so before the planned celebrations in Fraumy. The only tiny problem, hardly worth worrying about, was how to actually get there.

Chapter Twenty

He could return to The Red Duck and hope Louise and Philip were not completely intoxicated by the brandy. They had guided him willingly before. He looked down at the newspaper, which had uncrumpled to show his face beaming up at him. It would not be safe to use public transport. If a nun, a blind serviceman and a schoolboy truant could recognise him, others could too. He could make his way to the river and hope to find an aquatran. He did not imagine that even a subterranean tributary of the Seine would run through Fraumy, but an aquatran would take him underground, which was half the battle.

The plan was not without danger and he paused to evaluate the risks before setting off. On the short walk to the river, he could still encounter a police officer. He needed to be invisible. Monsieur D'Haricot snapped his fingers. He could become invisible. All it would take was smoke and mirrors.

He had instructed Otocey's manservant to collect the contraption that Victoire had offered him in exchange for the beautiful Clodette from the riverbank. The man seemed competent, if somewhat impudent for a butler, therefore he assumed the chargeur should now be outside Otocey's residence. Keeping his head bent low and stooping to become anonymous in the Parisian melee, he exited the alley and made his way in a circumspect manner to Otocey's house.

The machine was where he expected it to be. A transport officer had stuck a ticket on the handlebars, warning that the vehicle was causing an obstruction and would be removed. The given date had come and gone and the chargeur remained on the pavement, forcing pedestrians and prams to circle around it.

Monsieur D'Haricot walked past it, giving a mere distasteful glance, until the dog walking couple moved on and the pavement was empty. He returned to check if the contraption was locked. As he circled round it, he became aware of movement at one of the ground floor windows of Otocey's house. The Vicomte's manservant was watching him from behind the curtains. Monsieur D'Haricot marched to the door and rapped the knocker.

The door was answered by the manservant. Before he could speak, Monsieur D'Haricot was ready with his own question. 'Is Nicolas at home?' he demanded.

'I am afraid not,' the man replied. 'He will be absent for several days. Do you intend breaking in and searching the house while he is absent?'

It was an odd thing to say and Monsieur D'Haricot was taken aback. 'Do you take me for a criminal? I am Monsieur Louis-Philip D'Haricot. I was here as a guest of Nicolas not so long ago.'

'Indeed sir, I remember the occasion. However the newspapers inform me that you are a violent enemy of the country, who has attacked government officials and kidnapped a senior member of the security staff. That being the case, and knowing that the senior member of staff in question would never divulge secrets to any enemy of France, it is logical to assume that you would wish to get your hands on Nicolas's interrogation devices.'

Monsieur D'Haricot ran his tongue round his mouth while he worked out what the manservant was saying. 'I am not an enemy of France,' he declared. 'It is your master who has kidnapped the General and I intend going to Fraumy to save him. What interrogation devices?'

'It is no matter. I see now that your intention is to steal the chargeur.'

'That vehicle belongs to me,' Monsieur D'Haricot reminded him. 'It was a gift from Victoire Chapleau.'

'Then perhaps you would care to pay the parking fines,' the manservant said, producing several sheets of official documents from his trouser pocket. Monsieur D'Haricot snatched them from him.

'I shall deal with them in my own time. Now, perhaps, you shall allow me to continue with my business.'

'It was you who knocked on the door,' the manservant answered, somewhat peeved.

Monsieur D'Haricot strode to the chargeur. The manservant waited a moment, then followed him. He stood on the kerb with his arms folded. It appeared Monsieur D'Haricot was to have an audience while he mounted and prepared the vehicle.

'The celebrations begin in—' The manservant consulted a pocket watch attached to a gold chain clipped to his top pocket. '—three hours and forty-seven minutes. You would be advised to use the boost facility.'

Monsieur D'Haricot looked blankly at the dials.

The manservant pointed to a green lever. 'You do know how to work this machine?'

'Yes, of course, I have ridden bicycles since before wearing long trousers.'

The manservant rolled his eyes. Monsieur D'Haricot squirmed in the chair, stretched his legs and pressed as many buttons as he could find.

'Move over,' the man said, in a voice lacking its usual haughty tone.

Monsieur D'Haricot did as he was instructed, allowing the man to sit on the armchair beside him. He expected to be squashed, but the chair expanded to fit them both. The manservant activated the blue smoke and pointed to a gauge that appeared in front of him. 'FRAUMY' was marked in capitals ninety degrees from 'V C's BOUDOIR' followed round the clock face by 'SEINE' then 'PARADISE'. He didn't ask where paradise was.

'Hold onto your breeks,' the manservant said. Monsieur D'Haricot had sufficient faith in his belt and braces not to take the warning literally.

At the age of six, Monsieur D'Haricot had ridden behind his father on a bicycle belonging to the local butcher. Although he had gripped his father's waist like a young monkey hanging on to its mother's back, when the bicycle juddered over cobbles he had slipped. His legs had tangled in the back wheel and the bicycle was brought to the ground in a muddy puddle. The humiliation, the butcher's anger and his father's unjust reaction had affected him ever since. Technically he was not currently riding behind the manservant, but having two people on one bicycle was something he had vowed never to repeat.

The manservant was happy to take the controls. Monsieur D'Haricot felt his heart slow to a more reasonable pace and his stomach contents settle and grudgingly admitted the man knew how to control a chargeur. The familiar Paris streets became suburban boulevards and then fields of happily grazing cows.

'We don't have time to stop off at my favourite vineyards,' the manservant bemoaned. 'Perhaps we will manage on the way back.'

They seemed to fly past farms and villages and Monsieur D'Haricot had to check the wheels remained on the ground. 'What is your name?' he asked as they startled a line of ducks on a pond. The birds took to the air in a panic and their droppings narrowly missed Monsieur D'Haricot's shoulders.

'Robert,' the man answered. Monsieur D'Haricot had a vague recollection of Otocey using the name. Robert gave a laugh. 'In Nicolas's house, it is more usual for someone to ask what zodiac sign you are rather than what name you use.'

'And what sign are you?' Monsieur D'Haricot asked.

'You shall have to work it out, if you are interested,' Robert answered.

Monsieur D'Haricot liked a puzzle, especially when it was put forward as a challenge. He was silent while they continued their journey through a small town, with Robert honking the chargeur's horn at cars that were unable to see them through the blue mist. They reached a railway crossing and the signal indicated that the barriers were about to descend. Monsieur D'Haricot was relieved when Robert stopped the machine. He turned to face Monsieur D'Haricot.

'Otocey believes you are a Sagittarian,' he said.

'That implies you don't,' Monsieur D'Haricot replied.

Robert tapped the side of his nose, the train whisked past and the barriers rose. On the other side Robert stuck his hand out to veer right, missing Monsieur D'Haricot's nose by a hair.

'No-one can see us,' Monsieur D'Haricot complained, fearful of a recurrence of the signal which might set off a nose bleed.

'Habit,' Robert answered. 'In my profession, it isn't proper to let standards slip.'

They left the road and followed a dust track at the side of a field running alongside the railway line.

'Would you like me to do my share of the pedalling?' Monsieur D'Haricot asked, belatedly.

'If you wouldn't mind,' Robert answered. 'The chargeur boost keeps the speed up, but it's necessary to turn the pedals to keep it charged.'

Monsieur D'Haricot smarted at having to be told how the machine worked. He made sure he kicked Robert's ankles as they changed feet positions.

'Have we far to go?' he asked.

'No. In fact, it is time we delved underground,' Robert replied. He pointed towards a railway tunnel cut through a hill. 'We can make use of that.'

Monsieur D'Haricot was no longer shocked, or even mildly surprised, by anything people said to him. 'Should I close my eyes?' he asked by way of a droll remark.

'Gracious, no. I'll need you to change the points,' Robert answered. 'It can be a tricky manoeuvre. They no longer employ point masters in the provinces. Madame Chapleau and her cabinet feel it is an unnecessary expense, especially with the plans to acclimatise the population to life above ground.'

'How is that plan coming along?' Monsieur D'Haricot probed.

'Very well, thank you for asking. Madame Chapleau's twin is now able to remain above ground for significant periods of time before melting. On average it takes six months of constant exposure to sunlight, with reduced reliance on readjustment biscuits to acclimatise. I doubt, in Mala Kai's case, she will be able to live above ground permanently. I use the pronoun "she", but it is interchangeable.'

Monsieur D'Haricot hadn't expected such a detailed answer, and it crossed his mind that Robert might be an automaton. He hadn't let out even the slightest yelp when his ankle had been kicked. Monsieur D'Haricot thought about repeating the action, with more force, but that seemed impolite and unwise since Robert was in control of the vehicle.

'What percentage of your population is now functioning above ground?' he asked.

Robert turned to give him a questioning look. 'What do you mean by "your population"? I was born and brought up in Nice. If you mean my employer's kind, then I would say less than a quarter of a quarter percent.'

'Then your employer will need a good many readjustment biscuits for his plan to take effect.'

'That is not my business,' Robert said curtly, returning his attention to the track ahead. They had reached the tunnel and were about to enter. Robert pressed a button and amber headlights were turned on.

'When should I look out for the points' lever?' Monsieur D'Haricot asked.

'Now,' Robert said, uncharacteristically raising his voice.

Monsieur D'Haricot's reflexes were not up to the speed of the chargeur. Robert stuck a hand across Monsieur D'Haricot's face to reach out of the seating area and grab a stick. As the chargeur ran forwards the lever was pulled into position. When it clicked, Robert let go. Monsieur D'Haricot's nose and mouth had been blocked by Robert's forearm during the operation, preventing him from breathing. His face had turned purple and he lost consciousness.

He was out cold for less than five seconds, but when he came to the chargeur was underground, following a narrow track along a tunnel. He could see ahead by the light of the headlamp, but the tunnel was unlit. The walls seemed to be pressing in on them like a scene from a horror movie and the echo from the chargeur sounded like laughter. He pulled at his collar.

'Can you smell something?' he asked Robert.

'Nothing unusual.'

Robert's voice was muffled. Monsieur D'Haricot stuck his fingers in his ears to pop them. He yawned, having been told that helped restore balance on the eardrums. It worked and his hearing was restored.

'Something rotten,' he said.

'There is a trace of hydrogen sulphide in the tunnel. I wouldn't advise you to light a cigarette until we are in Fraumy.'

'Which will be?'

'In five minutes.'

Had his pocket watch been working, it would have been too dark for Monsieur D'Haricot to check it. From Robert's optimism he was sure there would be time to freshen up and devise a plan before the celebrations were at their critical point. The tunnel widened and lamps appeared on the walls, giving off a purple light. By it, Monsieur D'Haricot could see a station with uniformed guards.

'Will there be problems at the border?' he asked. 'I don't have travel documents with me.'

'Neither do I,' Robert answered.

'Are we in any danger? Do you have a gun or a knife?'

'I have a clothes brush,' Robert replied. 'I was attending to Nicolas's dinner jacket when you arrived. Do not sneer. I once knew a man who died from an asthma attack after breathing dander from a clothes brush.'

'You had better allow me to do the talking,' Monsieur D'Haricot decided. He had stopped pedalling and the chargeur slowed to walking pace as it approached the checkpoint.

'They insist on speaking Flemish,' Robert answered. 'They call it Fraumish, but my grandmother was from Belgium and she spoke the same way without ever having heard of Fraumy.'

'You can translate?' Monsieur D'Haricot was hopeful.

'My grandmother's vocabulary was limited, at least in my hearing. If they say "dinner is ready", "time for bed", "brandy or champagne?" or use selected swear words popular forty years ago then yes, I can translate.'

'I'm not sure how far that will get us.'

'It serves Nicolas well whenever he visits Fraumy.'

'He visits often?'

'Why wouldn't he? He is the son of Baron Friedrich van Lüttich's sister. The Baron was Dauphine van Lüttich's late husband.'

'How did he die?'

'You don't want to know.'

They had reached the border station and Robert pulled on the brakes and greeted the guards. One of them scowled while the other broke into a fit of laughter.

'What did you say?' Monsieur D'Haricot asked.

'I meant to say we are here for the celebrations, but I may have said assassination. A slip of the tongue,' Robert answered jovially.

'That guard may have a slip of his trigger finger.' Monsieur D'Haricot did not share the humour of the situation. He reached for the chargeur's boost lever and pushed it. The brakes were still on and the machine creaked, but it jolted forwards. The guards were quick to jump out of its path.

'What are you doing?' Robert tussled with him for control. A shot was fired over their heads, ricocheting against the tunnel walls. It was sufficient to convince Robert to release the brake and proceed at full speed ahead.

'The guards will have informed the capital of our arrival,' Robert said, once they were safely free of pursuit and were heading into the centre of the city.

'We don't have time to worry about that,' Monsieur D'Haricot answered. 'Do you know where Otocey has taken the General?'

Robert slowed the chargeur as it reached a junction into a main street. He pulled in to the side and applied the brake. Monsieur D'Haricot was slow to stop pedalling. The momentum thrust him forwards against the handlebars. The knock wasn't hard, but when he

195

regained his position blood was dribbling from his nose onto his upper lip. Robert offered him a handkerchief.

'Your system hasn't got used to the differing pressures underground,' he explained.

Monsieur D'Haricot accepted the handkerchief. The letters 'N.O.' had been embroidered in gold thread at one corner and at the opposite corner a coyote had been stitched into the silk. Its red eyes gleamed at Monsieur D'Haricot.

'This is your master's handkerchief.'

'I didn't pilfer it. He lets me have his old ones. I collect handkerchiefs the way less imaginative people collect autographs. Would you prefer this one?' Robert pulled a second handkerchief from his pocket. It had the initials EvL and in the opposite corner there was a scorpion.

'You have Edgori van Lüttich's handkerchief?'

'Gori has been at the house several times. Borrowing money from Nicolas is a regular occurrence. They are related, as I mentioned.'

'What other handkerchiefs do you have?' Monsieur D'Haricot was intrigued.

'Victoire Chapleau and Mala Kai use the same design, with llamas in the corner – something to do with the double 'l' and Latin. Angelique has two designs. I have the dark angel, but not the... other one.' Robert paused, aware that Monsieur D'Haricot had picked up on his reluctance to say what it was. 'The Arch-duke has—'

'Yes, thank you. I don't suppose you have one with the Queen of Diamonds?'

Robert snatched back the handkerchief. 'You are either trying to get me sacked or killed. No-one is permitted to handle that gentleman's clothing except his personal attendants. This is Brudamberg, the capital city of Fraumy. The central square is that way.' He gave Monsieur D'Haricot a nudge, implying he should dismount.

'You are not coming?'

'I have work to do in Paris.'

'Brushing clothes?'

'There is no need to be facetious.' Robert waited until Monsieur D'Haricot was surefooted on the pavement, then handed him his hat which had fallen onto the armchair. 'The chargeur will be waiting outside the house when, or should I say if, you return.'

Monsieur D'Haricot watched as a puff of blue smoke rose from the bottom of the chargeur and it and Robert disappeared.

The buzz from the central square was growing louder. Monsieur D'Haricot recognised the rhythms of steel bands with the drones of alpine horns competing in the background. There was no time to concern himself with Robert. There was serious work to be done. He lodged his hat firmly over his ears and made his way to the street corner.

Monsieur D'Haricot considered himself to be above the shallow pleasure seeking activities of his fellow citizens, but like any curious individual he was drawn to a parade. Even before he spotted the band major leading the procession with his baton twirling, his foot was tapping. Spectators tossed handfuls of coloured confetti at the marchers. He assumed it was a Fraumy custom and, to avoid looking conspicuous, he searched in his pocket for change to purchase a bag from the young sellers.

As a fringe to the main parade, the streets were taken over by musicians and artistes demonstrating their prowess. Above the calls of a juggling yodeller, Monsieur D'Haricot was able to distinguish the strains of a Spanish guitar. He looked across to see Juan leaning against a lamppost, an overlarge pink sombrero concealing most of his face. He knew it was Juan because he was wearing the suit St. John St. Clair had on when they first met. Monsieur D'Haricot walked towards him.

'I do not know you, señor,' Juan said in a lazy drawl.

'I didn't say you did, although you do,' Monsieur D'Haricot answered. 'I am looking for Otocey. You know him.'

'No, señor. I know only my music.' He strummed a chord and let out a pitch perfect wail in A minor.

Monsieur D'Haricot covered his ears and moved on towards a street stall selling crepes smothered in colourful syrup. The server looked so much like Maulise, in appearance and mannerisms, that Monsieur D'Haricot had no doubt it was the artist.

'Delisooky,' Monsieur D'Haricot said.

The man eyed him as if he were a stranger talking nonsense. Monsieur D'Haricot accepted his crepe without further conversation. When he spotted Philip balancing two dancing girls, one in either hand, he deduced that the entire zodiac gang was here incognito. His job was to find the General before the van Lüttichs did.

With the help of the sugar rush from the crepe syrup, Monsieur D'Haricot engaged his brain once more. If an assassin expected the General to be on show, waving to his people from the middle of the parade, he would have to be hidden from security, but with a clear view of his or her target. A roof or upstairs window seemed the likeliest positions. Monsieur D'Haricot looked up at the ornate gables and carved stonework of the town's architecture. It would have been impressive above ground. To have been carved in what was, for all intents, a cave was mind-boggling. Monsieur D'Haricot had been trained not to have his mind easily boggled. He ignored the fine construction and scoured the windows for the barrel of a gun.

The parade was nearing the corner. The crowd were moving with it, dictating the speed. Monsieur D'Haricot was jostled to the back of the pavement and crushed in the doorway of a closed hardware store. An elongated, white Mercedes Benz with an open top was progressing at the pace of the walkers. The General was sitting in the back, dressed in his splendid Arch-duke's uniform adorned with so many medals and badges of honour it could have been chain mail. He clanked every time he raised his hand to wave. One of his awards looked suspiciously crablike in form and size and when it waved a pincher at him Monsieur D'Haricot was convinced it was Marina.

The driver was the only other person in the car. Two armed guards walked alongside, one on either side of the vehicle. It seemed inadequate protection until Monsieur D'Haricot noticed the flicker of metal at the belt of one of the jugglers and when the acrobat performed a somersault the handle of a pistol was clearly visible stuffed into his Harlequin tights.

'Are you enjoying the show?' a female voice spoke from beside Monsieur D'Haricot. He twisted to see Angelique, dressed in combat gear with her hair cropped and a military cap low over her face. 'If you are searching for Werner, you won't find him here.'

'You mean that treacherous automaton is in place to fire at the Arch-duke?' Monsieur D'Haricot asked.

'You are a clever boy. A tad slow, but you seem to get there, which is why I am surprised to find you on the street. Wouldn't it be more helpful to search the upstairs rooms?'

'I was about to do that,' Monsieur D'Haricot replied. 'I have only just arrived.'

Angelique glanced at her palm. Enmeshed in the skin was a circular clock face with dials that glowed. 'It must have taken longer for the tranquiliser to wear off than Victoire calculated,' she said.

'Victoire? She is not involved in the plot to kill the General, is she?'

'That would upset you, would it?' Angelique pouted, putting on a voice fit for a five year old.

'I do not believe Madame Victoire Chapleau is a killer.'

'No? That is why she works for a secret government security department.'

'Victoire deals with expenses, the office paperwork and procuring foreign biscuits.'

'Is that what she told you? It is no matter. You are wasting time. Forget about Werner, you need to find Otocey.'

'Do I? I thought Van Lüttich was the danger.' It appeared they were playing cat and mouse, which was a game Monsieur D'Haricot excelled at.

'I have the situation with the General under control. You are needed elsewhere. I'll give you a hint. Start by locating the—' Angelique replied.

Monsieur D'Haricot thought she said the town hall, but the marching band was upon them and drowned out the conversation.

'I'm afraid I have to fly.' She blew him a kiss as she sped off in a whiff of jasmine and bergamot. Monsieur D'Haricot had wanted to ask about the dark angel symbol on her handkerchief, but the matter had slipped his mind.

The Mercedes had reached the corner. The General had a broad grin on his face. It was the first time Monsieur D'Haricot had seen him smile and he had suspected the man's tight facial muscles restricted any expansion of his lips beyond that necessary for drinking.

'Duck!' A German accented voice spoke from behind him. Monsieur D'Haricot acted on instinct. His forehead had reached the level of his knees when he heard the shot, followed by a ping. The screams began before he could pick his hat up from the kerb where it had fallen. 'Run!' the voice warned.

Monsieur D'Haricot swirled round to see the back of a figure in work breeches and a worn shirt with what appeared to be apron strings tied round his waist disappearing down a side alley. Monsieur D'Haricot had the feeling that it might have been Delanoir.

'That way.' Monsieur D'Haricot gave instructions to a horde of security guards who had materialised from the crowd and were dashing towards him. A path cleared and five of the men raced after the gunman. A sixth stayed with Monsieur D'Haricot. It was Gustav, the aquatran captain. 'The General, was he hit? Is he hurt?' Monsieur D'Haricot gasped.

'It is quite a sight. The shot took his head right off,' Gustav replied.

Chapter Twenty-one

Monsieur D'Haricot gaped at the car. The General's head drooped at a ridiculous angle, revealing two springs attached from his body to his guillotined neck. His head bounced as the vehicle progressed.

'That is not the real General. What have you done with him?' Monsieur D'Haricot demanded.

'You had better come with me,' Gustav said. Monsieur D'Haricot hesitated and Gustav raised his pistol to make the point.

'Are we going to the town hall?' Monsieur D'Haricot said, intending to show he was ahead of the game.

'Why? What is happening there?' Gustav asked.

His ignorance seemed genuine. Monsieur D'Haricot didn't answer. He put out his palm to indicate Gustav should lead the way to wherever he was going.

After the initial horror of the attack, the crowd recovered. Assuming the 'assassination' was part of the show, they were happily throwing the remainder of the confetti at the automaton Archduke. The tail end of the procession was made up of circus performers and people dressed as animals. Marina had disentangled herself from the General's sash and Monsieur D'Haricot recognised her dancing on two legs a little behind the last performer. She was followed by laughing children, encouraging her by throwing titbits.

Monsieur D'Haricot paused to wait on her. 'Marina, what are you doing?' he chided.

She stopped when she heard her name and sidestepped towards the waiting Monsieur D'Haricot and Gustav, using her pinchers to nip ankles in order to clear the way. When she reached Monsieur D'Haricot he picked her up and she gave him a wink.

'To the tower walls,' she declared. 'Allons enfants!'

Away from the celebrations, the deserted streets were strewn with scraps of paper and puddled with spilt alcohol. Monsieur D'Haricot picked his way carefully through the debris left by the celebrants. They were entering an older part of the town. The stone work, although once ornate, was crumbling. Monsieur D'Haricot could see the clock tower ahead of him. Gustav marched towards the arched gateway. Looking up, Monsieur D'Haricot could see the Fraumy coat of arms carved on a slab of sandstone at the centre of the arch. He recognised the design from one he'd seen in the General's office. Two fish with their tails entwined in the manner of Celtic artwork.

Cold air blew on Monsieur D'Haricot as he crossed the threshold into the building. The damp from the walls crept under his skin and dribbled through his tissues. A pale-skinned lizard scrambled out of his way. Monsieur D'Haricot expected the clock to strike thirteen, but it remained silent with the hands dangling limp. The entrance hall was not large, but managed to accommodate the members of the zodiac elite.

An elaborate circle had been painted on the floor in gold, complete with astrological symbols, mythological beasts, arcane writing, religious quotations and Latin numerals in a mishmash of traditions. It had been divided into twelve segments, with an additional section overlapping Scorpio and Sagittarius. At the head of the room was a throne, covered in velvet and furs. Monsieur D'Haricot expected the real Arch-duke to be seated on it, but he had taken his place on the circle next to a scowling Dauphine van Lüttich.

At least Monsieur D'Haricot assumed that was who it was. The woman looked nothing like either the hag with the pups, or the elegant duchess in Dieppe, but she stood in the section marked as Aries. Otocey was beside Louise, attempting to keep control of proceedings. He spotted Gustav and Monsieur D'Haricot's entrance and clapped his hands to gain attention.

'All stand.'

Everyone was already standing, but they fell silent and bowed their heads. Monsieur D'Haricot put Marina on the ground and she scurried across the floor to the empty space between the Chapleau twins and Otocey. Gustav ushered Monsieur D'Haricot to his position beside a bored looking Edgori van Lüttich.

'Watch whose toes you are standing on,' Olivier Hector complained as Monsieur D'Haricot took his place, as far from Gori as possible.

'Keep to your own square then,' Edgori answered.

'Gentlemen, please,' Otocey interrupted. 'Silence for the Queen of Diamonds.'

Monsieur D'Haricot thought he was beyond being astonished by anything that happened, but he had to look twice at the person marching into the room, draped in a purple velvet cloak with red diamonds embroidered on the ermine collar. The second glance confirmed his suspicion that it was not the late Emperor Napoleon Bonaparte taking his seat on the throne, but a lifelike automaton of the great leader.

Otocey bowed to the machine and Monsieur D'Haricot heard Gori snigger.

'Let proceedings begin,' Otocey declared.

Maulise began marching on his spot. Gustav had taken his place in the vacant segment next to him, and after a few seconds he also began marching. The General was less enthusiastic and Dauphine kept her toes on the ground and barely lifted her heels. Next to her Philip was like a veritable infantryman, swinging his arms and whistling. As Victoire and Mala Kai joined in, then Marina and Otocey himself, Monsieur D'Haricot realised he would have to do his part when it came to it. Louise nudged Juan who, having reverted to his St. John persona, was not impressed by the ostentation. Edgori stood defiant, but a gesture from Otocey, running a finger against his neck, persuaded him to comply. Finally Monsieur D'Haricot began marching on the spot.

'Wait for me, you idiot,' Monsieur Hector put in from the extra segment.

The noise of fourteen marchers echoed around the walls, circling around the domed roof. Otocey chanted weird words. They may have been old French, Latin or Shakespearean English, but Monsieur D'Haricot didn't try to understand them. He kept an eye on Napoleon.

'How long do we keep this up for?' the General complained. 'My knees won't take it.'

'All this thumping will waken the Core Worm,' his sister said, with more than a hint of glee.

Otocey's cross-eyed glare managed to pierce them both. 'Candles, we need candles,' he said.

'Cannons would be better,' Gori answered. 'We've tried your way. Now do I get to kill him?' He pointed across at the General.

'Nobody is killing anyone,' Monsieur D'Haricot stepped out of his segment. 'This farce is finished. I am taking the General back to Paris, where I feel he is in need of a sojourn in a health sanatorium.'

'I am the one who gives the orders,' the General rebuked him. The others began mumbling.

'Patience,' Otocey argued. 'These rituals take time.'

'You said this was the right time,' Dauphine objected. 'Now you say it is the wrong time.'

'The time is never wrong,' Monsieur D'Haricot reminded the Vicomte.

'That is true,' Otocey snapped back.

'Something is wrong,' St. John/Juan said. 'Is the clock on the tower fast?'

'That clock has been broken for over a century,' the General said.

'Oh, ah, yes.' Monsieur D'Haricot wiggled his index finger in front of him. Everyone looked at him, expecting an explanation for his uttering. 'My father's clock was fast. He put it fifteen minutes ahead deliberately.'

'I am not interested in your father's clock,' Otocey said.

'You should be, because it means that I was not born five minutes after midnight, but ten minutes before, on the previous day as marked on my birth certificate.' Otocey's jaw dropped before Monsieur D'Haricot could finish.

'You aren't a Sagittarian,' Victoire said.

'No, it would appear I am a Scorpio.'

'Traitor! I knew I couldn't trust you.' Otocey stamped his foot.

'You don't need me then.' Gori examined his watch, as if he had a vital prior engagement he might just manage to keep.

'Can't we find a real Sagittarian?' St. John/Juan suggested.

'There was one here not so long ago, a man you could have recruited at any time,' D'Haricot continued.

'Where is he?' Otocey demanded.

'I sent him home.' Standing outside the circle, the mismatched group seemed ludicrous. Monsieur D'Haricot could not hide his amusement.

'Who are you talking about?' Victoire asked.

'The Vicomte's manservant, Robert. He brought me here.'

'Robert?' Otocey struggled to recall which of his servants Robert was. 'He told you he was a Sagittarian?'

'He asked me to guess. He is a fiery optimist; a travelling adventurer with a sideways sense of humour. He knew I wasn't a Sagittarian and, as they say, it takes one to know one. I will wager my apartment Robert is a true Sagittarian.'

Otocey stood with his mouth open, unable to find the words. Mala Kai stepped across the circle boundary to address the others. She was wearing a chain of office declaring her to be the Primus of Ecnarf.

'Since Nicolas's idea is dead and Gori isn't permitted to kill the Arch-duke, it is time for my proposal,' she said, rubbing a mark from the metal amulet on the chain. 'We have three suitcases full of corporal readjustment accelerator biscuits. That is sufficient for an army to take over Belgium and the North of France. Once we have persuaded the locals to join us, we can march on Paris.'

'I'm up for that,' Gori said. 'Where do we find our army?'

'There is a rabble outside who would follow any parade with a sparkly banner and good music,' she answered. 'Louise and Juan can play for them and Philip can sing. They have drunk enough cheap wine to believe the Queen of Diamonds is their reborn general.'

'I'm the General,' the Arch-duke protested.

'That was never our plan, Kai,' Victoire held out an arm towards her twin.

'It was always mine,' Mala Kai answered.

One by one, the group had stopped marching. Only Marina was twirling on the spot, snapping her pinchers together and demonstrating elegant dance movements with her free legs. She seemed oblivious to the discussions going on above her head, but Monsieur D'Haricot imagined he saw a twitch of her feelers when Mala Kai mentioned the biscuits.

'Where are the cases?' Gori demanded. 'You had them, mother, didn't you?'

'Someone tried to steal them from me in Dieppe.' She glowered across at Otocey.

'They were mine to begin with,' Otocey replied. 'Gustav unloaded them at the wrong pier.'

'Don't blame me. You should print your instructions in legible writing,' Gustav objected.

'The cases are safe.' Otocey cleared his throat. 'Friends, Our Primus has the true Ecnarf spirit. It is time to fulfil our destiny.' He clapped his hands three times and the automaton of Napoleon rose from the throne. In mechanical movements, he lifted the throne with outstretched arms and moved it aside to reveal the cases Monsieur D'Haricot had seen belonging to the Duchess in Dieppe. Otocey adjusted his shirt cuffs before making a show of undoing the clasps of the nearest case. He threw open the lid with a dramatic flourish and a superfluous adage in Latin, then stepped back with a gasp.

Everyone could see that the case was empty. Not a crumb of the biscuits remained. Otocey opened the second case and the third. There was nothing in either of them.

'I don't understand,' Otocey stuttered. 'They were full when I checked them in Dieppe. Mala Kai can vouch for that. You were also in Dieppe, D'Haricot. What do you know of the cases?'

'The duchess asked me to see they were transported to her hotel room,' Monsieur D'Haricot answered.

'You did that personally?' Otocey demanded.

'I left it to the hotel staff.'

While they were talking, Marina had stopped dancing and was crawling towards a shaded corner.

'Where is the crab going?' Dauphine van Lüttich pointed a crooked finger at her.

'Marina, what do you know about this?' Monsieur D'Haricot asked.

'Liberty! Equality! Fraternity!' Marina raised a cheer. No-one joined in. 'All crabs are equal and free,' she declared.

'What is she talking about?' Mala Kai asked.

Louise walked towards Marina and bent down to address her. 'What did you do with our biscuits, dear?'

'Did you give the readjustment biscuits to your fellow crabs?' Monsieur D'Haricot pictured the scene on the beach.

'I had to free them,' Marina explained. 'They didn't understand their danger. I knew the biscuits would help.'

'You used all the biscuits on a few market stall crabs?' Mala Kai's voice caught.

'No, no. There were lobster and shellfish too,' Marina answered. 'Afterwards I tossed the remaining crumbs in the sea for other crabs to find and enjoy the benefits.'

'Does this mean we can't live above ground?' Maulise asked.

'We still have a few packets of biscuits in Paris,' Victoire answered. 'Not enough for an army.'

'It took years to manufacture the biscuits,' Otocey lamented. 'The chance may never come again in our lifetime.'

'We were promised,' Maulise raised his arms to urge the others to support him.

'I told my superiors in Madrid there would be positive developments,' St. John/Juan said. 'This will be something of an embarrassment for me.'

'It is the crab's fault,' Gustav said, shoving past Otocey. 'I knew we should have served it up as bisque.'

'Nobody touches the crab.' Louise put her body in front of Marina. 'I blame him.' She pointed at Monsieur D'Haricot. 'He was the one looking after her.'

The zodiac gang were angry and even Philip, who Monsieur D'Haricot had regarded as a friend, had his sleeves rolled up.

'The Updweller was never on your side, Otocey,' Gori said. 'He has his own agenda, which I suspect involves a secret treaty with England.'

'Typical, treacherous, sting in the tail Scorpio,' Otocey grumbled.

Louise was pushed aside as unfriendly hands advanced towards Marina. Monsieur D'Haricot acted quickly, diving between legs to seize the crab and secure her in the folds of his jacket. He was being pressed into the corner. The others had taken up Otocey's complaint, blaming Monsieur D'Haricot for rickets, pleurisy, photophobia and all the ills they suffered underground. Gori was armed with a duelling sword and Gustav waved his pistol as he moved closer at the head of the pack.

It was pointless trying to reason with them. Monsieur D'Haricot had reached the wall and felt its coldness through his clothing. He freed a hand to tap the stonework in a forlorn hope that a secret trapdoor would open.

He closed his eyes and felt something reach out and grab his shoulder. It was an ordinary hand, but it had the grip of an eagle's talons and the strength of a buffalo. Monsieur D'Haricot dug in his heels, but he couldn't prevent the arm dragging him through the mix of bodies towards the gateway. The others were slow to react and he was outside, beyond them, before they could retaliate. It gave him a moment to see his rescuer. It was Angelique.

'This is not the time for questions,' she said before he could ask.

Marina was shaking from the mention of the bisque. Her pinchers were clicking together like castanets. Monsieur D'Haricot dampened his concerns and followed Angelique at a fast jog around corners and down alleys until she was satisfied they had lost Otocey and his gang. Monsieur D'Haricot caught his breath outside a haberdashery shop.

'That was a lucky escape,' he said.

'There was no luck involved,' Angelique corrected him. 'Wait here.' The shop displayed a sign informing customers it was closed, but Angelique managed to unlock the door and enter. She returned with a trench coat and a wig. 'Put these on,' she instructed.

'They are stolen,' Monsieur D'Haricot objected.

'Borrowed,' Angelique replied. 'I shall have them returned when you no longer need them.'

Monsieur D'Haricot put on the coat. It trailed on the ground and the wig tickled his ears. He was afraid it might be harbouring lice. 'You knew Otocey's plan would fail,' he said.

'Of course.'

'You never believed in the zodiac prophecy?'

'Whether the prophecy is true and whether I believe in it are of no consequence. You should not have been a part of it. Victoire was wrong to have involved you. You have odd moments, but you are the most unlikely Sagittarian I have met. Victoire realised her mistake and tried to warn you at her party. When she found out you had taken my fan, which would lead you to Otocey, she went to speak with him. He and Mala Kai kidnapped her and took her to Sark in the four hours he stole from you at your first encounter. Mala Kai was able to take over her mind. You saw her in a transitional stage at Otocey's mansion the following day.'

'If you knew this, why didn't you stop it?'

'I did what I could. I reminded Victoire that her sister cannot tolerate the levels of alcohol that she herself can. She made sure Mala Kai overindulged in Le Crotchet and was able to free her mind while her twin suffered from her hangover.'

'When did you remind her?'

Angelique made a clicking sound with her tongue. It took a moment for Monsieur D'Haricot to identify the sound.

'Estelle's cast? That was you?'

'I go by many names. Estelle, Angelique, Madame Jouet and several others.'

'I knew I recognised the toilet water in the bistro. My nose never lies.'

Angelique nodded. 'Victoire tried to prevent you coming to

Fraumy. You wouldn't take her note in the General's office, which is why she drugged you at The Red Duck. She apologises for that. She was not aware, as I was, that even if the prophecy had worked and the ground had opened up and knights flooded through to follow their Queen to glory, the biscuit cases were empty. An army could not have survived above ground for long.'

'How did you know about the biscuits?' It seemed a silly question, as Angelique appeared to know everything, but he had to ask.

'You don't believe a crab, even one of Marina's unique abilities, could be capable of emptying the contents of three heavy cases into the sea. She needed a helping hand.'

'Who do you work for?' Monsieur D'Haricot asked. 'Surely not the van Lüttichs?'

Angelique laughed. 'Do not insult me. I am my own agent and have been working to stop their plan, as well as Otocey's and Mala Kai's. I run a secret organisation which I cannot tell you about, unless I eat you afterwards. Our aim is to maintain a balance of power. My interest in St John St Clair has nothing to do with Otocey's astrology. Losing my fan was not part of the plan. It threw a cobblestone into the pond. I now fear that keeping peace above ground may not be possible in the coming years, but my remit is in regard to those civilisations below it.'

'You regard this as a successful mission?'

'It will take Otocey years to rethink the meaning of the prophecy, Mala Kai will be forced to resign as Primus and Gori's plot to form an alliance with Germany is finished. The whole of Fraumy knows that a German – Werner – tried to shoot their Arch-duke.'

'Wait, I thought Delanoir was responsible.'

'He fired the shot, but my agents will make sure Werner takes the blame. No-one will know he is an automaton and he will be dismantled before he can stand trial. The Germans have been told that it was Gori and his mother who thwarted the attempt. They will no longer be trusted in Berlin.'

'The people of Fraumy should surely be told of their treachery towards the Arch-duke,' Monsieur D'Haricot protested.

'That would not serve my purpose. It is not the first time Dauphine and her son have tried to take over Fraumy, and it will not be the last. All there is left for me to do is return you to Paris.'

'What about me?' Marina piped up.

'Where would you like me to take you, madam?' Angelique answered.

It was a Tuesday morning, two weeks after his adventures, and Monsieur D'Haricot was at home in his apartment in Montparnasse reading the situations vacant page of his newspaper. He had been dismissed from his position. Quite unreasonably, the General had filed a report claiming he was no longer suitable for the job. Both he and Victoire denied all knowledge of Fraumy. The Vicomte's house was boarded up with a 'for sale' sign outside. According to official reports the Vicomte had gone abroad, researching the Mayan culture of Central America, and would not be in Paris for several years.

Monsieur D'Haricot circled a number of possibilities he could consider applying for. He had the knowledge to act as a Tour de France mechanic and the pedantry to work as a curator at the Louvre, but those positions were not currently available. He put the newspaper on the table and was about to make a pot of coffee when his doorbell rang. He was not expecting company. The silhouette was that of a lady. He opened the door to find Victoire on his doorstep. She stepped inside, uninvited and unapologetic for her part in his dismissal.

'I have no time for pleasantries,' Monsieur D'Haricot said as politely as he could muster. 'What do you want?'

'I have come to return your bicycle,' Victoire replied.

'I have no desire to see that pile of scrap ever again.' Monsieur D'Haricot was about to usher Victoire out and close the door when he spotted the beautiful Clodette leaning against the railings. He couldn't help proclaiming her name aloud and moving past Victoire onto the pavement to examine her. Victoire joined him.

'I have a friend who is a bicycle mechanic,' she explained. 'He was able to fully restore it.'

'It? It? It is a she.' Monsieur D'Haricot's voice rose.

The bicycle looked newer than new. Monsieur D'Haricot wanted to mount it and freewheel down the street with his arms in the air, but not with Madame Chapleau looking on. He hoped a thank you would be sufficient to see her on her way, but she was insistent on having a drink with him.

'You didn't really expect anyone to believe your fanciful dalliances,' she said, once she was ensconced on his sofa with a glass of fine cognac. 'How can anyone live underground, never mind build cities there? How would they power them? Wouldn't there be problems with pressure and toxic gases. You didn't think of that, did you? I can't believe anything would grow without adequate light. What do the people you claim you met there eat? Blind lizards, algae and albino rats?' She gave a laugh. 'And what of the Core Worm?'

'You can mock if you want. I know what I saw.' Monsieur D'Haricot answered.

'I'm not making fun of you, Louis. It is an excellent story for one of my cocktail parties.'

Monsieur D'Haricot didn't answer. Victoire's eyes caught sight of his newspaper. She lifted it up. 'Ah, here is the perfect position for you.' She handed him the paper with her finger against one of the smaller advertisements.

'Assistant to a puppet master? I don't think so,' Monsieur D'Haricot replied.

'Not "a" puppet master,' Victoire said. 'It is "the Puppet Master".'

Monsieur D'Haricot looked at the advertisement. The lettering became illuminated and danced along the page. He thought he heard the tingle of a music hall tune rise from the paper.

'Never heard of him,' Monsieur D'Haricot said, forcing his eyes to look away.

'Her,' Victoire replied. 'You must come to my next party.' She removed a card from her purse and laid it on the table. Monsieur D'Haricot could see it was an invitation, with a date and time marked in purple calligraphy. 'I'll invite her along and you can discuss terms. You can also return her fan.' Victoire rose and put her empty glass on the table. 'We would be delighted if you brought your little friend too. Where is she?'

'She's in the bath,' Monsieur D'Haricot answered. 'She spends a good deal of time there.'

'I have a present for her.' Victoire opened her bag and brought out a box of patisseries. 'These are Monsieur Boucher's finest macarons. The pistachio ones are to die for.' She kissed her fingertips and fluttered them in the air, then fished in her bag for a brown paper package which she set beside the box. 'She will also enjoy these biscuits. They may not taste as scrumptious, but they are guaranteed to keep her conversation flowing for a good ten years at least.'

Lightning Source UK Ltd.
Milton Keynes UK
UKHW040649030322
399515UK00001B/168

9 781913 387396